Vera turned her gaze on to Bea. 'You never learn, do you? Your past riots have been disastrous. What makes you think this will be any different?'

Bea's voice was super cool. 'This isn't a riot, Vera. It's a peaceful sit-in until we talk to Mrs Davidson.'

Phyllis chipped in smartly. 'You screws got what you wanted when you went on strike.'

'Watch your tongue, Hunt.' Vera was tense now, ready for any sign of real trouble, but she couldn't resist the jibe. 'That's the difference between officers and prisoners . . . we have rights, you have none.'

PRISONER CELL BLOCK-H

A Dangerous Affair

Betty Quin

Thames Mandarin

A Thames Mandarin Paperback

PRISONER CELL BLOCK-H: A DANGEROUS AFFAIR

First published in Great Britain 1991
by Mandarin Paperbacks
Michelin House, 81 Fulham Road, London SW3 6RB
in association with
Thames Television International Limited
149 Tottenham Court Road, London W1P 9LL

Mandarin is an imprint of the Octopus Publishing Group
a division of Reed International Books Limited

TM © 1988 Grundy International

Copyright © 1990 Grundy International Distribution BV
Based on the Grundy Organization TV Production
from an original concept by Reg Watson and based on the
scripts of Denise Morgan, John Wood, George Mallaby,
Margaret McClusky, David Worthington,
Ian Bradley, Ray Kolle, John Upton, Sheila Sibley,
Marcus Cooney, Bryon Williams, Barbara Ramsey,
Chris Milne, Coral Drouyn and Alistair Sharp.

A CIP catalogue record for this title
is available from the British Library

ISBN 0 7493 0930 X

Phototypeset by Input Typesetting Ltd, London
Printed and bound in Great Britain
by Cox & Wyman Ltd, Reading, Berks

One

The breakfast bell was still ringing as the women, in their drab prison uniforms, shuffled miserably towards the dining room.

'Move it, Smith.'

Officer Vera Bennett's voice grated on Bea's ears; how much longer could she take waking up to the sound of that cold, hateful voice? She said as much, as she ambled alongside her cell mate, Ros Coulter.

Ros gave her a cheeky grin.

'Look on the bright side. You've got another ten years to go Bea. Someone's sure to have bumped off old Vinegar Tits by then.'

'Ten years!' For a moment, the character the other prisoners called Queen Bea, she of the quick wisecrack and the fearless swagger, disappeared. In her place, a woman of forty who'd murdered twice, lost her only daughter Debbie to drugs (what could she do about it from behind bars?) and now looked down the barrel of another decade in Wentworth Detention Centre.

But it was only for a moment. Big Margot Gaffney was always on the watch, waiting for Bea to show some sign of weakness, so that she could muscle in and take over as Top Dog.

Bea sized up the weary group ahead of her. Cavelli, whingeing about the food before they even got to the dining room. Stokes, who somehow always managed to look even grubbier after the morning shower, and Chrissie Latham, poor little bugger; six months gone and God all to look forward to. Even if she made it to full term – pretty unlikely the way they still had her pushing those weighty laundry trolleys around – what then? A year with her kid, maybe, then they'd snatch it off her and stick it in a home and that'd be the last she'd see of it.

Then she noticed the kid up front.

'Who's the new chum, Vera?'

Officer Bennett slid thin lips over sharp, pointed teeth, the nearest she would ever manage to a smile.

'Someone I'm sure you'll enjoy meeting, Smith'.

Ros shot Bea a warning look.

'She's baiting you, Bea. Watch it!'

'Take more than that sour old bitch to get me stirred up on an empty stomach.'

But Bea was watchful as they were herded into the dining room to join the noisy line of prisoners already queuing up for their food. There was something extra smug about Vera Bennett as she led the new kid to the head of the queue. The women turned as one to Bea. No one jumps queue in stir, so what is she going to do about it?

'She takes her bloody turn, Vera. There's others been here since the gong.'

Again the snakelike lips, more a sneer than a smile. 'Thank you for reminding me, Smith.'

The women quieted at once. A sense of tension, just the way Vera wanted them to feel.

'This is Sharon Gilmour. She missed out on food last

night. I'm sure just this once, you won't mind her getting preferential treatment.'

Aware of the others waiting for a lead, Bea swaggered up to the new girl to join her at the head of the line.

'Don't know that we're doing you a favour, Sharon. This bloody swill will turn your stomach anyway.'

The girl shot a nervous look at the other women.

'I can take my turn.'

'That's OK. But I'd better stick with you; catch you when you keel over.'

A grumble from the women, but mostly good-natured. Trust old smart-arse Bea to jump the queue under the pretence of helping a mate out.

'Get yourself a plate, Gilmour.'

Sharon glanced questioningly at Bea as Officer Bennett moved back to the door, apparently no longer interested in proceedings.

'Here.' Bea thrust a bowl into the girl's hands. Poor kid, she looked terrified. What would she be? Eighteen? Nineteen at most.

'Thanks.'

Sharon smiled a mixture of relief and gratitude. Maybe this tough woman could be her friend? Obviously she was the leader and that had to mean some kind of protection.

And she'd need it for sure.

'Won't be a sec, Bea. Gotta get more hot milk.'

Phyllis scurried off with the empty steel milk container.

Bea smiled at Sharon.

'Not exactly the Hilton when it comes to service.'

'You can bloody say that again. Wonder we're not

all dead from malnutrition with bloody Phyllis dishing out the grub.'

'Reckon you could live off your fat for six months without noticing, Margot.'

Bea turned her back on the grumbling line as Phyllis came back with a new supply of steaming hot milk.

'What are you in for, Sharon?'

'I'm on remand. Ten days.'

Bea was faintly amused at the naive answer.

'Yeah, but what are you charged with?'

Sharon hesitated, darting a rather anxious glance in Officer Bennett's direction. But Vera, it seemed, was engrossed in conversation with another officer.

'I got busted for drugs.'

She was instantly aware of the quiet in the room. But why? People got busted for drugs all the time, didn't they?

There was a new edge to Bea's voice.

'Pushing or using?'

Sharon forced a small laugh.

'Using? Do I look that dumb?'

'No love, you don't.'

There was no mistaking the steel that had come into Bea's voice.

'You look quite bright, actually.'

Sharon almost screamed in fright at the suddenness with which Bea slammed her plate down on to the hard, metallic counter, the noise ringing in her ears, and the threatening expression on Bea's face, now frighteningly close to hers.

'And it's bright bastards like you who get innocent, stupid little kids hooked!'

Bea waved her arm angrily as she spat out the words.

Sharon only saw the arm swinging towards her, and panicked. She picked up the bowl of steaming milk and cereal which Phyllis had doled out for her and threw it in Bea's face, with all her force.

A sharp scream, as Bea reeled back, clutching at her face, and pandemonium broke out among the women. Sharon, reading the ferocity in the faces all around her, grabbed a heavy metal tray from the counter, ready to protect herself! For sure, Vera Bennett wasn't going to do it. 'Hold that bitch!' Bea's voice was almost a scream as, writhing in pain, she made a lunge at Sharon.

'Back to your places, all of you.'

Officer Bennett was almost smiling as she stepped quickly between Bea and the terrified Sharon. Things had gone just the way she'd hoped.

'Put that tray down Gilmour.'

She turned a disdainful glance in Bea's direction.

'Officer Barry, take Smith to the Examination Room and get those burns treated. Gilmour, the Governor will want to talk to you.'

'She started it!'

Some of Sharon's bravado had returned now Bea was safely in the care of Joan Barry. But there was no mistaking the feelings of the other women.

'We'll get you, you little bitch.' It was a snarl from Big Margot.

'I'm on remand. I won't be staying.' Sharon searched Vera Bennett's face for confirmation. There was none.

'Get moving, Gilmour.' Vera's face was expressionless as she marched Sharon to the door.

Still clutching her burning face, Bea turned and gave the nod to the other women.

'She'll keep, girls.' There was a general murmur of assent as Officer Barry walked Bea out of the dining room.

It was Margot who broke the silence.

'They ought to stick that rotten little slut in solitary and throw away the key.'

Phyllis, mopping up the mess on the floor, shook her head miserably.

'Yeah, but bet your life, it'll be Bea who cops it. Old Vinegar Tits'll make sure of that.'

In the Governor's office, Vera was certainly doing her best to achieve just that end.

'I'm sure Smith started the whole thing. You know how aggressive she always is. She ought to spend a few days in solitary.'

Erica Davidson looked at Vera with a patience she did not feel.

'Thank you for your advice, Miss Bennett. I'll make my own decisions. And as for you Gilmour, you've been in Wentworth less than twenty-four hours and already you're in trouble.'

Sharon, unsure how to handle the composed woman confronting her across the desk, reverted to the 'little girl lost' routine that had worked so well for her on many occasions.

'She threatened me, Mrs Davidson. I had to defend myself.'

Erica's clear blue eyes reflected the dislike she instinctively felt for such a blatantly insincere performance.

'You are on remand, Gilmour. Therefore you do not

have to work with the other women. I shall also arrange for you to have your meals separately.

Sharon reacted angrily. Who did this upstart of a Governor think she was anyhow?

'Why don't you just lock me up in my cell, on bread and water?'

Erica's voice was icy smooth as she replied.

'That can be arranged.'

There was no mistaking the authority in those words and Sharon realized too late she'd been a fool to show her hand so quickly. She lowered her eyes and there was no hint of arrogance when she spoke this time.

'Can I have a visitor, from outside I mean?'

Vera's lips tightened. No doubt the Governor would allow it. She ran the place as though it was a holiday camp, not a prison.

'Anyone in particular?'

Vera couldn't restrain herself any longer.

'Surely, after what's just happened . . . ?'

She let the words hang but her tone was clearly disapproving. Erica emitted a small sigh; Bennett was an efficient officer but she could hardly be said to have the women's welfare at heart.

'Well, Gilmour?'

'My sister, Judy Bryant.'

Erica pushed a pad and pencil across the desk.

'Write down her name and phone number.'

Sharon hastily did as she was told. Jude would soon get her out of this hell hole.

'And meantime, Gilmour, stay out of Smith's way.'

Erica reached across and retrieved the pad and pencil.

'That will be all, Miss Bennett.'

Vera's lips were a hard, thin line as she opened the door of the Governor's office and bundled Sharon hastily outside. She didn't quite slam the door, but at her desk Erica noted, with a wry smile, the disapproval inherent in that firmly closed door.

'How's the face, Bea?'

Officer Meg Jackson stepped into the cell and cast a sympathetic glance at Bea's inflamed cheeks.

'I'll never make Playboy now, Mrs J.'

Meg gave a small chuckle. She probably knew more about Bea Smith than anyone in the prison. Tough, gutsy, aggressive, but under the dry wit and the raunchy exterior, there was a loyal and caring woman who'd helped out many a friend over the years.

Certainly, Bea's kind of justice wasn't played by the book, but when the chips were down, it was pretty good to have her on your side. And Meg knew from long experience that while it didn't always pay to stick your neck out for the prisoners, you got a lot more co-operation from the soft sell than you ever would from Vera's dictatorial approach.

'I reckon Vera set the whole thing up.'

Meg tut-tutted, but they both knew it was just a formality.

'I can't discuss a fellow officer. But you know, Bea, things could be a lot easier for you in here.'

Bea cracked a smile, but it didn't last. Her face was killing her.

'You wouldn't be offering me a deal, would you, Mrs J.?'

Meg laughed.

'You're an intelligent woman, Bea. A born leader.

12

The other women respect you. If only you'd stay out of trouble.'

'You know how I feel about drug pushers. They got my kid.'

'I know.' Meg had heard the story many times and it never failed to bring back memories of her own son, Marty.

'But it's the law's job to deal with the likes of Sharon Gilmour, not you.'

Bea nodded but Meg knew from of old that she hadn't really made any ground on that score.

'Got any more new girls?'

Meg nodded, a small frown creasing her brow.

'Bit of an odd couple, mother and daughter. I can't quite make them out.'

'How come?'

'Well,' Meg was searching for words. 'The mother's quite a frail little thing. And the daughter, Caroline; you just can't imagine someone like her ending up in here.'

'Sometimes the classy ones are the real dark horses. What's she up for? Murder her old man?'

Meg met Bea's amused glance steadily. 'As a matter of fact, yes.'

If Meg was finding Caroline Simpson puzzling, the prison social worker, Paul Reid, was even more baffled. He hadn't pressed her mother, Vivienne Williams, with too many questions. The older woman was obviously unwell and still in shock over the whole business. But Caroline – why was she so tense? So unwilling to say anything in her own or her mother's defence? The gutter press had branded them as accomplices who'd

13

killed a stalwart husband and father to get at his insurance money. It didn't make sense.

He had expressed his thoughts to the Deputy Governor, Jim Fletcher. Jim was a firm officer, but there was a compassionate side – not quite in the same category as the warm hearted Meg Jackson, but he certainly sought to give the women a fair hearing and an unbiased judgement. Maybe Jim would be able to make a bit more progress.

But after Jim had released Caroline from solitary, where they'd put her after admission, and managed to persuade the Governor to let her mother spend at least another day in the infirmary, he too seemed to find himself beating his head against a brick wall.

If these two women had killed for the money, why hadn't they gone about it differently? They'd just sat there and literally waited to be picked up by the police. Real criminals would have planned the crime with cold-blooded logic. They were covering up, the pair of them, but what? Was Caroline trying to take the rap for her mother? Then why let both of them be incriminated?

He tried to tell himself he was just taking a professional interest. But was he? Caroline was a dammed attractive woman and she had the one quality you rarely saw in Wentworth – class. As a married man, he shouldn't even be admitting the instant attraction he'd experienced when he first laid eyes on her. He didn't kid himself there was anything left in his marriage but the two little boys. Leila had made it clear long ago she was simply sticking it out for the kids.

But it was breaking every rule in the book to even think about associating with a prisoner. Still, these women needed help. And it was part of his job to see that they accepted all possible help both from Reid, the social worker, and legally.

At least they had each other, for the moment. That would put paid to any revolting lesbian advances a woman like Caroline was sure to receive in a place like Wentworth. Thank God!

Jim admitted to himself that he'd never come to terms with that kind of relationship. It revolted him. And if one of those predatory dykes so much as got near to Caroline Simpson, they'd find out just how tough Jim Fletcher could be.

Caroline's thoughts were running in much the same direction as she sat on her bunk, staring at the cold grey walls of the cell she'd been assigned to. While her mother was in the infirmary she felt doubly vulnerable in this ghastly place.

God, what a mess it all was. Her marriage to Michael in tatters, her father dead, and now the two of them flung into this terrifying institution with very little hope of ever getting out of it. Vivienne would never make public the fact that her husband was a violent man who had abused her throughout their long and seemingly respectable marriage. 'A careless fall', she'd tell the doctor when she turned up with yet another suspect injury. Too proud, and now it was all too late.

'Penny for them.'

Caroline was brought back to the present with a shock. She gave a small shudder as she looked up into the shrewd blue eyes summing her up. The reaction was not lost on Bea.

'I look like the back of a bus at any time, but right now I'm carrying a couple of extra battle scars.'

Bea's hand touched her inflamed face fleetingly.

Caroline didn't want to talk to this tough-looking woman. She didn't want to be within a mile of her or any of the other creatures she'd laid eyes on. But an instinct that if she kept talking maybe nothing worse would happen prompted her to reply.

'Did you have an accident?'

'Yeah, something like that.' The blue eyes took on a steel glint.

'Rotten little bitch. But she'll get hers. It's an eye for an eye around this joint.'

Caroline tried hard to suppress another shudder when suddenly the air was rent by a shrill, hideous scream.

'My God! What's that?' Caroline was on her feet but Bea stayed immovable in the doorway, blocking her exit.

'Nothing to get excited about. Just someone learning a little lesson and getting a haircut at the same time.'

But even as Bea spoke, Margot came lumbering along the corridor, breathless and shaken. Bea frowned. 'What's up? Did you do the job?'

Margot nodded but it was clear something had gone very wrong with the plan to teach Sharon a lesson.

'We done Sharon over. But there was a struggle. I didn't see Chrissie. Gawd Bea, I reckon she's losing the baby!'

Two

'How long they gonna keep you in here, Bea?'

Phyllis couldn't keep the anxiety out of her voice as she set down the lunch tray from the food trolley.

'If the Governor has her way, could be for keeps.'

'It was Margot and the others who give Sharon the haircut.'

A small chuckle escaped Phyllis.

'Reckon you're the one who scored. They're in the pound.'

'You reckon wrong, Phyl.'

Bea looked around the sterile cell with distaste.

'You feel like you've got the plague or something, getting stuck here in the Isolation Block. Nothing to do, no bugger to talk to.' Bea glanced over her shoulder. At the end of the corridor she could see Meg Jackson talking to Officer Barfield.

She lowered her voice, anyway. You could never be sure old Vinegar Tits wouldn't jump out of the woodwork when you least expected it.

'So what's happened? Is Chrissie OK?'

'Yeah.' Phyllis automatically lowered her own voice too. 'They say she had a pretty rough time. But she's all right.'

'What about the baby?'

'Not so good.' Phyllis tried to choose her words carefully; no point in making Bea feel worse than she already did.

'Seems like it's got respi . . . respa . . . aw, something wrong with its lungs. Has to stay at the hospital till it gets stronger.'

'What are you holding back?'

Phyllis was quick to recognize the building aggro in Bea's voice.

'Nothing. It's just too little and too crook for Chrissie to bring it to Wentworth.'

'Bet she's upset. She's been living for the day when she'd have that kid here with her, in Maternity.'

'Yeah.'

A tight smile twisted Bea's lips.

'And when she gets back, she'll want my guts for garters.'

There was no point in denying it.

'She's called the kid Elizabeth, after Lizzie.'

Lizzie Birdsworth! Bea smiled at the thought. Old Lizzie would be thrilled when she got the news. Bea wondered fleetingly how her old mates Lizzie and Doreen were making out at the Halfway House. Pretty hard for those two leopards to change their spots! Doreen forever getting herself into scrapes and Lizzie with her lifetime love affair with the bottle! Well, it was to be hoped neither of them would wind up back in Wentworth . . .

Phyllis took a furtive look down the corridor.

'I'd better get back. I've still got to do the lunches for C Block.'

'Who's calling the shots while I'm stuck in here?'

Phyl was hoping that subject wouldn't come up, but it was never any good trying to stall with Queen Bea.

'That stinking little Gilmour tart. Got herself a load of pills from somewhere so most of the women are sucking up to her for all they're worth.'

Bea brought her fist down hard on the metal tray and food splattered all over the place.

'They've got to let me out of here! I've got to stop that bitch.'

Bea would have been even more concerned if she'd known that at that very moment, Sharon, supervised by Meg, was enjoying a visit from her 'sister' Judy and putting the word on her for a further supply of drugs.

'I've got to have the stuff, Jude. It's the only way I can keep those big dykes off my back.'

Judy shook her head. Would Sharon never wake up!

'Drugs got you in here, Sharon. Aren't you ever going to learn your lesson?'

'That's right, preach to me!'

Sharon put her hands to her cropped head.

'They did this to me. Three bloody great bitches came at me with a pair of scissors.'

A look of sheer horror crossed Judy's face.

'You mean the warders just let it happen?'

'They don't give a stuff about me. And neither do you.'

Judy looked at the young, rebellious face. Why did she care so for this selfish, headstrong girl? I've told myself a thousand times that she's a taker, a user . . . but the love is still there, and there's not a damned thing I can do about it.

'Honey, you'll be out of here in a few days. But you have to stay out of trouble till you go to court.'

'OK. If you won't help me I'll just have to find myself another "friend" – someone who'll protect me from the other freaks.'

She kept her eyes on Judy's face, secretly confident that this would push Jude over the brink.

'In return for a few favours, of course, and I guess I can manage that. Gets pretty lonely in here.'

Her confidence wasn't misplaced. Defeat was in Judy's eyes as she gave an almost imperceptible nod. Sharon moved closer and her voice was a whisper.

'Over there. Near the main entrance. See those shrubs? Aren't they pretty?'

Judy's eyes swept around the garden – a pleasant place if it wasn't for that towering steel fence and the guards at the gate, reminders that the women were just as imprisoned outside as they were locked away in their sterile cells.

'It's a hell of a risk.'

'If you don't love me enough . . .'

A defiant shrug that said it all. No drugs, no future.

'OK. I'll try for tomorrow.'

Judy reached out and stroked the ragged, cropped head.

'I'm sorry. No physical contact.'

Meg managed a small apologetic smile in Judy's direction.

'Sorry.'

'Time's up anyway, I'm afraid.'

Judy nodded and with a last wistful glance began to slowly walk away. Meg watched her, thoughtfully.

'I take it your sister hasn't been able to raise the bail money for you?'

'You don't earn a fortune driving a taxi.'

'Is that what she does?'

'Yeah.' Sharon fell into step alongside Meg.

This Jackson woman was just too goody-two-shoes to be true! But she'd flip if she knew the real story. Why not find out?

'She's not my sister. She's my lover.'

If she'd hoped to shock Meg, she was disappointed. Meg's expression was enigmatic.

'You prefer older women do you, Sharon?'

Bitch! She'd get back at her for that.

'Is that a come on, Mrs Jackson?'

To her annoyance, Meg laughed out aloud.

'No, Sharon, it's not. Try the Magistrate. Maybe you'll have better luck with him.'

Sharon gritted her teeth! She'd get even with this mealy-mouthed screw before much longer!

Lizzie Birdsworth was thinking along similar lines as she walked out of the prison reception area and into the grounds. That bitch Bennett, she had no right to refuse! What if Bea was in Isolation? No rules to say she couldn't have a visitor. Lizzie didn't spend twenty years inside without learning that!

'Hello Lizzie. How are things going on the outside?' Lizzie's scowl turned to a quick smile as she looked up to find Jim Fletcher beaming down at her. Good old Fletch the Letch, he'd always treated her pretty right.

'G'day Mr Fletcher. Came to see Bea but old Vinegar . . . er . . . Miss Bennett said no go.'

'Did she now?' Vera Bennett! Forever taking out her

own personal frustrations on the women! Sour bitch, no wonder she was a lonely spinster and the most unpopular officer at Wentworth. Well, Jim was Deputy Governor and he'd soon set Miss Bennett straight on this one.

'Wait here, Lizzie. I'll sort things out.'

'Thanks Mr Fletcher.'

Lizzie watched the tall, straight figure march purposefully towards reception. Easy to see Jim Fletcher had been an army man. Lizzie grinned to herself. If she wasn't pushing seventy-two she could go for him herself. She'd always liked 'em tall, dark and handsome.

Funny to be back at Wentworth, as a visitor. Gawd, she'd spent most of her life there and in the end it turned out she should never have been convicted, and a Governor's pardon thank you very much! Not to mention the Compo to come. Funny though, with all that good news, how Wentworth still felt like home.

She could hear the end-of-work bell ringing. The women'd be coming out for their daily airing now. Might see a few familiar faces. She screwed up her eyes, searching the faces as the women filed past. None of the old mob, although there was something about that pair that just passed her. She'd have to ask Bea, she'd know. Lizzie chuckled as she ambled towards reception. Bloody Bea! Bugger always knew everything, or thought she did!

But it was Lizzie who was doing all the talking when she and Bea settled down in the interview room, under the watchful but friendly eye of Officer Barry.

Barry had been around Lizzie too long not to be up to every trick in the trade the old girl might pull. As for Bea Smith, all right, she might be in for murder and she was a pretty tough cookie; but Joan Barry had found out long ago that, given a fair go, Smith could be a very co-operative prisoner, and, most of the time, a damned good influence on the other women. No drugs around Wentworth when Queen Bea was in charge. And personally, Barry had her reservations about the Governor's decision to isolate Smith.

Ironical, really. To look at the two of them, both so obviously delighted to see each other, they could be a couple of housewives taking the weight off their feet after a bout at the supermarket.

'Did you hear that, Mrs Barry? Our Doreen's got herself engaged. Kevin's his name, lovely young bloke.'

'I'm pleased to hear that, Lizzie.'

Bea couldn't resist stirring her old mate a little.

'You mean to say he didn't take fright when he clapped eyes on you?'

Lizzie's snort was very indignant.

'Thinks I'm Dor's Aunt *and* he's asked me to live with 'em when they get hitched. What do you think of that?'

'Great.' But there was a worried crease between Bea's eyes.

'Does he know Dor's done time?'

'She told him the lot. Well, he sort of found out, but it didn't make a scrap of difference. Mind you, I thought at first maybe he was after her money. I mean, he's just got this delivery van and an ordinary job.'

Bea exchanged a wry smile with Officer Barry.

'You're getting bloody protective in your old age, Lizzie.'

'Yeah'. But thank God Lizzie had been wrong.

23

When Kevin had found out Doreen's mother had left her the house, he'd even backed off a bit. Real independent that boy, and good as gold.

'I got it!' In her excitement Lizzie jumped to her feet.

'Got what?' Bea looked at her with mild surprise. Always hard to follow the old girl's chit chat . . . like trying to keep up with a grasshopper, the way she switched subjects.

'Them two women I saw in the garden just now. Thought I knew their faces, and I did. They come to the Halfway House once. I remember the old girl had a black eye. Seems the old man had been beating her up for years. They was both as jumpy as hell.'

Bea held up a hand to slow the conversation down a bit.

'Slow down, Lizzie. What two women?'

'Dunno that I can remember their names. Mother and daughter, real silvertails they was.'

A thoughtful expression had come over Bea's face.

'One of them by the name of Simpson?'

Lizzie screwed her face up in an effort to concentrate.

'Couldn't be sure. But yeah, I reckon it might have been.'

Joan Barry stepped forward. She never enjoyed doing this to the women.

'Sorry Lizzie. Time's up.'

'Aw.' Lizzie turned appealing eyes on her. 'I haven't told her half the news yet.'

Bea got up from her chair, resigned.

'Write to me. It'll help to pass the time in Isolation.'

24

'Aren't you still doing that craft work? You know, making moccasins and all that?'

'If I see another slipper I may just throw up.'

That wasn't quite the reaction Vera Bennett had when she visited the women to collect the craft work for the week. By the time practically every prisoner in H block had failed to return one item of finished work, she was white with fury.

That'd show that wet-behind-the-ears social worker, Paul Reid, what these women were really like! If he knew the number of projects that had been started in Wentworth over the years, maybe he'd realize it was a lost cause and a waste of Government money. Hard work and doing it by the book, that's all that scum really understood.

She said as much to Jim Fletcher. But he knew she was still fuming because he'd overruled her and let Smith have her visitor. Let her find someone else to wrangle with. Besides, his thoughts were occupied elsewhere.

Birdsworth was a bit vague most of the time, but she was still an observant old girl. And if, as Smith had told him, Lizzie had seen Caroline and her mother at the Halfway House – well, it threw a whole new light on the matter.

But why had Smith told him? Well, she was a shrewd one. Not much got past her. He'd just have to hope none of the other women had noticed his special interest in Caroline Simpson – Vera Bennett in particular! Just the same, he had to find out the real story.

But there didn't seem much hope of that at first. She listened with obvious scepticism when he caught up

25

with her outside her cell. The police would hardly accept the evidence of a hardened ex-crim like Birdsworth.

'She wasn't the only one present. Surely it's worth a try.'

Caroline looked at him for a long moment.

'My mother's kept it to herself for years. It's too late.' She took a deep breath and there was something about the proud lift to her head that touched Jim's heart.

'It's true. My father was a violent man. I begged her many times to do something about it, or leave him. But there was always too much pride . . . for what that's worth now.'

'As things stand it'll be at least ten years inside for both of you. Do you think your mother could survive that?'

He knew he was hitting below the belt, but the thought of this sensitive woman even spending twenty-four hours in Wentworth caused a revulsion he'd never felt before, regarding any other prisoner. He ought to stop now, before he got in any deeper. Or was it already too late?

Caroline seemed to read his thoughts.

'Why is it important to you?'

'It's not.' He already knew that was a lie. 'I'm interested in seeing justice done. And I'm extremely worried about your mother's health.'

A beat, then.

'Are you married, Mr Fletcher?'

'Yes. Why do you ask?'

'Oh – just curious.'

The cynical note had crept back into her voice.

'Let's hope your marriage is a little more successful than mine's been.'

Was this the moment? To tell her the way things really were? No. He mustn't rush her. She'd lose even the faint thread of faith she seemed to have in him.

But it was hard to keep that controlled approach when her husband, Michael, made his official visit the next day and Jim had the misfortune to be the duty officer in the prison garden. How had this woman – attractive, intelligent, sensitive, married a man like that? There was such obvious weakness in the slack lips and almost colourless grey eyes. He might be wearing an expensive suit and trying to present himself as the successful man of business, but Jim had met too many of this type before.

The male prisons he'd worked in had more than their share of the white collar failures who blamed everyone but themselves for the mess they were in, and spent their lives convinced the world owed them a living.

Ironical that it should be Caroline behind bars, and this lily-livered creature on the outside, masquerading as a useful member of society. And Michael's words were certainly not doing anything to change Jim's opinion.

'Why can't we talk in private?'

Caroline glanced fleetingly at Jim, just a hint of apology in the expression, and Jim was well aware that her husband had noticed and resented the interchange.

'I'm just doing my job, Mr Simpson. I don't particularly enjoy this type of eavesdropping.'

'No?'

The colour rose in Caroline's cheeks as Michael

turned his back deliberately on Jim, raising his voice at the same time.

'Only the lowest form of life would do a job like that.'

Jim knew he was deliberately baiting him but he tried to keep his voice even.

'Do you want to talk to your wife or not, Mr Simpson?'

It was Caroline who rushed in, breathlessly, to stave off the difficult moment.

'You've already refused to testify for me, Michael. Why are you here?'

'I've changed my mind.'

Caroline looked at him for a long moment. What had she ever seen in this man? If she'd thought he'd be a good provider she'd been sadly mistaken. The endless rows they'd had over money! P'raps it was true, that accusation he'd so often made. She'd been desperate to get away from her father and the ugly endless scene that was her mother's marriage. She was to blame too.

Instinctively her eyes flew to Jim Fletcher. She'd been trying to fight the attraction she felt for him. But looking at him – so much a man, such a burning contrast to the weak man who called himself her husband . . .

'So that's the way it is.'

Michael's sneering voice tumbled her back to the reality of the moment. His lips were close to her ear now.

'You think if you suck up to an officer you'll get special treatment, is that it? Well, there's a price, believe me! He's got the key to your cell and he'll use

28

you and dump you like I bet he's done to hundreds of women like you!'

Something chill seemed to touch her heart at those words. Was it true? Had Jim Fletcher just been softening her up? Was it just a routine he'd used on plenty of other unsuspecting prisoners? Whatever might be the truth, one thing was certain – she wanted no more to do with Michael, inside or out of the prison.

'I'd like to go in, Mr Fletcher, please.'

It was impossible for Jim to keep the concern from his face. What had that creep been whispering into Caroline's ear to distress her so?'

'As you wish, Simpson.'

'Oh yes, all you have to do is say the word, Caroline, and he'll come running, and you'll be a sitting duck.'

Before Jim's anger could explode, Caroline had hurried off towards the main building and Jim, with one last disgusted glance at Michael, was obliged to follow her.

Neither of them saw the look of sheer hatred that passed over Michael's face. If they had, they would have realized that this was a man obsessed. If he couldn't have Caroline for himself, he'd make sure, by fair means or foul, no other man could!

Three

'MacNally's been brutally beaten up and Edwards nearly died from an overdose. I'd say that's a fairly serious situation.' The atmosphere in the Governor's office was tense to say the least. And Erica, Meg, Jim and the other officers, hurriedly called to an emergency meeting, had to acknowledge the truth of Vera Bennett's words.

Nevertheless, Erica's voice took on an icy edge as she turned towards Vera.

'I'm aware of the gravity of the situation, Miss Bennett. That is why I called this meeting.'

'I'm inclined to agree with Meg. The drug problem's only come up again since Smith got sent to Isolation.' Jim addressed the words to the Governor but his gaze was on Vera. He knew what her reaction would be even before she spoke.

'The officers run the prison, Mr Fletcher, not a convicted murderer by the name of Smith.'

Erica passed a weary hand over her brow.

'We're all well aware of the rules and regulations. But I don't see that we have a lot of other options.'

Meg hesitated then chose her words carefully.

'I'm not by any means making an accusation, but it's certainly a coincidence that all the trouble started around the time Sharon Gilmour was admitted. And she *has* been charged with pushing.' Erica nodded briefly but her expression was still baffled.

'We've stepped up security. We've conducted a thorough search of the cells and the grounds and we've come up with nothing. So how on earth is the stuff getting inside?'

Jim shrugged, as puzzled as Erica.

'I guess that's the sixty-four-thousand dollar question.'

'And for my money, the only one who'll come up with the answer is Smith.'

There was silence after Meg had spoken. For the moment, even Vera was at a loss to find a better idea.

But pacing up and down her sterile cell in Isolation, Bea, in fact, was currently as baffled as Erica. Obviously, the Gilmour kid was handing the stuff out to the women – a sure way of getting them on her side and buying protection. But how the hell was she getting it inside?

Pat O'Connell, busy collecting Bea's breakfast dishes, couldn't throw much light on the situation either. Although she felt pretty sure that Chrissie Latham was in it up to her neck.

This was a mystery in itself. Chrissie had to keep her nose clean if they were going to let her make baby visits to the hospital. Pat gave a small grunt of disgust.

'Strikes me that Chrissie and Sharon are a lot more than just good friends. Can't keep their hands off each other. Don't reckon the second bunk gets used too often in their cell.'

Bea shook her head. That Chrissie. Just about the

most oversexed female she'd ever come across. Any port in a storm for that one, baby or no baby. But she was really sticking her neck out getting in with the Gilmour bitch.

'Keep your eyes open, Pat. We've got to work out a way to put that kid in solitary where she belongs.'

'I don't want any trouble, Bea. I got my kids to think about. If I was to lose their visits, I don't know what I'd do.'

'At this stage, I just want you to play along, let her think she's the Queen Bee. Try and get her to confide in you. Strikes me she's the sort that can't help bragging about her little exploits.'

'OK. Hey, did I tell you? We've lost our cell mate. They've transferred Ros to J block, reckon she'll get more chance to study there.'

Bea nodded absently. Nice enough kid, Ros, but she'd never been the company old Lizzie and Doreen were.

'One thing's for sure. They won't be moving Gilmour in to share with me, eh?'

A grin creased Pat's tired face. 'Not bloody likely. Gotta go, Bea. See you later.'

As Pat trundled her trolley down the corridor towards the security gates, Bea's face took on a thoughtful expression. Maybe it was time to talk to the Governor; make a deal?

In the prison grounds, Sharon was putting the word on Judy for a very different kind of deal. And Judy was not reacting in the way she'd hoped.

'I've stuck my neck out for the last time, Sharon. No more d . . .' Judy broke off quickly, very aware of

32

Officer Barfield strolling along just a short distance behind them.

'Come on, you'll be going up before the judge in a couple of days, then you'll be out of here.'

'I could be dead before then.'

Judy looked hard at the angry young face. But she mustn't give in this time. Sharon had to kick the racket, once and for all.

'You know how much I love you, honey. There's nothing I wouldn't do for you. But I won't let you destroy yourself.'

A burst of shrill, derisive laughter from Sharon brought a slight frown to Officer Barfield's face.

'That's just so noble, Jude! I mean, I'm really touched!'

Judy flushed with humiliation. 'Don't be like that.'

'I won't.' Sharon turned on her brightest smile. 'I won't be anything at all to you. Who needs you, you hulking old dyke? I've got Chrissie now. She's so pretty, with that soft, blonde hair and those big, sparkle-blue eyes. And her skin, it's so smooth . . .'

She never took her eyes from Judy's face, savouring the hurt and anger which she saw there.

'She was kind of depressed after they wouldn't let her bring the baby back here. I couldn't just stand by and see someone so sweet going through such a bad time. She's a great cell mate too. Really spoils me – makes my bed, knows just how I like my coffee; and she's got really loving ways, Jude.'

For a moment, Judy felt a wave of dizziness. Do you just fall over and die when someone breaks your heart? She shook her head to try and clear it.

'You really know how to hurt me, don't you?'

33

'I don't want to, truly.'

Sharon actually smiled as though her words of a moment ago meant nothing. 'But when you won't help me, Jude, I feel rejected and I just lash out. I don't really want to be that way.'

How can I go on and on, buying this little girl act, letting this kid wrap me round her little finger? How long's forever, I guess.

'OK.' Judy glanced apprehensively over her shoulder. Barfield was engrossed in conversation with another officer.

'But how?'

Sharon gestured briefly towards the main entrance.

'I like working in the garden, Jude. But do you know I think I like working in the kitchen garden best of all.'

Judy nodded, getting the message loud and clear.

'My friend Pat doesn't like it, but that's because she has to empty the rubbish every morning.' Then, suddenly, as if acting quite spontaneously, Sharon's hand darted out to touch the thick coil of hair which Judy wore pancake-style on the top of her head.

'You're losing your hairpin.'

Judy's hand had instinctively gone to her head and in the fleeting moment that their hand touched, she felt the sharp edge of the tiny spill of paper which Sharon was passing to her.

'What's going on Gilmour.'

Officer Barfield had hurried forward, catching the brief moment of physical contact.

'Sorry.' Judy clenched her fist, palming the note. 'I've got such a mane of hair. I'm always spraying the world with hairpins.' Barfield seemed satisfied and Judy decided to make her exit while the going was good.

'I've got to get back to work. Taxis don't make any money in the parking station. See ya, hon.'

'Bye Jude. I'll be counting the hours till I hear from you.' Sadly, Judy made her way towards the main building. She'd have to go through with it. She couldn't give Sharon up. And all that talk, just bravado. The kid needed her more than ever now. Or did she? Just who do you think is kidding who, Jude? She didn't know the answer to that one and she wasn't about to try and find it.

There was nothing of the little girl lost about Sharon as she resumed work in the prison laundry and told Chrissie and Pat, in hushed tones, that she'd have good news for them when they talked later. She'd have the rest of the women eating out of her hand after this little lot was dropped off. Passing the note had been a breeze.

As the end-of-work bell sounded, the three lingered behind briefly. Chrissie had done the pick-up from the garden last time, but there was no way she'd be able to convince the screws at this stage that she still needed walks in the fresh air to regain her strength. Anyone who'd been shoved back in the laundry to work was definitely not considered an invalid!

Sharon smiled smugly. The pills would be in a rusty beer can. Jude would toss it over the back fence really early tomorrow morning. When Pat took the rubbish out, she'd collect the can and – bingo! Back in business! Pat feigned an enthusiasm she didn't feel. She was secretly worried sick about her kids, but she had to know the scam so she could get word to Bea.

As it turned out, that little scheme nearly went off the rails. Lil went off sick and Barry tried to recruit

Pat for full-time kitchen duty. But it was Meg Jackson who intervened and persuaded Barry to make other arrangements so Pat could stay on meal trolley duty.

As an officer, she couldn't come right out and say that she felt sorry for Bea, but she did know there was a real friendship between Smith and Pat O'Connell, and anyone locked away in Isolation certainly needed the sight of a friendly face occasionally.

Meg said as much in the privacy of the staff room to Jim Fletcher. But it was plain his thoughts were taking a very different direction. Indeed, if Vera Bennett hadn't just signed off for the day Meg suspected she might have been witnessing a real bun fight.

'I'm just fed up with her endless innuendo.' Jim slammed his empty coffee cup back on the trolley.

'You have been taking a pretty keen interest in Caroline Simpson's problems.'

Jim gave an exasperated sigh. 'Don't you start, Meg.'

'You know the rules about officers associating with prisoners, Jim. And you also know the inmates have got us under the proverbial microscope every breathing second we're on duty.'

'I feel sorry for them. A woman like that shouldn't be in a place like Wentworth.'

Meg's eyebrows were raised in genuine surprise.

'The charge is murder.'

'I know.' Jim hesitated, then, 'There are extenuating circumstances.'

'Isn't that for the Court to decide.'

'Naturally.' He was trying to sound matter of fact but it was clear to Meg that Jim had got himself emotionally involved. 'But it's not a crime to lend a sympathetic ear. You of all people would agree with that.'

'I do.' Meg met his gaze squarely. 'But a lot of people, officers and prisoners, might mistake that compassion for something different.'

Jim remained very thoughtful after Meg had quietly left the room. He'd told Leila only last night that he was fed up with all the overtime the officers were being forced to work. But it wasn't strictly true.

When he was at the prison he had a hard time trying to keep his distance from Caroline. When he was home he spent his time worrying about her, agonizing over some way he could perhaps help her; and her mother of course.

He knew Leila already suspected some kind of involvement. He'd never been much good at hiding his feelings from her. And even though she was long past being jealous, it didn't help the home atmosphere and that was bad for the boys. There had to be some kind of solution. But what?

The Governor was putting much the same sort of question to Bea as she faced her across the desk. Strictly speaking, she wasn't sure she should have agreed to this *tête-à-tête* with Smith. But after the information that Bea had passed on to her, obviously something had to be done, and immediately.

'No names no pack drill, Mrs Davidson?'

It wasn't a statement but a question.

'Of course.' Erica managed a faint smile. 'I know the rules about lagging just as well as you do, Smith. It's one of the things that makes my job so difficult.'

'Then it's a bargain?'

Erica stood up, a diminutive figure in her elegantly tailored suit. But no one could underestimate the strength of character in the clear, blue eyes and the firm set of the mouth.

'I don't make bargains. I appreciate co-operation. Shall we leave it at that for the moment?'

'Sure.' But Bea could afford a small smile. You'd never get the Guv. admitting you had her over a barrel. And you'd never get her going back on her word either. Queen Bea would be back with the fold in no time flat!

Pat was out and scouring around the rubbish heap bright and early next morning, and sure enough the rusty beer can had been thrown over the fence as arranged. It took only a moment to palm the bulk of the pills inside, then she quickly tossed the can into a slightly more prominent position and scurried back into the prison kitchen.

A half-hour later, the prisoners were stunned to find the place in turmoil. Cells were turned topsy turvy, dogs patrolled every inch of the grounds and there was a sense of tension and urgency throughout the building.

As Jim and Meg made yet another fruitless cell search, Pat pushed her trolley slowly along the corridor. She'd passed the pills on safely to Bea – no worries there, and the screws would find out soon enough that they were wasting their time. Meantime, good old Bea was back from Isolation, slamming down the steam press in the laundry as if she'd never been away! That Gilmour kid had better watch her step!

'If Gilmour's been the problem, which I strongly suspect, she'll make a mistake sooner or later. Meantime, Latham's baby visits are to be suspended and Gilmour loses all privileges.'

Erica looked at Jim for confirmation.

'Not much else we can do for the moment. Apart from the few pills in the beer can, we haven't found a thing.' He frowned, a niggle at the back of his mind. 'Hardly worth the risk, throwing the can over I mean.'

'Well, our information was accurate. We're just going to have to be doubly vigilant.'

When Judy learned Sharon could no longer have visitors, a feeling of desperation came over her. A kind of premonition that this was the beginning of the end, that Sharon was slipping away from her. Well, Judy glanced down at the coin machine in the taxi. Only one thing for it, as they say back home in America – 'if you can't beat 'em, join 'em.' And that decided, she even managed a smile!

She was still smiling when she faced Meg in reception and was told her visit to Chrissie Latham was approved.

'But I get to be searched, yes?'

Meg nodded, finding the American accent and phraseology rather attractive. 'OK.' Judy plonked the coin machine on the counter in front of Meg. 'Want to start with me or this?'

'Officer Knox will take you behind the screen, Miss Bryant.'

Judy nodded, the smile still intact, as she moved towards the screen.

'I've always been fascinated by these things.'

Meg was idly sliding coins out from the ten cent slot as Jim passed through en route to the garden. He paused a moment, and then a sharp intake of breath as a soft plastic packet flew out from the slot.

'What on earth?' Meg looked at him with round eyes.

'Marijuana.'

'That's right. About four ounces.' Judy was smiling broadly at them, no trace of remorse in her voice.

Meg looked at her curiously. 'You knew it was there?'

A quick shrug. 'Just following orders. It's for Chrissie.' For a moment they could only stare at her in astonishment. She seemed to find this even more amusing.

'Shouldn't somebody call the cops?'

There was no smile on Chrissie Latham's face as she fronted Sharon.

'Your bloody cow of a girlfriend shopped me!'

'What are you talking about.'

Something very close to fear crept into Sharon's eyes as Chrissie told her the score. God, Jude must be pretty desperate to get herself nicked on a drug charge! Why the hell had she run off at the mouth about Chrissie and her baby blue eyes. They could both be bloody well in for it now. But she tried to keep her voice casual as she reassured Chrissie.

'Don't worry. I can handle Jude.'

Chrissie looked at her angrily.

'Yeah, well just don't handle me any more, right? Bad enough I lost my baby visits without the bloody great lesso mate of yours getting stuck into me.'

But it was a very benign Judy who confirmed to Meg she'd refused bail and had deliberately set herself up so she could be with Sharon. As Meg cynically remarked later to Jim, there was no accounting for tastes! She personally found the Bryant woman very pleasant and certainly much too intelligent for a stupid little chit like Sharon.

Jim looked at her in disbelief. 'How can you talk like that? The woman's a lesbian.'

Meg gave a dry chuckle. She was all too aware of Jim's sentiments on that subject. 'A sexual preference doesn't necessarily affect the mind, Jim.'

'Where's she been allocated?'

'You're not going to like it, but when Simpson and Williams get back from their hearing, they're going to find someone in the third bed.'

'Bryant? You can't do that! Not to Caro . . . those women.'

'The Governor's already done it.' Meg touched his arm gently. 'Jim, if Bryant thinks enough of Gilmour to get herself gaoled, Simpson and Williams have got nothing to worry about.'

But when Caroline and Vivienne returned to the prison in the late afternoon, still in shock at the enormity of the bail set for them – $5000 each – they treated this invasion of their privacy (if it could be called that) as yet another hurt and humiliation. And with no hope of raising bail, what was there to look forward to but more of the depressing same?

In the recreation room, Bea was feeling pretty depressed herself. She was glad to be back in the thick of things. But the Gilmour kid was still carrying on as though she owned the place and any time now the storm would break, and big Judy would be thumping the daylights out of Chrissie Latham. And Bea figured she owed Chrissie. Her baby was still on the critical list and, thanks to Gilmour, she wasn't even getting her visiting rights.

She said as much to Pat. Reluctantly, Pat confided that Bryant had already been heard saying that if Gilmour didn't steer clear of Latham there'd be all hell to pay. And any more trouble and Chrissie could kiss goodbye to ever seeing her kid again.

Bea was thoughtful for a moment. Lagging just wasn't her scene but there had to be a way and she did still have those pills stashed safely. She bent her head closer to Pat's.

'Reckon you could make a delivery on tomorrow's trolley rounds?'

She looked a bit dubious. 'I gotta stay clean, Bea.'

Bea nodded. She knew how much Pat worried about her kids outside.

'You just deliver. I do the rest.'

It was a very nervous Pat who pushed her trolley along the corridor next morning after the women had been summoned to their various assigned duties. She checked quickly as she rounded the corner and halted the trolley. All clear. She darted quickly into the two-bed cell. In the cupboard under the wash basin she found what she was looking for. A distinctive toilet bag with the name Sharon lovingly embroidered on it. In a flash, she'd planted the packet of pills, zipped the bag shut and replaced it. Nothing to it.

She turned quickly. Just her luck for old Vinegar Tits to appear! But it wasn't Vera standing in the doorway. It was big Judy Bryant; this was probably it!

'Looking for something?'

Pat's mouth was dry but she managed to keep her voice casual.

'Just checking for dirty linen.'

For a moment it seemed Judy was going to move in on her. Then to Pat's astonishment she simply turned and walked away. What was that all about? She must have seen Pat plant the stuff in Sharon's bag?

There was no time to think about it. Even as she hurried back to her trolley and started off down the corridor she could hear Bennett's voice loud and clear.

'Latham, Gilmour, follow me.'

Now what? But she wasn't going to hang around to find out. If Bea had done her part of the job, the search would be on and the farther away she was the better.

And the search really was on. Jim and Vera were leaving no stone unturned this time. They'd had the tip-off and this time they surely must nail Gilmour.

Chrissie and Sharon watched, horrified, as the two officers literally tore the place apart. And there it was. Jim, reaching into the cupboard, unzipping Sharon's toilet bag . . . and coming up with the plastic bag of pills.

'Don't know where they came from or how you managed to hide them before, Gilmour, but this time you've been caught red-handed.' Vera's lips were twisted into a particularly nasty smile. 'Anything to say?'

Sharon wanted to scream but she kept her voice under control.

'I don't know anything about them.'

Vera exchanged a quick glance with Jim. How many times had they heard that one?

43

'Something wrong here?'

Sharon turned sharply at the sound of Judy's voice.

'Mind your own business, Bryant.'

At the sight of Judy, something snapped inside Sharon.

'You did this, you rotten bitch!'

'That'll do, Gilmour.' Jim glanced at Vera. 'P'raps a stint in solitary will help to calm you down.'

'I want to see the Governor, I know my rights.'

Vera gave a dry laugh.

'I'm sure she's looking forward to seeing you.'

Sharon turned furiously on Judy.

'Smart, aren't you? They'll stick me in the bloody pound now so you've got yourself nicked for nothing, you stinkin' dumb dyke!'

But as Jim and Vera marched a defiant Sharon and an obviously bewildered Chrissie off to the Governor, there was a small smile on Judy's face. True, Sharon would be locked away. And that way no one, including Chrissie, could get to her either!

Four

'Caroline! You don't mean it!' Vivienne's words were an anguished wail.

'I'm sorry, mother. The terms were just not acceptable.'

Judy looked curiously at her two cell mates.

'I'd have thought anything was better for you than being stuck in here.'

Caroline turned on her sharply.

'My dear husband Michael agreed to bail us both out on condition that we went and lived with him. Believe me, Wentworth doesn't seem so bad with that as the alternative.'

'Bad news, huh?'

'Bad!' There was so much venom in that one word. 'He's a loathsome, snivelling little creep and I hope I never have to set eyes on him again.'

Vivienne reacted, shocked by Caroline's outburst, especially in the presence of a comparative stranger. Pride dies hard.

'Caroline. Please!'

'It's OK.' Judy smiled at the older woman, realizing her embarrassment. 'We all have to let off steam occasionally.'

'Speaking of which, Bryant, take this trolley load of linen to the laundry.'

Jim's voice took them all by surprise.

'I know my rights, Mr Fletcher. I don't have to work.'

Jim's mouth twisted in a wry smile.

'It hasn't taken you long to learn the ropes.'

'You get pretty wised up, driving a taxi.' Judy moved to the doorway. 'But since you've asked me so nicely I guess I'll oblige just this once.'

She gave a quick wink in Caroline's direction and moved off with the loaded laundry trolley.

'I heard your good news, about the bail.'

Jim had been surprised at how mixed his reaction had been, but he tried to keep his tone light.

'We're not accepting. Mr Simpson's terms were – too demanding.'

'I see.' Again, his feelings were in disarray. He couldn't bear to see her in here, but the thought of not seeing her at all was getting harder and harder to bear.

For a moment their eyes held. Then Jim turned abruptly away, Meg's words of warning ringing in his ears. But there must be a way. Caroline, locked up all night with that Bryant creature – it was too awful to even think about.

The fact that Judy was a lesbian was of little concern to Bea. But as she watched the big woman unloading the soiled sheets into the machines, her curiosity was aroused.

'Volunteered for work?'

Judy chuckled. 'Mr Fletcher asked me, ever so nicely.'

'You're a Yank.'

'Is that an offence?'

46

Bea shrugged. 'Just curious.'

'You know what that did to the cat.'

Bea could feel Bev, Lil and the other women watching, enjoying this little sparring match; wondering if Top Dog Bea would be able to handle this new challenge.

'I don't think Mr Fletcher likes me very much.'

Bea allowed herself a small grin. 'He's got big eyes for Caroline. Probably thinks you're some kind of threat.'

Judy looked amused. 'Seems a lot of people feel threatened.'

Bea could hear Bev's sharp intake of breath.

'Meaning?'

Judy leaned back against the driers, seemingly totally relaxed.

'Reckon someone thought Sharon was getting a bit too much influence, so they set her up to get her out of the way for a while.'

Bea met the direct gaze from the big, brown eyes without a flicker.

'I wouldn't know about that.'

Judy straightened and made her way leisurely towards the door.

'Funny; I thought you called the shots around here.'

Bea heard the faint snigger from the women. Was Queen Bea going to take that lying down? For answer, Bea slammed the steam press down with a force that made the others jump. Maybe that would answer the question – for the time being.

But if Judy seemed to be taking the situation in her stride, Erica Davidson had not given up by any means.

Chrissie Latham, with her future as a mother at stake, was the obvious key. But so far the Governor had made little headway.

'It amazes me that, because your baby daughter is out of sight, you've transferred all your "love" to someone like Sharon Gilmour.'

Chrissie looked puzzled. What was the Gov. getting at?

'Libby means more to me than Sharon, you know that.'

'Does she?' Erica gave the girl a long, shrewd glance. 'You seemed prepared to go to solitary for Sharon's sake. Would she do the same for you? Especially now her friend Judy is here.'

Chrissie frowned, trying to make sense of Erica's words.

'I don't want to take your visiting rights away from you Chrissie.'

Libby did mean everything. So what the hell . . .

'Judy got the stuff in, for Sharon to sell inside.'

Erica nodded but that didn't answer all the questions.

'But how come more drugs were found after the first search?'

'They were already here. I s'pose that Judy heavied someone into hiding them. She seems to like making trouble.'

'I see.' Erica stood up and gestured to Officer Knox.

'You've been very helpful, Chrissie.'

'Do I get my visits back?'

'I'll let you know.' But Erica's smile was reassuring and Chrissie determined that somehow she'd have to steer clear of Judy Bryant and stay out of trouble.

*

Chrissie might have been reassured if she'd heard what was going on between Bea and Judy at that moment, as they queued up for their midday meal in the dining room.

'I've been trying to get Sharon out of the drug racket for as long as I've known her. Maybe a little stint in solitary will do the trick.'

'I thought you were in it with her?' Bea still looked a bit unconvinced.

'I guess everyone does, including the Governor. But believe me, I feel the same way about it as you do.'

There was a ring of sincerity to the words and Bea was pretty sure she knew the truth when she heard it.

'Want to sit here?' She indicated the table where Pat was already seated.

Judy grinned, registering the concern in Pat's face as she unloaded her tray.

'Don't look so jumpy, Pat. I'm not the sort who goes around trying to buy a fight. Or make it to Top Dog.' The words were not lost on Bea. 'Just so long as they leave disciplining Sharon to me. OK?'

Bea nodded. That's the way the game was played, inside.

Bea glanced up as Vera Bennett moved from the doorway and started to make her way slowly towards their table.

'Just when I thought a meal might be edible for once, up pops old Vinegar Tits and everything goes sour.'

Judy followed her gaze and registered the unpleasant smile on Vera's face. Pat noticed too.

'Something rotten's happened to someone. Vera's practically smiling.'

There was an ominous silence as Vera stopped by their table.

'I'm surprised to see you've still got an appetite, Bryant.'

Judy looked up, questioningly.

'Why's that, Miss Bennett?'

'Your friend Gilmour's with the V.J. at this moment.'

Bea cocked a cheeky eyebrow in Vera's direction.

'Too bad he didn't ask you along, Vera. You're probably missing all the juicy bits.'

Vera's lips tightened but there was still the gleam of satisfaction in her pale eyes.

'I simply like to see justice done, Smith. Another week in solitary will no doubt help Gilmour to mend her errant ways.'

'A week!'

Judy was on her feet, stunned at the very thought. The poor kid would never survive it.

'That's just a guess.' The unpleasant smile was back. 'I'd say more likely two weeks minimum.'

The fury that was mirrored in Judy's face was frightening. Bea was on her feet in a moment, laying a restraining hand on Judy's arm.

'Take it easy, Jude.'

For a moment, time seemed to stand still, then Judy's right arm came thrashing out and her clenched fist struck Bea fair and square in the jaw.

'Gawd!'

Pat looked down in alarm at Bea's unconscious body sprawled on the floor.

'Barfield.' Vera's voice rang out sharply and Officer

50

Barfield hurried forward. 'Arrange for a stretcher. I'll deal with Bryant.'

She turned to Judy, quiet now, just breathing deeply and looking with something almost like regret at Bea's unconscious form.

'You'll get solitary for this.' Vera grabbed the unresisting Judy by the arm and marched her towards the door. And only she heard the gentle reply. 'Thank you.'

Unaware of the uproar in the dining room, Jim was making a routine cell check when Caroline came hurrying towards him. He could see at a glance how upset she was.

'What is it Caro . . . Simpson?'

She checked abruptly. Even in her short time inside the prison she knew better than to name names or talk too freely.

'I'm just going to check on my mother. I got permission for her to sit in the garden. She's not feeling well.'

'Something's upset you.'

'No. It's just . . .' She glanced along the corridor and something very like fear came into her eyes. 'This place . . . it's . . .'

'Step into your cell.'

Very gently he reached out and propelled her forward.

'Why won't you let anyone help you? You're frantic to get out of this place.'

She kept her voice controlled but he knew it was an effort.

'Our family has never accepted charity.'

'Stop being so bloody priggish! Can't you see what it's doing to your mother?'

For a moment she was too shocked by his words to answer. When she did it was strangely matter of fact.

'The second offer for bail, the anonymous offer?'

He met her gaze squarely.

'Well?'

'It was you, wasn't it?'

'Of course not!'

A touch of bitterness crept into her voice.

'Do you want me to come and live with you, like my husband does?'

He wasn't ashamed of the gentility he knew she could hear as he answered.

'I don't like to see a woman like you in a place like this. You don't belong.'

'So it was you.'

No good trying to go on denying it.

'Yes. But I can't be named – my job. We have to find a relative willing to be nominated.' He put a gentle hand on her shoulder.

'Caroline, at least accept for your mother.'

A moment of tension, then she was leaning against him, no longer able to hold back the sobs. His arm went around her instinctively.

'Just for my mother.'

'All right.' Footsteps sounded nearby and he hastily moved away from her. 'I'll speak to the social worker, Paul Reid, immediately. He'll make all the arrangements.'

'How can I ever repay you?'

His eyes were caressing as he looked down on her tear-stained face.

'You just did.'

'We're due at the Classification meeting, Mr Fletcher.'

He turned abruptly to see Meg waiting in the corridor.

'Right.'

Without another glance at Caroline, Jim joined Meg and fell into step beside her.

'Simpson looked upset.'

He was only too aware of Meg's curiosity, and concern.

'She'll be all right now. She's had good news. The bail has been put up for her mother. Mrs Williams will be going home.'

Meg received his words in silence but a worried frown clouded her brow. Jim was sticking his neck out for Caroline Simpson, and just how far could he go before the Governor caught up with him and his job was on the line?

The door clanged shut on Judy and looking around she knew why the women hated solitary so much. The barest essentials, a sterile cage, and that poor kid Sharon had already spent forty-eight hours in the filthy place. Quickly, she moved to the wall dividing the two solitary cells.

'Sharon. It's me honey.'

Silence. The walls were probably pretty thick.

'Sharon. It's Judy. Hey, kiddo, I'm your new neighbour.'

She tried to project the warmth and love she felt; if this didn't prove the depth of her feelings, what would? She smiled wryly – no one in their right mind would purposefully get put into the pound. It wouldn't be easy explaining to Bea later, but that would have to wait.

'Sharon. Listen. I have to explain. It was Pat who planted those pills on you. I let it happen and I didn't do her in because I wanted to get you away from that slut Chrissie Latham. Do you hear hon?'

'Yeah.' Sharon's voice was faint but there was no mistaking the loathing in it. 'I hear and I hate you, you big stupid cow.'

'Sharon . . .'

'Get lost.'

It was almost a scream of rage. Slowly Judy sank down on to the hard, narrow bunk. She'd just have to give her time, and, she thought ironically, right now she had lots of it!

'But *why* did she hit you, Bea?'

Pat wrung out the cold flannel and handed it to Bea as she lay on her bunk nursing a very sore jaw.

'I don't know. But when I bloody find out, she'll get hers believe you me.'

'They chucked her in solitary.'

Pat frowned, trying to figure something out.

'She didn't do it just to be near that bloody Gilmour kid, eh?'

'Who cares. She did it and she'll pay for it.'

Bea fingered her jaw carefully. 'She's got a mean right but at least she left my teeth intact.'

'Geez, Bea, what's up?'

At the sound of the familiar voice Bea sat bolt upright.

'Doreen! What the hell are you doing here?'

54

'That's a nice old welcome.'

But Pat was smiling broadly.

'Good to see you Dor.'

Bea shook her head then wished she hadn't – it didn't do a lot for her bruised jaw.

'OK. Spill it.'

Doreen sighed and plonked herself down on the bunk in which she'd slept so many times before.

'I had all this trouble with Kev's Mum, she's a real snob, Bea, and then Lizzie talked to her and fixed it and then we both felt so good we went out and had a few drinks and . . . we nicked a couple of bottles 'cos we were out of cash and then I run smack into these two cops . . . and that was it.'

'On probation and you go and nick a couple of measly bottles of booze.'

'It was Scotch, good stuff too.'

Bea and Pat exchanged rueful smiles. 'So where's Lizzie?'

'They let her off with a forty cents fine. That's all she had on her.'

'Oh Gawd.' Bea brought her fist down hard on the bed.

'You got yourself a job, a good bloke and you muck it all up.'

Doreen shyly held out her left hand.

'He give me a beaut ring too.' She looked down fondly at the modest diamond in its simple setting. 'Mrs D said I could keep it on. That was nice of her, wasn't it?'

'Yeah. Well,' Bea grinned across at Doreen. 'Nearly lights out. Better make yourself at home.'

Doreen looked around a touch wistfully.

'I'm real sorry I've messed things up, but you know, in a way, it's nice to be back.'

Bea looked at her old friend – plump and pretty and after all the time in stir still as naive as the day she was born! Dopey Dor – but it was good to see her again.

The end-of-work bell was ringing next day as Jim hurried towards Caroline as she moved out with the other women into the prison grounds for exercise.

'Simpson. Over here.'

He kept his voice formal, even terse, aware that Bea Smith and her cronies were keeping an interested eye on him.

Caroline smiled. 'Did you manage to get someone to call in on Mother? How is she?'

If only she hadn't smiled in just that way. It made it even harder to break the news.

'Paul Reid went to see her.' He glanced down tenderly into her upturned face. 'It's not good news. She's in hospital.'

'Oh no!' There was instant panic in her eyes. 'How bad?'

'It's early days . . .' It was no good trying to deceive her with those beautiful green eyes so intent on his face.

'She's pretty bad. She took an overdose.'

For a moment she was stricken to silence. Then . . . 'I must go to her.'

She turned as if she would run to the prison gates and he put out a hand quickly to stop her.

'Wait.' He could sense the women alerted to what was happening between them. 'I'll speak to the Governor, arrange a visit as quickly as possible. Trust me.'

56

She took a moment to steady.

'You know I do . . . Jim.'

He would have given anything to put his arms about her and comfort her. But as it was she read the compassion and much more in his eyes. She watched him walk away. How ironical to meet this man at this time, no future in it for either of them. But at least for the moment he was her one source of hope and comfort – and he'd made her feel a woman again.

Watching the action from nearby, Bea drew her own conclusions, confiding to Pat that Old Fletch the Letch looked like he'd got it pretty bad. Pat looked disapproving. Men, all the same. Grab all they can, lumber you with kids then dump you.

Bea listened, unsmiling, 'Tell me about it!'

As they started to make their way back towards the main building under the watchful eyes of the officers, Doreen came hurrying towards them.

'How did you go, Dor?' Pat looked anxiously at her. 'No go?'

'They give me another two weeks on top of the six months.' Doreen managed a smile. 'S'pose it could have been worse.'

'If he's worth a crumpet he'll wait for you.' Pat didn't believe her own words for a moment but hopefully Doreen would.

The bell for the evening meal was ringing as they neared the building. Suddenly, Bea stopped and Pat and Doreen saw what had caught her eye. Jim Fletcher emerging from reception with Caroline Simpson in tow.

'Reckon they're eloping?' Bea couldn't resist the crack.

'Her Mum's real crook, I heard them talking in

reception.' Doreen's face mirrored the sympathy she felt. 'Maybe the Gov.'s letting her visit.'

Bea gave a small, cynical smile.

'Maybe the Gov. would be having second thoughts if she knew Fletch the Letch was trying to get into Simpson's knickers.'

Pat chuckled. 'Reckon she'd screw a screw?'

Bea shrugged. 'Been a long time between drinks for her. But if she does give the green light, he'll be out on his ear and we'll be fronting up to a new Deputy Governor.'

Doreen frowned. 'But Mr Fletcher's got a wife and kids.' Bea shook her head; talk about the voice of innocence!

'Why should that make a difference?'

Doreen looked down at the diamond, sparkling on the third finger of her left hand. It ought to make a difference. Or was Kevin just like all the rest of them, after all?

Five

Doreen had always enjoyed working in the prison garden and she decided she liked big Judy Bryant. Beaut sense of humour and she seemed to really enjoy Doreen's company and her tales about the old days with Franky and Marilyn and Wonky Warner and all.

But as Judy walked across to her Doreen looked up in dismay.

'Whatever happened to your hair, Jude?'

The thick coil of shiny brown hair was dripping with watery sludge that ran down her cheeks and into her collar.

'Guess I used the wrong shampoo.' Judy's smile was enigmatic. OK, so Bea Smith had jumped her in the toilet block and given her a dunking in a bowl of filthy, disgusting water. She had something coming to her after she'd floored Bea to get into solitary. And a lot of good that had done her relationship with Sharon. Doreen gave her an old fashioned look.

'Come clean, Jude.'

Judy laughed and touched her wet head. 'Wish I could.'

She gave Doreen a friendly pat on the arm. 'Let's say a score's been evened and hopefully that's the end of it. OK?'

'OK.' Doreen smiled. 'I won't let the name Bea Smith so much as pass me lips.'

They enjoyed the joke together as they went back to work. Sharon, reluctantly carrying out garbage duty, was a witness to the by play. She was already fuming over Judy's obvious liking for Doreen Anderson. Much more and she'd have to do something about that bitch. Judy was her property.

The fact that Sharon had rejected all overtures of friendship with Judy during their solitary stint didn't count. Sharon expected to get what she wanted when she wanted it, no questions asked. Anyway, she was getting pretty fed up with on again, off again Chrissie Latham.

In the laundry, as Bea slammed the big steam press down with a bang, Chrissie's thoughts were a long way from Sharon. The Governor had just confirmed that she could have her baby, Elizabeth. As soon as they got hospital clearance, she and the baby would move into Maternity.

'You'd better steer clear of Gilmour, Chrissie. One more run-in and the Gov. might change her mind.' Bea gave Caroline a lewd wink, 'She might have blabbed to Narcotics but she still got two years, and you can bet your life Bryant'll stick with her like glue now she's pulled off a twelve-month sentence.'

'She's nothing to me.' A very tender expression flitted over Chrissie's young face, 'I just want my baby and no one and nothing else.'

'Well, you'd better get that trolley load of linen to the kitchen quick smart or Vinegar Tits'll be on your back.'

Chrissie nodded and disappeared with her load with alacrity.

Bea glanced towards the doorway. 'Keep an eye out, Pat. I've got a bit of news.' Bea fished out a cigarette and lit up. Seeing Queen Bea had declared official smoko, Bev and Lil did likewise.

'I've been talking to Reid, the social worker bloke. Told him we weren't interested in all that junk about our own radio station.'

Bev looked disgusted. 'Those bloody do-gooders sure come up with some screwball ideas.'

'Yeah.' Bea inhaled deeply, building up her little moment of triumph and authority. 'I told him we'd only go on with his craft stuff and making the toys *if* we get the cash from the sales.'

There was a general chorus of approval.

'Yeah, well, it won't be cash in hand.' A murmur of disapproval at that. 'It'll be chalked up along with our regular pay. *And*,' she looked around the interested faces with just a touch of smugness, 'told him we were fed up about security. He's working on the Gov. to leave the gates open.' The approval was very definite this time. 'So, keep your noses clean and don't blow it before we get it, OK?'

But even as she handed out this advice to the women, Judy Bryant was lying unconscious on the floor of her cell. A grim faced Vera was looking from a shaken Chrissie to a scared Sharon.

'Well Latham, you've really blown it this time. I don't think even the Governor would think you were a fit and proper mother if you go round bashing people over the head with chairs!'

'It wasn't like that!' Chrissie looked appealingly at Sharon.

The latter put on a bravado she didn't quite feel. 'I'll tell it how it happened, Chrissie, no worries.'

Vera smirked unpleasantly. 'Why don't we all go along together.'

Chrissie looked at the inert figure on the floor.

'What about her?'

Vera looked at the unconscious form with studied distaste.

'She's not going anywhere for the moment, is she?' It was at this moment that Meg Jackson rounded the corner.

'What's going on here?' She moved quickly into the cell, knelt beside Judy's body and quickly felt for a pulse. 'We must get her to the infirmary immediately.'

Chrissie's voice was a whisper 'Is she . . . ?'

Vera gave her a rough shove. 'Get moving, the pair of you.' Chrissie gave a last pleading look in Meg's direction. An almost imperceptible shake of the head; at least Judy wasn't dead! But her chances of having her baby most certainly were. God, if only she'd never laid eyes on Sharon Gilmour.

Both the Governor and Jim Fletcher were expressing much the same sentiments as they talked over the latest incident. Jim's mouth was grim. 'I imagine Bryant is rueing the day she decided to get herself into Wentworth to be with her "girlfriend".' He literally spat out the word. Erica sighed.

'Vera's convinced Chrissie Latham started it all. But doesn't it strike you as odd that, whenever Gilmour is involved in trouble, she is never to blame.'

Jim hesitated but fairness would always win through.

'I don't approve of the Bryant woman but she's the one we'll get the truth from. And I'd say ten to one she backs up Chrissie's version.'

'Why so strong in Latham's defence, Jim?'

His face softened a little. 'I saw the way she looked when you told her she could have the baby. You can't tell me that was an act, or that she'd willingly do anything to jeopardize that happening.'

'I'm inclined to agree.' Erica paused a moment then chose her words carefully.

'Caroline Simpson requested leave to see her mother again. I'm afraid I had to refuse.'

Jim knew he was on dangerous ground and tried to keep his face expressionless. 'That seems a bit hard. The mother's very ill.'

'She's been taken off the critical list.' Erica watched him closely. 'Rules are rules, and they're there for everyone's good.'

Jim looked up sharply. Erica's way of giving him the message – back off from Simpson.

'Too bad someone didn't bail her out as well as the mother.' It was more a question.

'I believe there's still a chance.' Jim kept it casual. 'Paul Reid's looking into it.'

It was much later in the day before Jim had a chance to talk to Caroline. She was moving down the corridor, returning from the dining room. Even the ugly prison uniform couldn't disguise the grace of her figure or conceal the shapely legs and finely turned ankles. God, he cared about this woman.

'I'm sorry you're not allowed to visit.'

'It's inhuman.' There was a tiny break in her voice.

'If you were out on bail you could see your mother as often as you liked.'

She nodded and took a deep breath. 'If I'd listened to you my mother would be all right now. If the offer still stands . . .'

He wanted desperately to put his arms around her but instead he said simply, 'it does.'

'Thank you Jim.'

For a moment they stood looking into each other's eyes.

Her voice was very gentle.

'The wrong time and the wrong place for us.'

He nodded; then, a question. 'I'd like to see you – outside of here.'

'It won't get you into trouble?'

He smiled down at her. 'Some things are worth the risk.'

After all the heart searching and hesitation, Caroline couldn't believe how quickly things happened. She was disappointed she would not be allowed to go home but Reid's suggestion of the Halfway House was a small price to pay for freedom. As she walked towards the main gate with a silent Jim at her side, she took a last, long look at the bleak line of buildings and a small shudder ran through her.

'What is it.'

Jim had sensed her moment of panic.

'There's still the charge of manslaughter. If I'm sentenced . . .'

Instinctively his hand went out toward her, but aware of the guard he quickly withdrew it.

64

'Take one day at a time. And if you need anything, you know where to find me.'

She nodded and as the moment of parting arrived, she leaned towards him and kissed him lightly on the cheek.

'Thank you.'

An emotional moment and Jim could only just handle it.

'Just don't say goodbye.'

She smiled rather mistily, turned and was gone. He was relieved to note that the gate guard seemed totally uninterested. And a little shaken to realize just how much that light, fleeting kiss had meant to him.

Jim was further shocked the following morning when Erica called him into her office and told him about the anonymous phone call she'd received.

It seemed he'd been seen visiting the Halfway House on the previous night. Jim admitted he had called on Caroline Simpson to ensure she'd settled in and, indeed, was there, honouring her bail. Erica accepted his explanation but he was left in no doubt as to just how disapproving she was on the subject. And when Meg suggested that the only way they'd keep Gilmour out of trouble was to let Bryant share her cell, he didn't have the heart to rise to the bait as he would normally have done. Erica was a bit reluctant but since Bryant had told her the true story of her bashing she could see little alternative.

If Gilmour was so jealous that she would threaten to beat up someone as naive as Doreen Anderson – and according to Bryant that was what had happened – there seemed no other answer. Erica had been amazed that Doreen could be involved at all. But as Meg had pointed out, once someone like Bryant had been fingered as a 'dyke' then even the simplest overtures of friendship were completely misunderstood.

Bea was going through rather different overtures at that moment. The idea of a theatre group had been muted before but this time old Reid had taken the bull by the horns and got the show, literally, on the road. Ken Pearce was the guy nominated to knock them into shape.

Bea looked at the neatly dressed man sitting opposite her. The getup didn't fool her. That face, attractive as it was, had seen a lot of action. He seemed to read her thoughts.

'Robbery with Violence.' He grinned. 'Did my full stretch, too.'

Bea gave a cheeky grin. 'Takes one to know one.'

'What do you say? Going to give the theatre thing a go?'

Bea shrugged. 'The women aren't that keen.'

'Bet you could get them going.'

She gave him a measuring glance. 'Got a lot of people going in my time.'

'Who's surprised.' He was really giving her the once over and to Bea's surprise (she'd long ago labelled herself as 'forty, fat and finished') he obviously liked what he saw. Well, she wouldn't rush her fences, but the truth was, she liked what she saw – a lot.

'Fancy old Reid letting us have a *tête-à-tête* like this in his office.'

A chuckle from Ken. 'Maybe he thought an armed

robber and a lady in for two-time murder would have a bit in common.'

Bea raised an eyebrow. 'Checked me out, did you?'

'I like to deal with number one.' He was sucking up to her of course, but she didn't mind.

'OK. I'll let the women read this stuff first. But I reckon we can do business.'

There was a very definite message in his final words.

'We're gonna make a good team, you and I.'

There was a new spring in Bea's step when she joined Doreen, Pat and the others in the dining room later. Plenty of teasing too. But it was good natured. Hell, if a woman got a chance for a bit of hanky panky or even a mild spot of flirtation with a bloke in this place, good luck to her. And as Doreen innocently pointed out, Bea wasn't really over the hill – yet.

Bea made a playful slap in her direction and instantly noticed.

'Where's your ring, Dor?'

'I give it to Lizzie to give back to Kev.'

Bea was exasperated. 'You silly bitch.'

Doreen shook her head. 'He's too good for me. And I'd probably only mess things up again when I did get out.'

She could see that Bea was angry with her, so hastened to change the subject.

'Eh Bea, Lizzie passed on a bit of dirt.'

Pat sniggered. 'She probably made it up.'

'No.' Doreen leaned closer to Bea. 'Fletch the Letch has been calling on Caroline at the Halfway and Lizzie seen 'em, out of her window, kissing goodnight.'

'Jeez, he's really asking for it!' Bea shook her head.

67

A screw was a screw, but Fletcher wasn't a bad guy. They could do a hell of a lot worse.

Pat shrugged. 'Told you, they're all the same.'

Bea gave Pat a hard glance. 'Something's been bugging you all day. Out with it.'

Pat sighed, fed up with the endless miseries that seemed to be bugging her. 'That Reid fellow's been at me to appeal, reckons I might get something off me two years.'

'Worth a try.' Doreen looked at Bea questioningly.

But Pat was matter of fact. 'They already said I've got about a one in a hundred chance. I don't want to go through that again.'

'That's not all, is it?' Bea had known Pat for too long.

'Me boy, Andrew, he's run away from home.'

'Gee, I'm sorry.' These were the really tough moments, the moments when they all knew they were prisoners, and someone else was in control of their lives.

Jim Fletcher was feeling in something of the same boat. He'd had a blinding row with his wife, Leila, when he got home. She'd had an interesting phone call, from Caroline's husband. She'd been filled in on his every move and the state of his bank balance. In vain he had tried to explain, to reassure that the bail money would be put back, but no. Leila really laid it on the line. She'd known for a long time that he was only hanging in there for the kids. She could handle the lack of interest, the endless double shifts, let alone risks, that his job involved both him and his family in. But another woman! No thank you. And a gaol bird at that. He could pack his bags and get out!

He looked around the seedy hotel room. Just the bare necessities but he couldn't afford any better. God, he never thought he'd wind up in a dump like this. But even as he rose wearily to unpack the few bits and pieces he'd hastily shoved into his suitcase, he knew there was no going back. That bloody swine, Michael Simpson. If he could just get his hands on him!

But that wasn't the way. Somehow, he had to hold on to Caroline, and his job and his boys. Right now, he didn't know how. But at the thought of Caroline and the absolute trust he'd seen in her eyes he felt a new determination. What had she said? 'The wrong time and the wrong place for us.' And that had told him all he wanted to know. She felt the way he did. And somehow, they'd work it out together.

Six

Lizzie Birdsworth's elation at getting herself back into Wentworth was short-lived, when Vera locked her firmly into a single cell with no chance to even say hello to her old mates, specially Bea and Doreen.

But Meg couldn't conceal her amusement when Erica confided the charge to her. It seemed that Lizzie had gone on a rampage of shop-lifting, even to walking off with a mink coat, in her efforts to escape the loneliness of the Halfway House, once Doreen had been arrested.

So, when it looked as though she'd get off, she'd sneaked into the Magistrate's rooms at the Court, snaffled the precious memoirs he'd told Erica and Lizzie he'd just finished writing (after a considerable number of years of effort), and stuffed them down the lavatory. He'd been very sympathetic to the old girl prior to this and it had been plain to Lizzie that she'd have to do something desperate. Well, she'd pulled it off. The old bloke had been beside himself with rage and very happy to tag Lizzie as a public nuisance who belonged inside!

Erica was disappointed that Birdsworth's rehabilitation had failed. But Vera was in complete agreement with the Magistrate and had enjoyed a certain sense of satisfaction as she locked the old girl in.

As she confided to Meg, these women were criminals and Wentworth was not a holiday camp. Meg listened in silence, she'd heard Vera's sentiments on the subject too many times over the years they'd worked together.

'And O'Connell, wanting to make a phone call at this hour of the night!' Vera snorted at the very idea.

'She's worried about her kids, Vera. The boy's run away. It's natural she'd want to speak to her daughter and at least assure herself that she's OK.'

Vera was tight lipped. 'She can do it at the proper time through the proper channels.' She hesitated, but curiosity got the better of her.

'You were looking a bit grim when I came in. Was the phone call bad news?'

'You could say that.' There was no trace of a smile on Meg's face now.

'It was Geoff Butler.'

'That animal.'

Meg nodded. 'Trying to assure me he'd mended his ways and would I care to go out to dinner with him.'

'My God! The nerve! After the way he beat you up!' Vera was visibly bristling. 'His type don't change their spots!'

'I'm well aware of that.' Meg frowned. 'But I'm a bit uneasy to hear that all the charges against him have been dropped except for the attack on me.'

'You've got Jim Fletcher as a witness.'

'I know. But I still dread the thought of having to appear in court.'

Meg would have been more disturbed if she'd known

that at that moment Geoff Butler was calling on Leila Fletcher, trying to track his old 'mate' Jim down.

Leila was experiencing the same apprehension. There was an air of suppressed violence about Butler and she was quick to sense he wasn't looking Jim up as an old army mate from Vietnam. He'd have an ulterior motive for sure, and, even as she thought it, she slid the telephone book over the notepad where she'd jotted down the name and address of the hotel where Jim was staying.

They might be separated, and Leila might be more upset about his affair with Caroline than she'd admitted, but as the wife of a prison officer, she'd many times had to face the realization that all too often Jim's life had been in danger.

She simply fed him the story that she and Jim had had a final blazing row and Jim had walked out – she didn't know where he was and she didn't care. He seemed to accept the story and as she closed the door behind him she breathed a sigh of relief. Maybe she'd better phone Jim and warn him. But then, Butler knew where to find him at work, so there wasn't much point. She'd let it go for now.

Her thoughts might have been a little less charitable if she'd known that at that moment Caroline was making coffee for herself and Jim in the Halfway House kitchen.

She was still furious that Michael had rung Leila and told her what was going on. Typical of the snivelling little coward! Jim was more philosophical. 'Our marriage had nowhere to go, anyway. But,' and there was deep concern in his voice, 'she can use it as an excuse to stop me seeing the two boys.'

'But she wouldn't do that? She knows you love Mathew and Nick.'

'She could get a court order to stop me, while we're waiting for the divorce to go through.'

Caroline watched him for a moment, then . . .

'Maybe we should stop seeing each other for a while?'

His expression was almost wistful. 'I don't want that.'

'But, if there's a scandal you could lose your job. And that would only exacerbate the problem.'

She was right of course. Erica had already given him a gentle warning and you couldn't keep anything from the prisoners for long. They didn't have much in life except their daily routine and their gossip. And he knew from experience one careless word or look and the rumours would be flying around the prison in seconds!

The next morning dawned bright and sunny and Doreen hummed to herself as she busied herself in the prison garden, weeding a patch of newly planted petunias.

'I love petunias. When I was little me Mum told me that's where the fairies lived, inside them little bell-shaped flowers.' She giggled, remembering. 'I went around peering into the bloody things for years'.

'You never discovered any fairies?'

'Not the kind she meant!'

Judy chuckled with her, but it was an effort and she paused in her raking to take a deep breath and steady herself.

'You not too good, Jude?' Doreen looked at her anxiously.

'Bit tired is all.'

'S'pose Sharon kept you awake all night, complaining. Gee that kid's a whinger.'

'I guess that's my fault. I've spoilt her.'

'Yeah?'

Judy nodded. 'I've always had this big thing about protecting her.'

'What from?'

Judy frowned. That was quite a question.

Doreen looked at the big woman leaning thoughtfully on the rake. She was kind of handsome in a way. That beaut thick brown hair and the big eyes. And she had a fantastic smile.

'You got any family back in the States, Jude?'

It wasn't just curiosity. An American was something of a novelty to Doreen and it was hard for her to imagine just cutting off from the country you were born in, and landing up thousands of miles away from everything.

'Maybe. Haven't heard from my family for twenty years.'

Doreen was quite shocked. She'd had it pretty rough, but gee, twenty years!

'Being "gay" was the worst crime in the book, specially in a hick place like Norris Town. I had an affair with an older woman, a school teacher.'

'Funny. I never thought about a teacher being, you know . . . they always seem so square. So, what happened?'

'Word got round the town. My father chucked me out. So I got as far away as I could, came to good old Oz. I wrote to him later but he never answered.'

'What happened to your friend?'

'Lost her job. Then she hung herself.'

Doreen stared at her, wide-eyed. Gawd! What a thing!

Judy shrugged, putting the past back where it belonged.

'I decided then, no one's ever going to hurt anything I love again.'

'Gee Jude. I'm really sorry.' Doreen was going to continue but she broke off as she heard the sound of a dog whining gently. She looked around quickly then hurried across to a small shrub near the pathway. Crouched beneath it was a very small dog, probably the dirtiest one she'd ever seen.

'Jude, look.' Doreen picked the bedraggled little creature up and cradled it. Judy moved across to her, smiling at the joy in Doreen's face.

'It's a girl, Jude.'

'It's also in desperate need of a bath.'

'Yeah.' Doreen looked at the dog lovingly.

'We can't keep it, Doreen.'

Doreen raised her head defiantly.

'What the screws don't know won't hurt 'em. Besides, she needs a feed and I'm going to make sure she has one.'

But when Judy and Doreen smuggled the dog into the laundry in the tool box, Doreen's worst fears were realized. The women were fussing delightedly over the dog and already arguing about who would have the privilege of bathing her when Vera burst in on them.

Doreen quickly returned the dog to the box and closed the lid while the women crowded around her, obscuring Vera's vision, at least for the moment. But there was nothing they could do about the soft whining coming from the box. Like a well-trained sniffer dog, Vera made a beeline for it, opened the lid and looked down at the dirty little creature inside.

'How did this filthy thing get in here?'

Doreen looked at her hopefully. 'It was in the garden. We just wanted to give it a wash and feed, true.'

For answer, Vera glared back at her. And to the astonishment of Bea, Judy and Doreen, the dog jumped out of the box and wagged a feeble tail in Vera's direction. It was worth another try. 'She likes you Miss Bennett.'

'No accounting for tastes!' said Lizzie, but she kept her voice too low for Vera to hear her.

'Make a leash out of something.' Vera glared around the laundry.

'The rest of you get on with your work. And I'll need to know later, Bryant, why you and Anderson saw fit to leave your gardening duties.'

There was a resentful murmur from the women as Doreen tied a remnant of sheeting around the dog's neck and handed the other end to Officer Bennett. Far from being intimidated, the dog did its best to jump up on Vera, making it very clear it would be happy to give her a nice friendly lick or two. But it cut no ice with her and she marched it from the room without another word.

Doreen looked miserable. 'She could at least've let us bath it.' A small cackle from Lizzie. 'With a bit of luck it'll show it's got some class, and piss all over old Vinegar Tits' shoes.'

Vera's hopes of making it into a serious incident were

dashed when Erica laid eyes on the little creature. 'It's a bit smelly, but I'd say it's a pedigree and most certainly has an owner.' She stroked the dog's head a moment, her expression gentle. 'You know how starved the women are for pets, Miss Bennett.'

Vera's lips tightened. 'If Security was working properly it would never have been able to get on the premises.'

'I'll be the judge of that.'

There was no doubting the authority behind those words. 'Tie it up in the garden for now. And let Bryant and Anderson clean it up. Meantime, I'll call the RSPCA.'

Vera quickly passed on the instructions to Officer Knox. She wasn't going to let the women think she'd backed down over the wretched animal.

Knox was only too pleased to pass on the good news. It was her belief that a few animals around the place would do a lot to promote harmony amongst the prisoners. Judy and Doreen had the time of their life bathing the little creature and discovering what a pretty creature it really was, once the grime was gone. Knox smiled benignly and determined that the women could enjoy the dog's company for as long as it took the RSPCA to call and collect it.

On the far side of the garden, a very different scene was taking place. Leila had been right in thinking Geoff Butler would seek Jim out at work. He'd lost no time in laying his cards on the table. He'd given Jim a second chance in Vietnam – he needed Jim to do the same for him now. Without Jim's evidence that Geoff had attacked Meg, there was no witness, no proof. Geoff would be cleared and he vowed he'd be out of the country on the next flight. Jim eyed him closely. They'd fought side by side once. But how could he trust Geoff Butler?

He was still mulling over the question when the phone call came through from Michael Simpson. And as he listened, Jim could hardly believe his ears. The man was actually offering to pay him, in cash, to stay away from his wife.

'You're a sick man, Simpson.' Jim fairly spat the words into the phone.

'You want me to beg, Fletcher? All right, I'm begging you. Name your price.'

Without another word, Jim slammed the phone down. God, no wonder the fellow sickened a woman like Caroline. What must her life have been like, married to the turd?

He was sitting over a coffee in the staff room, lost in his own gloomy thoughts, when Meg and Vera entered, the latter fuming and Meg obviously amused.

'We were made to look fools. The RSPCA arrived and we can't find the dog.'

Meg shook her head. 'For heaven's sake, it's no big deal Vera. I have it on the best authority that the dog will turn up in the garden in the morning and that'll be the end of it all.'

'Who told you that?'

Meg's eyes twinkled. 'For the life of me I can't remember. One of the women I daresay.'

A more serious expression crossed Meg's face.

'I'm dreading Geoff Butler's trial, Jim.'

He looked up, trying to get his troubled thoughts in order.

'You simply have to tell it the way it happened, Meg.'

She hesitated for a second, then . . . 'We both do.'

His eyes met hers squarely.

'I know.' Was there just a trace of uncertainty in the words?

Meg felt sick at the very thought. Without Jim's backup, Butler would get off. And after the brutal way he'd treated her, that was just too much to stomach.

But she need not have worried. Jim's evidence was clear and concise. He confirmed her story and his own involvement as a witness. 'Yes, Butler had proved violent with him too, and with the two arresting officers.'

Meg's reaction to the sentencing was cynical – a good behaviour bond and five hundred dollars. Farcical in her opinion.

Jim agreed, and he wasn't much comforted, after the hearing, when Butler verbally abused him of betraying a 'mate' and ruining his future.

He would have been even more alarmed if he'd seen Michael Simpson approach Butler and obviously make some kind of overture of co-operation with him. 'We've got a mutual cause' was how Simpson put it. 'You've got the know-how and I've got the money.'

That was the kind of offer Geoff Butler would find too good to refuse. He'd planned on getting back at Jim Fletcher some way, anyhow. If he got paid to do it, so much the better.

Seven

Next morning, as the women were finishing their breakfast in the prison dining room, there was a general sense of gloom. Judy seemed uninterested in her food, and the company. Sharon was bitching about things in general and Doreen and Lizzie were still frustrated and angry that the little dog which briefly brought so much joy into their lives had been snatched from them and undoubtedly put down by the RSPCA.

Only Bea, who'd just heard that Ken Pearce would be coming back to talk over plans for the proposed drama group, was on top. But even her efforts to cheer Pat O'Connell fell on deaf ears.

After her boy Andrew had been found and returned to the home, Pat had decided to go through with the appeal against her sentence. But she held out little hope and was haunted by the fact that her kids would have flouted the authorities and disappeared again before she would ever get out of Wentworth.

The atmosphere wasn't helped when Sharon announced to all and sundry, and Bea in particular, that she thought the drama thing was a dumb idea and they all knew Bea was only doing it because she had the hots for Ken Pearce and was hoping to get herself a lay or two – 'Some hopes,' she added bitchily.

That really put the fat in the fire. Bea had been wanting to teach that kid a lesson for too long.

'You do one thing to muck this up, Gilmour, and I'll thump the living bloody daylights out of you.' There was so much pent-up violence behind the words that Sharon experienced a moment of real fear. She turned quickly to Judy.

'You going to let her talk like that to me, Jude?'

As Judy rose slowly to her feet, Bea grabbed the front of Sharon's uniform. 'Fight your own battles you snivelling little slut.'

Sharon's eyes darted to the doorway. Old Vinegar Tits was studiously looking the other way. She was just waiting for Smith to step out of line so she could crush the drama idea. There'd be no help there.

Pat, Lizzie, Doreen, Phyllis and a couple of the other women had risen and were now making a small human shield between the doorway and Bea. Bea's other hand reached out and grabbed Sharon's wrist in a painful grasp.

'Jude!' Sharon's voice was shrill. Judy jumped up quickly from the table as if to lunge forward and grasp Bea. But even as her arm reached out, she caught her breath in a sob and slumped to the floor.

'Gawd.' Doreen's eyes were round as she looked down on Judy's inert body.

'What's going on here?' Vera pushed them aside abruptly. 'What happened?' Her eyes were riveted on Bea who'd hastily released Sharon. And she was surprised when an upset Sharon fell to her knees beside Judy, her words just above a whisper. 'She just – collapsed. Get a doctor, someone, quick!'

There was no mistaking the sincerity and the shock.

*

Sharon was even more upset when, later, the Governor explained to her that Judy, according to the doctor's preliminary examination, had severe cardiac problems. It appeared there was something of a family history – Judy's mother had died of a heart attack at the age of forty-five. Probably one of the reasons she'd been trying to cover up the fact she was sick.

'She's been a bit tired. And the nurse gave her some pills.' Erica nodded. 'For her blood pressure. The thing is, she refused to have the tests which are absolutely essential for her.'

Sharon looked scared. 'And if she doesn't?'

Erica chose her words carefully. 'There is a seventy percent chance she will drop dead on the spot.'

The girl's face was chalk white. Big Judy, who'd always been there, protected her, thumped, pushed, persuaded, whatever . . . Suddenly, she was someone with a bad heart who could die at any time.

It had been a long time since Sharon had put aside her self-centred approach and examined her real feelings for Judy. In her own way, she loved Judy. So why hadn't she noticed she was really ill? Why hadn't Judy told her? Because she'd worry and everything had to be just right for little Sharon. A sense of guilt and shame swept through her. 'I'll try and persuade her, Mrs Davidson.' Erica nodded briskly. 'Good; the sooner the better.'

But Judy was adamant. She wasn't going to die on the operating room table like her mother. A bit of rest, a few pills, and she'd be fine. It was Pat who suggested maybe Lizzie could give Sharon some advice. The old girl might not have much time for the Gilmour kid, but when you got sick inside, you had to stick together, lend a hand.

Since Judy had been released from the prison infirmary, she'd been resting in her cell. Lizzie hesitated for a moment in the corridor. Judy was lying on her bunk resting and Pat O'Connell, on trolley duty, was putting her lunch tray on the bench.

Lizzie propped herself in the doorway. 'G'day Jude. They tell me you got my trouble – a dicky ticker.'

Judy managed a smile. 'They just want to play guinea pigs with me Lizzie.'

Pat looked at Lizzie, slightly puzzled but, at a sign, left the cell to go back to her trolley, where she had a lunch tray for Bev in the adjoining cell. That Bev! More sickies than a cat could eat canaries.

Lizzie stayed leaning against the grill. 'They can't do nothing for me, just pills. Wish they could. They reckon I could go any time.'

'All gotta go sometime.' Judy grinned but there was no conviction in the words.

'Yeah, but I tell ya. You get a real heart attack, it's a bloody awful way to go. I been there. Jeez, the pain.'

Lizzie suddenly bent, as though to pick something up.

'What's that?'

And as she straightened, she gave a small, anguished cry and clutched at her heart, gasping for air as she fells slowly to the ground, obviously in terrible pain.

'Pat!' Judy rushed to the doorway as Pat came hurrying back.

'Gawd. Lizzie's had one of her turns. They'll have to get her to hospital. Get the screws.'

As Pat knelt down beside Lizzie to loosen her clothing, Judy hurried along the corridor. She was breathing hard. What she'd seen had shocked her deeply. Was that really the way to go? Maybe she'd just take those tests after all!

The word soon got around that Lizzie was in the prison hospital but a smiling Meg assured them she was fine – just one of her turns. And as she later told Erica, very coincidental that it happened in Judy Bryant's cell and that Judy had now agreed to tests. Erica felt perhaps they'd keep that information to themselves.

But something they could not keep under wraps was the incredible news that Vera had actually adopted the stray dog and had been caught out buying all sorts of expensive goodies for it. So old Vinegar had a heart after all! But woe betide anyone who let on that they knew!

It was after ten when Caroline and Jim returned to his hotel. They'd had dinner in a discreet little Italian restaurant and for the first time it had brought a sense of normality to their relationship. Jim looked apologetically around the seedy room.

'This makes things seem – sordid, somehow.'

Caroline moved across to him, taking off her jacket, kicking off her shoes. 'It's the only place we can be together. And that's what I want, Jim.'

Her arms were around his neck. He caught his breath. He'd waited so long for this moment.

'I do love you Caroline.'

As their lips met in the first real kiss they had shared, all the cares of the day, the dreadful complications of wife, home and family, seemed to pale into insignificance. They would make love, here, now, in this anonymous place. For the moment, nothing else mattered.

Alone in the house which she and Jim had built all those years ago, Leila quickly replaced the phone on its cradle.

She'd been nervous enough before, but that call . . . just the heavy breathing, deep, rhythmic, frightening . . .

She took a deep breath. She'd ring the police. But as her hand reached out the brick came crashing through the sitting room window, showering her with broken glass, and a scream of sheer terror she never knew she uttered came from deep down inside her.

When Jim told Caroline the next day what had happened to Leila, the joy and happiness she'd known the night before with Jim simply became a load of guilt. That they should have been in each other's arms and making love when it happened only made the whole nightmare more horrendous. And she realized that it was time she too confided about the intimidation that had been happening to her . . . strange knockings on the window, the constant feeling that there was someone lurking in the Halfway House garden, just waiting to strike. And the obscene note. Where was it all going to end?

Leila was thinking the same thing as she stared in disbelief at the wall of the sitting room. The glass had been cleared away, the window patched . . . but now, in huge letters and glaring red paint, the words 'HELLO LEILA' on the sitting room wall. Who had done this? How had they managed to get in? Dear God, what next?

Geoff Butler was planning, even as the thought went through her head. He had assembled a parcel of drugs, he told Michael. They were to be planted in Jim Fletcher's hotel room. That would put paid to his career and his affair with Caroline.

'Why do I have to deliver it?' Michael's voice was a frightened whine. Butler regarded him with disgust. 'You're in this up to your neck, like me. You'll do as I tell you.'

Michael looked at the hard eyes and cruel mouth. Why had he ever got involved with this man? But he'd do the delivery. He was more afraid of Geoff Butler than Jim Fletcher.

He was disconcerted when the hotel desk clerk told him Mr Fletcher had asked not to be disturbed. But of course, he had never meant to deliver them to the door himself, and the clerk assured him the parcel would be handed over the moment Mr Fletcher came down to the foyer.

Leila had had enough. There was no way she and the boys could stay in the house tonight. She parked the car expertly in front of the rundown hotel and hurried the boys through into the foyer. They were Jim's sons too and he simply had to do something about their safety.

The desk clerk passed on the same message he had to Michael Simpson but when he learned that he was addressing Mrs Fletcher, he shrugged and smiled. 'He's been working a lot of extra hours so I s'pose that's why he left the message. But I'm sure it doesn't apply to family.'

Leila smiled and turned to shepherd the boys up the stairs. 'Oh, there's a parcel. You might like to take it up.' The desk clerk was holding out the package. 'Save me the trip?' She nodded and took it from him almost absently, then headed for the stairs.

The boys were full of questions, about the place, why the passageway was so dark, why Dad had chosen to stay in such a horrid place. She made vague answers then found the number she was looking for, 32A. She raised her hand and knocked, three times.

Inside the room, a rather weary Jim was washing his face, trying to get the wretched soap out of his eyes. 'Just a moment.' He was cursing softly, he'd told them he wasn't to be disturbed.

Matty and Nick were excited at the sound of their Dad's voice. Matty grabbed the parcel. 'I want to give it to Dad.' 'No,' Nick tugged at it. 'Me.'

'Will you stop it boys.' Leila yanked the parcel away from their eager hands.

Jim could only stare in horror as the home-made bomb exploded with a roar, blowing the door off its hinges.

The news had spread quickly through Wentworth. While the staff recoiled in horror at the news, the women were subdued into fitful snatches of conversation. The radio details had been graphic. Both little boys killed instantly. The wife, critical, not expected to live. Old Lizzie shook her head. 'Caroline's going to feel pretty bad about this.'

Bea gave her a sharp look. 'So she bloody should, buggering around with someone else's husband.'

Caroline was, in fact, sitting trancelike in front of the radio. It couldn't be true. Things like that didn't happen to ordinary people. And those two little boys.

She knew how much Jim loved them. Dear God, why had she ever let him help? She should be back in prison. If she had been . . . She'd have to see Jim, at least tell him how sorry she was . . .

But it was a stranger she confronted. Numbed with shock, he could only stare at her. The hospital had just phoned. Leila was dead.

It was over for them, of course. They would blame themselves for the rest of their lives but that wouldn't bring back Leila or the boys. Caroline must honour her bail and then either face the prison sentence or just walk away.

But who had done this? Michael was weak, and a coward. If he was behind it, then he'd have left the dirty work to someone else. Well, she would tell the police everything she knew, and if it went against her, so be it. She would take what was coming to her.

Erica felt rather heartless as she hung up the phone and faced Meg. 'The Department will help out, temporarily. Someone called Jock Stewart. He comes highly recommended.' She sighed. 'It seems so awful to be talking like this after such a tragedy.'

Meg nodded compassionately. 'We still have to run the prison.'

'Yes.' Erica straightened tired shoulders. 'One bit of good news. Judy Bryant's come through the operation very well. And O'Connell's parole has been renewed. Since her sentence was reduced to six months that means she can be released immediately.'

'I'm so glad.' Meg smiled, remembering. 'I saw her with Andrew and Emma the other day when they visited. They love their mother very dearly and they need her now, not in two years' time.'

'Arrange it will you, Meg, and let me know how the Vincent woman has settled in.'

Meg nodded. 'I don't think Vera approves of her being allowed to go on with her painting.'

'Our instructions are to let her continue. And since I make the decisions as to what I consider beneficial to the rehabilitation of the prisoners, I shall be keeping a sharp eye on Vera to see she doesn't aggravate the situation in any way.'

Meg smiled her agreement as she turned and headed for reception. If Vera had her way she'd probably reintroduce capital punishment!

Jim was appreciative of Caroline's co-operation. Thanks to her, Michael Simpson had been picked up, and being the weakling that he was, it hadn't taken long to get the full story from him.

Jim might have known Geoff Butler would find a way to get even! Well, he'd nearly made a fateful error there. In his rage and grief he'd gone out and bought bullets for his old service revolver. He'd decided quite rationally to kill Butler. But thanks to Simpson, who'd been only too willing to try and curry favour with the police, they'd soon traced Butler.

A fool to the end, he'd tried to outwit the police and had finally fallen to a police sniper's bullet. A fitting end, though Jim could have wished he's suffered as Leila had. He tried not to think about the boys. That would come later when he realized the full dreadful impact of the loss.

*

The officers tried to act as normally as possible towards the women, but there was an inevitable sense of tension. Erica insisted that the drama group should continue as planned and she was even slightly amused to learn that, as a result of the conference she'd allowed between Smith and Ken Pearce, the women were studying Macbeth – p'raps that saga of violence and death might make their own lot seem rather more acceptable.

What Erica did not know was that, for all Vera's reluctance to allow a prisoner special privileges, deep down there was the same burning desire to paint that was so obvious in Kerry Vincent. Maybe that's why she'd been so tough on her at first. But now, as Vera stood in the doorway, watching Kerry put the finishing touches to a landscape in particularly beautiful pastel shades, she freely admitted to herself that this girl was no hack. She could really paint.

As Kerry laid down her brush she became aware of Vera.

'I always feel sort of sad when I finish a painting. It's like – saying goodbye to a friend.'

To her surprise, Vera nodded. 'I can understand that. But then, you do paint to sell, don't you?'

Kerry shook her head. 'My agent David Austin would like me to think that way. But the truth is, I don't care about that. I just want to paint. And if someone feels something special about something I've done, I'd rather give them the painting than sell it to someone who just wants to buy pretty pictures.'

'It's a wonderful gift.' Vera's eyes were riveted on the landscape. Kerry took advantage of Vera's softened mood.

'I didn't think you approved of my being allowed to do this, inside.'

'You give some of the prisoners an inch and they'll go berserk.' She searched for the right words. 'But if someone's got a real talent, then perhaps they should have the chance.'

Vera's eyes went back to the painting and Kerry impulsively picked it up from her easel.

'You like this a lot, don't you?'

Vera nodded. 'There's something about it. It reminds me of where I lived as a child. And the colours . . . they seem to evoke so many memories, good ones.'

'Please take it.' Kerry held out the canvas to Vera. 'But be careful. It needs to really dry off. And it'll have to be framed.'

'I couldn't.' Vera raised her arm, almost in a defensive gesture. 'It's . . . very kind of you, but no.' She managed a small laugh. 'I'm sure someone out there would pay a very handsome price for that painting.'

'I told you. The money doesn't interest me. You love this, it means something to you.' Kerry proffered the painting again.

'Well . . .' Vera was weakening. She wanted it so badly.

A small, tight smile was on Kerry's lips. 'I promise you I won't expect anything in return.'

Their eyes met for a moment. Kerry's honest and clear, Vera's just a little wary.

'I never make deals.' It was the voice of the 'old' Vera.

'Neither do I.' Kerry put the painting into Vera's

hands, turned and picked up a business card. 'My agent runs the gallery. He'll get it framed for you.'

'Thank you.' For a moment Vera just stood there, more deeply touched than she'd felt in a long time. 'I'll take great care of it.'

'Just enjoy.' Kerry turned away and began sorting through her supplies, looking for a fresh canvas to begin on. Vera turned and without another word left the cell. Bea and the other women would have been surprised to see the gentle expression on her face, and the tear that stole down her cheek as she hugged the canvas to her and walked slowly along the corridor.

Later, in the recreation room, the women discussed the good news of Pat O'Connell's release. Lizzie was positively ecstatic. She'd put the hard word on the Governor, and she'd got permission to move back in with her old mates Bea and Doreen.

'Oh Jeez, there goes any chance of sleep with you back, Lizzie. You snore like a bloody buzz saw.'

Lizzie took the ribbing in good part. Why not? She had even bigger news. She'd chatted to that nice Salvation Army bloke last time he came round, and found out if you 'get religion' and wanted to show willing, you could get the odd outing. And the Gov. had been very encouraging. With a bit of luck, she'd be getting an airing next Sunday. Doreen burst out laughing. 'Gawd, don't they know you're a bloody old klepto? You'll probably snaffle the collection plate.'

'That's a very unChristian thing to say.' Lizzie adopted her very best lady of quality manner. 'And I'd appreciate it if you'd moderate your language, the lot of you.'

'That's all we need, Lizzie going religious on us.'
They were still laughing when Meg Jackson came in.

'Evening, ladies. Just thought you'd like to know
that Bryant's come through with flying colours.'

There was a chorus of 'bewdy', 'good one', from the
women. What did they care if Jude was a lesso? She
was no stalker, and overall she was a pretty good sort.

Bea looked around the room. There was no sign of
Sharon. Curious.

Bea's unvoiced suspicions were remarkably accurate.
Lonely and frustrated, Sharon had been keeping an
eye on Kerry Vincent since she'd been brought in. She
was the antithesis of Judy in looks and build but there
was something about her, a hint of hidden strength, a
flash of steel that excited and attracted Sharon. She
was lounging in the doorway now, watching Kerry at
work.

'Don't you ever take a break?'

Kerry turned, with a quick smile. 'Only when the
lights go out.' Was that a subtle come on? Sharon
moved inside the cell. 'Gets pretty lonely, doesn't it,
when they lock you in and you're all alone in the dark.'

Kerry shrugged. 'I can still think in colour.'

'Maybe we could make beautiful pictures together.'
She reached out and slid her hand softly over Kerry's
long, shiny, blonde hair.

For a moment Kerry just stood very still, her brush
halted in mid-air. Then gently, but very definitely, she
removed Sharon's hand from her hair. 'My work's
enough for me, Sharon.'

Sharon gave a short, cynical bark of laughter. 'What
are you, some kind of weirdo?'

'No.' Kerry's face was very serious now. 'But when I do care about someone, I don't play around wherever I can get it, the moment my partner isn't on the scene.'

There was a hint of something very nasty in Sharon's eyes now. 'You leave Judy out of this.'

'And you leave me alone. Firstly, I'm not a dyke, and secondly, I wouldn't fancy you if I was.' Kerry turned back to the half completed canvas and calmly resumed her work.

'You're really up yourself, aren't you?' Sharon was fuelling her anger to cover the humiliation of rejection. 'Well you'd better watch it. We've all seen the way old Vinegar Tits Bennett's hanging round you and she only does that for one thing. When she's set up a spy, someone to lag on us. And nasty things happen to anyone who lags in this joint.'

Kerry managed to keep her cool until Sharon had slammed out of the cell and her footsteps were dying away along the corridor. But her hand was unsteady. She'd done enough time to know the truth of those spiteful words. She laid down the brush and wiped her hands thoughtfully. If word got out she'd given Bennett that painting, she could be in big trouble.

She'd have been even more unnerved if she'd known that at that moment the women had her under discussion. She seemed OK, but why all the special privileges? And Phyllis had just seen old Vinegar Tits looking like the cat who'd eaten the cream.

'Did you know she was real matey with Ken Pearce, Bea? Seems he was the one who helped get her the chance to go on painting while she was doing time.'

Bea's lips tightened. Well, well, Vincent had better not move in on that territory!

'Maybe we'd better just teach her a little lesson, eh?' Big Margot lumbered over to join the group.

'Better make sure you've got backup, Bea.'

'What are you on about?' Bea looked irritably at Margot. When she called the shots, that was it.

'Don't let the blonde hair and the baby-blue eyes fool you.' Margot spat out the words with relish. 'That chick's in for cold blooded murder.'

Eight

There was an indefinable air of tension in the dining room as the women sat eating their breakfast under the watchful eye of Vera Bennett.

The good news that Judy's return was imminent, complete with her new pacemaker, was overshadowed by the fear that in Kerry Vincent they did have a lagger in their midst. And, for all his apparently bluff and jovial demeanour, not all the women were convinced that the new officer, Jock Stewart, had their best interests at heart. Give them poor old Fletch the Letch any time.

Kerry, making one of her few expeditions outside of her cell, was careful to snub a friendly overture from Officer Bennett as she walked in. She had to avoid trouble at all costs or they'd stop her painting. And painting was her life.

The atmosphere was momentarily lightened as Meg Jackson entered with a handful of mail and a cheerful word for the women.

'I've got another letter from Kevin.' There was surprise, and a pleasure Doreen couldn't hide.

'Told you, Dor.' Lizzie sucked her teeth over her cereal in the way that set Bea's teeth on edge. 'He's true blue that fella.'

'Reckon you might be right, Lizzie.' Doreen was already ripping the letter open.

'Don't rush it, Doreen. They'll have cut out all the juicy bits.' Phyllis's wisecrack was received with a small ripple of laughter. Certainly if Vera had had anything to do with the censoring, she'd have cut out everything but the most bland information.

As Meg handed out the last of the mail, Kerry approached her. 'Mrs Jackson. I wondered if it would be possible for me to have a lamp? I'm trying to meet the deadline for the exhibition I've been promised, and the light's so bad in the late afternoon and evening.'

Meg smiled. This girl was a bigger workaholic than even Vera.

'I'll have a word with the Governor. It should be all right. She's always impressed with real enthusiasm.'

'Thank you.'

Vera looked on with a mixture of confusion and hurt. Why hadn't Vincent spoken to her? One minute she was handing over a beautiful painting that could have earned her hundreds of dollars, the next treating Vera like an arch enemy. Kerry moved back towards the serving counter, passing Bea on the way. 'Good morning.' It was addressed to the table in general, and, to Kerry's dismay, treated with a frosty silence. So it was true, what Sharon had said. They had tagged her as a lagger. She'd have to find a way to clear that up, and fast! Bea Smith didn't look like someone who'd make a pleasant enemy!

Jock Stewart was doing what appeared to be a routine check of the cells as the start-of-work bell rang and he heard footsteps approaching along the corridor. He stepped quickly into Kerry Vincent's cell. God, these do-gooders made him sick! A woman gets gaoled for murder and what do they do? Set her up like bloody Picasso and treat her like it was a bloody privilege to have her inside. He was about to step outside when he picked up a snatch of conversation that caught his attention.

'They've got everything set up in D Block for the sly grog scam.' It was Mouse, trying to keep her voice to a whisper but she was coming through loud and clear to Jock.

'Bewdy.' Phyllis gave a cackle of laughter. 'S'pose they'll charge us an arm and a leg, but it'd be good to drown our bloody sorrows for a few hours anyway.'

'Yeah.' Mouse lowered her voice still further, 'I'll keep you posted.' The rest was just a murmur of voices till the women had moved on to take up their duties in the laundry and kitchen.

He waited till it was quiet then stepped out into the corridor. So, they were up to tricks in D block, eh? He'd see about that, and boy would he make sure those bitches got what was coming to them!

Erica smiled across the desk at Kerry. 'I'm sure we can arrange a lamp for you.'

'Thank you.'

The Governor was secretly marvelling at this attractive woman, so gifted, so dedicated, yet she had killed a man! 'I've had a request that you should be allowed leave to be present at the exhibition Mr Austin, your agent, is arranging for you.'

Kerry's words came out in a rush. 'I think he wants

me there for publicity value. But it's not important to me. I just want to be left alone to paint.'

Erica nodded. 'We can discuss it again later.' She nodded dismissal and Meg indicated to Officer Knox that she should return Kerry to her cell.

After the door was closed behind her, Erica turned to Meg. 'Do you know why she killed?'

Meg shook her head. 'I only know the charge, not the details.'

'He insulted her work. She hit him over the head with the nearest thing she could find, a heavy brass ashtray.'

Meg couldn't resist a smile. 'Is that a hint that I should remain strictly complimentary about her work?'

Erica chuckled. 'It might be wise. But it wouldn't be hard. She really is extraordinarily talented.'

Officer Knox let Kerry through the security gates and left her to find her way to her cell along the deserted corridor.

She was pleased about the lamp. It had been so disappointing to have to stop work when the daylight faded. She had almost finished the painting on her easel – a lovely, fragile study of birds in flight over a misty, violet seascape. She turned into her cell and stopped in her tracks.

The painting had been brutally slashed from top to bottom – the canvas gaped like some wounded creature ripped and gutted by the bloodied hunter's knife.

Dear God! Who would do this! These paintings were her life, her reason for being. To do this was to kill part of her. A red, blinding rage rose up in her. Whoever did this would pay! And then the cold, hard light of reason came through. The women were testing her.

It was a cruel thing to do, but she'd been inside too long not to know the rules.

It was at this moment that Vera Bennett appeared in the doorway of her cell. She had come to find out the reason for Kerry's offhand behaviour. But the sight of the slashed painting stunned her. 'What happened?' There was genuine shock and concern in Vera's voice. She had thought the painting quite exceptional, had praised it highly. Kerry hesitated for just a moment, then eyed Vera coldly.

'I wasn't satisfied with it.'

Vera could hardly believe her ears. 'You did this?'

Kerry nodded, almost casually. 'I never keep anything I don't consider good enough.'

'But it was beautiful.' The words came out involuntarily.

'You're hardly an art critic, Miss Bennett.'

Ah, that hurt! Vera, so envious, so longing to have that kind of talent. But in a moment, she was back in control, the officer addressing the prisoner. 'Watch it, Vincent. Step out of line, and you'll lose your beloved painting privileges.'

Vera made a brisk exit. Kerry drew in a long, deep breath. She knew it would be very unwise to get on the wrong side of Bennett, but for the moment it was the women she had to convince and just maybe this would do it.

It wasn't that easy. Word soon spread that the sly grog scheme in D block had been blown wide open. And it wasn't long before Mouse remembered where she'd been when she told Phyllis about the scam. 'It has to be that bitch Vincent.' Phyllis agreed, there hadn't been anyone else around and they were right outside that cell! It was at this inauspicious moment that Kerry chose to front Bea.

Bea looked curiously at the black and white sketch which Kerry was holding out to her. 'I hope you like it.' It was a fine head study – clean, simple lines that somehow caught every nuance that was the woman they called Queen Bea. Mouse and Phyllis held their breath. Which way would the Top Dog jump. But for the moment, Bea registered something close to confusion.

'I'm not sucking up to you. But I'm not a lagger.' Kerry met the cold blue eyes very directly. 'I've been wanting to sketch you. Thought maybe you'd accept it as a kind of peace offering.'

'It's not bad.' Bea's non-committal answer didn't really give anything away. Lizzie had ambled up to them and was looking at the sketch over Bea's shoulder.

'Jeez, it's that real I bet it could talk. How about doing me?' She struck a pose that made them all laugh and for the moment the tension was gone.

'I'll do that, Lizzie.' Kerry moved off but she knew she hadn't solved the problem, not yet.

The women were pleased to have Judy Bryant back among them. There were lots of wisecracks about the pacemaker and some pretty lewd references to what it might do to her sex life. Jude took it all in good part and soon took the opportunity to let Lizzie know that she was grateful the old girl had 'staged' her heart attack for Judy's benefit. Thanks to Lizzie, she was feeling better than she had in a long time. Sharon's greeting was almost effusive. She'd missed Judy so much, the others had been mean to her . . . the list of complaints was long and detailed.

Judy listened, interested to find how little it all now meant to her. She'd really faced up to things when they were wheeling her along on that trolley, ready for the op. Sadly, she'd realized that, while she still cared for this girl, she was tired of the pettiness, the endless selfishness. Maybe she had encouraged it, but did she want to live with it for the rest of her life?

Sharon was oblivious of what was going through Judy's mind. She was too busy painting a black picture of Kerry Vincent. She hadn't got over that bitch rejecting her and she'd make sure, damned sure, she could convince the women that Kerry was a lagger. Then let *them* do the dirty work for her!

In the corridor, Bea heard the tirade and her face was thoughtful. She took a few steps and waited around the corner. Judy would want to rest and Sharon would have to come this way on her way to the laundry. After a moment, she did just that. And Bea pounced. She had taken Sharon completely by surprise and she decided to play her hunch.

'You've been making a play for Kerry, haven't you?'

'No.' But Bea could tell the girl was nervous and she grabbed her arm and twisted it hard behind her back.

'You made a play for her and she wouldn't buy, right?'

Sharon tried to bluff it out. 'What makes you think that?'

'Because you're an oversexed little slut who's been spoilt rotten and made to think she's little Miss Irresistible.'

'You're hurting me.' Sharon struggled to free her arm.

'No good calling for Big Jude, not any more.' Bea pushed her face close to the scared girl. 'She knocked you back and you slashed her painting.'

'No.'

Bea twisted harder, and Sharon knew if she screamed Bea would hit her harder and she'd end up in trouble with the women if she got Bea shopped.

'OK. Yes, I did it! Are you satisfied?'

Slowly Bea released the arm, her hard eyes boring into Sharon's defiant ones.

'That was just a warning.' There was real menace in Bea's voice. 'There's a lot of women in here would like to get even with you, Gilmour. Make sure there's not a next time.'

Before Sharon could reply, Meg Jackson rounded the corner. 'Why aren't you two in the laundry?'

The raging Queen Bea of a moment ago was nowhere to be seen. 'Had a toilet break, Mrs J., and just stopped for a sec to make sure Jude was OK.'

Meg didn't find the answer too convincing but further questions wouldn't evoke any answers, so she shepherded them towards the laundry, admitting privately to herself that Gilmour was still a problem, but a much lesser one since Bea had been let out of Isolation to keep things on an even keel. Vera might say the staff ran the prison, but Meg was wise enough to know that the pecking order amongst the prisoners was rock solid and any officer who chose to ignore that was just buying into trouble.

When Bea returned to the laundry the women were agog with quite another subject. Doreen, fresh back from the interview room, was big with news. Her mother's will had finally been processed. 'Mrs D says it's all mine, the house and all the stuff in it and after the legal costs and all that there's $4000 in the bank as well.'

'We'll have to start calling you Mrs Moneybags.' But Bea was delighted for her. Maybe this would make the kid try harder next time she was on the outside.

Doreen confided that the Gov. thought she ought to rent the house out, but she didn't like the idea much. Mum's house and all that. Lizzie knocked off folding sheets and lit up a fag.

'Why don't you talk to Kev about it, Dor?'

Doreen's face brightened. 'Yeah, maybe I'll do that.' She beamed happily at Lizzie. 'We can both go and live there when we get out, Lizzie.'

'You could start up a knocking shop. Lizzie's past it o' course but she wouldn't make a bad pimp.'

Lizzie glared at Phyllis. 'Don't talk so crude.'

Bea chuckled. 'Gawd, you've become a real pain since you got caught up with the Salvos, Lizzie.'

'They're good people, and don't you knock 'em. And anyone says different, I'll knock their bloody block off.'

There was a general burst of laughter from the women. Just as long as Lizzie didn't start singing hymns again! Voice like a foghorn, and boy did it have a rough passage out!

Kerry listened to the approaching footsteps with some trepidation. The women, work over for the day, were being taken out to the garden for a breath of fresh air. But as Bea, Lizzie and Doreen reached her cell they had a cheery greeting for her and Bea stopped long enough to admire the lamp.

'S'pose you'll work twenty-four hours a day now, eh?'

There was no future in asking questions. But clearly the women had proved for themselves that Kerry was no lagger. Better not to know the whys and wherefores.

There was a very different atmosphere in Erica's office. She was at boiling point, the afternoon newspaper in front of her. An article by Kerry's agent had spelt out in no uncertain terms that Kerry had been blackmailed into giving a Wentworth officer a painting in order to be able to go on working.

She looked around the room. Vera, pale and tense; Meg? Obviously news to her. Jim Fletcher, edgy on his first day back at work since his family tragedy; Knox and Barfield registering surprise, and Jock Stewart – hard to say, she hadn't got his measure yet and he wasn't displaying any particular emotion at this point.

'I'm waiting.' Erica's voice was sharp with authority.

'Vincent gave me a painting.' Vera was nervous but surely if she told the truth there was nothing to worry about.

'I'd admired it. But in no way did I ask. In fact, I was very hesitant. She was insistent, so I finally accepted. I took it to her agent to have it framed. Obviously there has been a misunderstanding.'

There, it was out. Was Barfield looking a touch sceptical? A slight smile on Stewart's face?

Erica broke the silence. 'I wish you'd mentioned it earlier, Miss Bennett.'

'I saw no need.' There was a slight edge to Vera's voice. 'I admit I was critical of Vincent being allowed to go on working, at first. But when I saw her work, and observed her attitude, I came to the conclusion that, in her case, the privilege was warranted.'

'Thank you.' There was an icy edge to Erica's voice. But she knew that for all Vera's bigotry she had never been accused of blackmailing a prisoner.

'Obviously a gutter press article to promote Vincent's work and the coming exhibition. Nevertheless, it's not the kind of thing we want discussed amongst the women. I shall take appropriate steps with the Department and the Editor of the paper. And naturally I shall be speaking to Mr Austin, Vincent's agent. That will be all for now.' They filed out of the room, Meg offering a sympathetic word to Vera, but the latter was so incensed and hurt at this point that she brushed Meg's effort aside and went briskly about her business.

She was striding towards the recreation room when Officer Martin caught up with her.

'Miss Bennett. It seems someone's taken the bulb from Vincent's lamp. She'd like a replacement.'

Vera's reaction was over-quick. 'If she's going to have a never-ending demand for extras and privileges, she'll have to earn them.'

It was simply an automatic reflex, but Jim Fletcher, rounding the corner at that moment, registered the words and a small frown creased his brow. But it was hard enough for him to get through this first day back at the prison. He wasn't going to start stirring up any hornets' nests.

Had he known the state of Vera's mind he might have changed his. She headed straight for Kerry's cell. She wasn't going to take that kind of rotten insinuation lying down! Let the girl face up and see what she'd got to say for herself.

Kerry was sitting despondently on her bunk when Vera walked in. She rose quickly. 'Do you know if someone is bringing a bulb, Miss Bennett?'

Vera's hackles rose. Twenty-four-hour service expected, was it? And who was to say this creature hadn't set her up. She'd given her the painting. She told her exactly where to get it framed – and from that very place and that Austin creep had come the newspaper story. It would seem Vera Bennett had been the dupe to spark off the publicity they wanted to sell this murderess's paintings!

'Wasn't it rather careless of you to lose the bulb, Vincent?'

Kerry eyed her narrowly. 'It was stolen.'

Vera's mouth twisted into a cynical smile. 'But you're the only person with a lamp. Why would anyone else want to steal the bulb?'

Vera's hurt and anger had put a cold, steely edge to her voice. And for Kerry, the penny dropped.

'It was you! Wasn't it?'

Vera kept her calm, almost a smile. 'And why would I wish to do that?'

'Plenty of reasons.' There was hatred in Kerry's eyes now. 'You hate me having these privileges. You envy me because I can paint and you can't.'

Vera's lips were tight. 'Your report stated that you were emotionally unstable, Vincent. I see now how obvious that is.'

Kerry held on to her rising anger with an effort. 'Was it you who slashed my painting? I wouldn't put it past you.'

'You've got a warped mind, Vincent.' Vera was keeping her eye on the woman. She'd murdered once. Who knew how close to the brink she was mentally?

'You wanted me to suck up to you because you knew that way the women would turn on me and do the job for you. Well, I'm smarter than that. That's why I let you blackmail me into giving you that painting.'

Vera's eyes widened in shock. 'You gave it to me.'

'Yes.' There was a manic light in Kerry's eyes now. 'I knew what would happen if I didn't. I haven't forgotten the way you treated me when I first came here. Well, now everyone knows and I hope they throw the book at you!'

She was breathing hard. Vera hesitated for a moment, then without another word turned and walked out. The woman was mad. But this wasn't the moment to push it further. No one would believe her of course. But Vera needed time to think things through.

As her footsteps died away along the corridor, Sharon stepped out of her cell and eased into Kerry's doorway.

'Looking for this?' She held out the lightbulb. 'I only did it for a joke.'

Kerry's impulse was to lash out, but she controlled herself with an effort. 'Looks like I owe Miss Bennett an apology.'

She put out her hand and Sharon, with a pretence of carelessness, dropped the bulb. It splintered into a thousand pieces on the hard cement floor. 'Sorry, accident.'

Kerry was on her feet in a moment. But before she could reach Sharon Judy was standing in the doorway.

'You did that on purpose.'

Sharon swung around. Judy had never spoken to her like that before. 'No, Jude, it was an accident, true.'

She smiled the smile that Judy had loved so well, but Judy's face was cold and set. 'You've done some rotten things in your time, Sharon. And I've always made excuses. I see now that was wrong.'

She turned to Kerry. 'I'll see things are explained, Kerry, and that you get another bulb.'

Sharon knew she'd gone too far. 'Jude, I'm sorry.'

Judy studied her dispassionately. 'Who cares? We're finished, Sharon.'

Sharon looked at her in utter disbelief. But only for a moment. There was a look in Judy's face that said it all. That special look in Judy's eyes . . . that special love . . . had gone.

Nine

'I've been suspended!'
Meg stared incredulously at Vera.
'I don't believe it.'

Vera was hurriedly wrenching things from her locker in the staff room. 'You saw that newspaper article.'

Meg frowned. 'But we all know that was a cheap publicity stunt.'

'It's not the first time Mrs Davidson's taken a prisoner's word against an officer.' Vera's voice was tight and bitter. 'The Vincent woman backed the story up and Mr Fletcher's evidence was all the Governor needed to suspend me.'

Jim moved uneasily in his chair. 'I simply repeated what I overheard. You have to admit that what you said was pretty damning.'

'I'll give you a hand with your things, Miss Bennett.' Jock's tone and expression were deeply sympathetic. 'Frankly, I'm appalled at the Governor's decision.'

It wasn't to be expected that the women would share his view. There was almost a party atmosphere in the laundry. Bea slammed the steam press down with a thwack. 'Got you at last, Vinegar Tits!'

Phyllis looked a bit puzzled. 'I got no time for old

Bennett but d'you reckon she'd really stick her neck out that far?'

'Who cares?' It was Mouse, shoving dirty linen into the washing machines and in high spirits. 'It was prob'ly her that blew the gaff on the sly grog scam.'

At this moment, Doreen fairly exploded into the room. 'Hey! Guess what? Some real estate joker just offered me seventy-five thousand dollars for Mum's old house.'

'Jeez Dor.' Lizzie gave a cackle of laughter. 'You and me's both gonna end up rich bitches, what with my compo and your house.'

Bea looked thoughtful. 'Reckon the offer's ridgy-didge?'

Doreen nodded. 'He had a contract and everything.'

'Bit fast, though?' Bea looked a question at the other women.

Lizzie nodded. 'Do you want to sell, Dor?'

Doreen was confused. 'Wouldn't mind the cash, but I dunno, it's Mum's place and you and me was gonna set up house when we got out, wasn't we?' Lizzie lit up a fag and exhaled a long cloud of smoke before she answered. 'Only one thing to do. Ring Kev, talk it over.' Bea gave Doreen a shrewd look. 'You're still pretty keen on that bloke aren't you?'

Doreen nodded affirmation. 'Had another letter. Wants us to get married just like we planned to.'

'Some hopes with you stuck in here.' Trust Phyllis to look on the bright side!

'It's been done before.' Bea grinned at the women. 'Might be just what we need to cheer up this dump.'

Doreen's face lit up. 'You reckon Davo would go for it?'

'Worth a try.' Lizzie looked at the others who murmured their agreement.

The mood was broken by the appearance of Officer Barfield with the news that Bea had a visitor – Ken Pearce.

Bea's reaction was a bit mixed. She was dead keen to see him again – that bloke really stirred up the old juices for her. But she hadn't forgotten Doreen's info, that Ken had some kind of involvement with Kerry Vincent. Maybe it was time he laid his cards on the table.

Ken was on the point of doing that as he chatted to Jock Stewart in reception, waiting for the all clear to see Bea. It amused Ken to find this guy Stewart, all affability and friendliness to all accounts, raving on about how tough it had been being an officer at Pentridge, and slapped into the maximum security section first off. 'Animals', he'd said those blokes were.

Ken couldn't let that pass. 'Maybe that's because of the way they've been treated.' He kept his eyes on the other man, waiting for the inevitable reaction.

'What would you know about it?' Jock looked him over. 'You do-gooders never see the other side of things.'

'I saw plenty.' Ken could hardly resist a slight grin. 'I did a twenty stretch. I mean, stands to reason I'd know the score.'

The reaction was classic. Jock's eyes were as cold as flint and the affable expression was replaced with a scowl that hinted at a streak of viciousness beneath the easy-going facade.

The look didn't go unnoticed by the social worker,

Paul Reid, as he ushered Bea through reception and invited Ken to join them in his office.

'I'll get an officer to stand guard.'

Jock reached for the phone.

'No.' Paul's tone was quite definite. 'That's won't be necessary. The Governor has given permission for our discussion to take place in my office.'

Stewart was furious, but he couldn't overrule Erica Davidson. Well, he'd make sure smart-arse Reid didn't leave those two alone.

But his resolve was thwarted. Jim came through at the double to tell him he'd have to take over garden duty – Officer Martin had had a bad turn and was already in the infirmary. Reluctantly, Jock accepted the order and made his way out of reception. One consolation: with a bit of luck those two bloody murderers might do each other in and save the Government a lot of time and money.

Paul excused himself from his office as soon as Bea and Ken had made themselves comfortable, coffees in front of them, and a packet of cigarettes within reach.

'Cigarette!' Ken pushed the packet towards Bea. Well, he wasn't going to perform any party tricks! She helped herself to a fag, then, when he made no effort, reached for the box of matches on the desk and lit up. He waited till she'd finished then went through the same little routine.

'How goes the play reading?'

Bea shrugged. 'It's not exactly the Royal Shakespeare but they're trying.'

Ken looked at her speculatively. 'You haven't lost interest have you?'

'Is it so important?' Bea flicked ash from her cigarette with a touch of defiance. 'You *have* got other projects. Kerry Vincent for instance.'

There was nothing slow about Ken Pearce. He knew the old green eye when he saw it! 'She's a talented artist. I'm trying to help her. That's it.'

Bea tried not to let the relief and pleasure show in her face. 'Not much future in getting attached to anyone anyway.'

She met his eyes steadily. 'My old man was shacked up with a floozy three weeks after they slammed me in here.'

'We're not all like that.' There was no doubting the sincerity.

Bea tried for a flippancy she didn't feel. 'Love will find a way, that's what the poets say! Bullshit.'

'Never had you pegged as a defeatist, Bea.' He grinned at her. 'I like "where there's a will" better.'

'Some hopes.'

He reached across and ran a gentle finger down her cheek. 'It's a challenge. I can never resist that, neither can you.'

Did he realize how quickly she'd responded? God, one fleeting touch and he'd just about set her on fire! Maybe there was a way. And if so, she'd bloody find it, that's for sure!

Doreen's interview was very different. She had been amazed when she was told she had another visitor about her Mum's house. She'd phoned Kev and he'd been a hundred percent behind her about not selling. And as she faced this stranger – Harry Bone he'd said his name was – under the watchful eye of Jock Stewart, her resolution grew.

114

She'd said yes to Kev when he'd pressured her again about getting married. Gee, it was beaut to have a fella like you that much, prison record and all. And when he'd talked about him and her and old Lizzie all sharing the home together, that clinched it.

'We're offering you eighty-five thousand dollars, Miss Anderson. That's a lot of bananas.'

There was something too smarmy about this bloke. She didn't like or trust him.

'How come it's gone up ten thousand bucks so fast?' She'd let him see she was no dummy.

'That's the way it is in real estate. Our client's just fallen in love with that place and he wants it at any price. But he wants it now.'

Doreen shook her head. 'I talked it over with my boyfriend. We're not selling.'

The thin smile was replaced by something bordering on the nasty. 'You're making a big mistake. Where are you ever going to get that kind of money again?'

'Kev's starting up his own business after we get married. We'll be OK.' Doreen stood up. 'I'd like to go back now, Mr Stewart.'

Harry Bone was finding it hard to hide his anger and frustration. Jock tipped him a quick wink, then smiled benignly at Doreen. 'It certainly is a lot of cash. Make life easy for a young married couple starting out.' But he recognized the obstinate jut of the chin and he knew better than to pressure the girl at this moment. She'd keep. He moved to the door.

'Mrs Barry, would you take Anderson back to the laundry please?' He ushered Doreen outside and shut the door.

Harry Bone's anger surfaced the moment the door

115

was closed. 'Silly bitch. You'd think she'd grab it. And if she doesn't, it's my neck. She'll have buggered everything up.'

Jock moved closer. 'I'm a bit of a father figure to the girls. She might listen to me.'

Harry looked at him warily. 'Why would you help?'

Jock shrugged. 'Like to help the girl.' He smiled blandly. 'We take the greatest care of these inmates; and the hours we work! And what do we get paid? A pittance.'

Their eyes met. Harry nodded, there was no need to spell it out any further. This bloke had a price like everyone. OK. The deal was on. But he'd better come up with the results in a hurry.

Jock, however, had another priority that had to be fixed first. Vera had told him how she'd taken the painting to David Austin, Kerry's agent, for framing. She'd been trying desperately to get it back but he kept fobbing her off with a cock and bull story about it not being finished. Well, he might react a little differently if Jock turned up.

Jock had good reason for wanting to help Vera out. The truth was he found the women prisoners beneath contempt. And the likes of Vincent being allowed to treat the place like some kind of extended university sickened him. And in Vera, he'd instantly recognized a soul mate, someone who shared his feelings about this scum and the sloppy way the place was run.

And if the truth be known, Jock Stewart was a vicious bully who enjoyed pushing other people around. It would be a pleasure to frighten the shit out of this Austin bum.

It was almost too easy. Austin was scared shitless. Jock enjoyed remembering it as he strolled down the corridor, the painting under his arm. He walked in unannounced through the open cell door where Kerry was working at her easel. Without ceremony, he threw the canvas onto her bunk.

'Miss Bennett doesn't need presents from the likes of you, Vincent.' She watched him warily. There was something about this man, a threat, a hint of suppressed violence.

She shrugged, pretending a nonchalance she didn't feel. 'It would have been wasted on her anyway.'

He moved closer. 'Nevertheless, it was a gift, wasn't it?' His voice was full of menace. 'And that's what you're going to tell the Governor.' There was hatred in his face now. 'Because if you don't, I'll see to it that you never paint again, in here or anywhere else.'

She thought for a moment he was going to strike her. But after a long, ominous silence, he turned and walked abruptly from the cell. She tried to pick up her brush again, but her hands were shaking so badly it clattered on to the cell floor. She stood there, staring at it, feeling that things were closing in around her.

Erica's reaction was swift. Vera was immediately reinstated and Jock received her profuse thanks with an apparent modesty. He couldn't see a good officer have her reputation smirched by one of the scum in Wentworth. And perhaps later she'd like to go out and celebrate. His shout of course. This moment surely called for champagne?

He was as good as his word. And Vera enjoyed herself. But she was just a little troubled next morning,

117

as her aching head confirmed that she had had rather too much to drink and she wondered just how garrulous she'd been. After all, she didn't know Jock Stewart very well.

But she couldn't dwell on it now. Of all the ludicrous things, Mrs Davidson was allowing the wedding plans for that Anderson slob to go ahead. A formal wedding in the prison grounds – disgusting!

Meg, on the other hand, had entered fully into the spirit of things. There were gales of laughter (and a wail of dismay from Doreen) when they discovered the lovely wedding gown Kevin had chosen for his bride was a size too small. Doreen finally confessed that she'd told him a smaller size.

Bea chuckled. 'He's going to find out sooner or later, fatso.'

Doreen looked crushed. 'I figured I'd have six months to lose weight before I got out.'

Meg comforted, arranged for the women in the laundry to let out the seams, assured Lizzie her contributions for the 'something old, something new, something borrowed', did not justify Lizzie pinching a pair of pantyhose and then it was Kerry with the final touch, a delicate little paper posie in red, white and blue, which she'd made herself.

Lizzie fussed about, muttering about 'happy the bride the sun shone on', and indeed it was a lovely day, but Doreen was getting more jittery by the moment. It was almost time when Jock Stewart appeared at the cell door with the news that there was someone to see Doreen about the sale of the house.

Meg demurred. 'Surely it could wait?'

Keeping it pleasant, Jock conveyed that it seemed

pretty urgent. But Doreen was quite definite. She and Kev weren't selling and that was that. Jock shrugged and walked away giving no indication of his own secret reactions. Meg declared the bride a picture, a hug from Bea and Lizzie, and a nervous Doreen was led out to the garden.

If the flowing full-length white wedding gown seemed a little incongruous in the prison setting, neither Kevin nor Doreen was aware of it. Erica, who'd promised to give the bride away, stood smiling, pleased to think that Doreen was taking a firm step towards real rehabilitation when she was released.

Kevin was looking at Doreen with adoring eyes as the Celebrant read out the simple, touching service. Lizzie was enjoying a good cry, Meg was lost in a sea of her own memories, and Bea was trying hard to look a little sceptical and failing completely.

The happy couple were oblivious to the two figures standing near reception, Vera and Jock, united in their scorn and disdain for what they felt was a farce being acted out before them. A cruel smile hovered about Jock Stewart's lips. The happy bride might be in for a surprise or two before much longer!

Ten

There was a natural let down in the recreation room later in the day. Doreen was looking wistfully at her wedding ring and thinking sadly that it wasn't much of a way to spend the wedding night. Bea tried to cheer her with a few ribald quips but her heart wasn't in it either.

It was Kerry who gave a lift to the proceedings. Her gift to Doreen and Kevin was the lovely landscape which she'd originally given to Vera. Doreen was quite overcome and sure that Kev would be thrilled, not just with the picture, but the thought that a real, famous artist would forever have one of her pictures hanging in their home. Kerry shook her head. All the talk about fame and exhibitions was beginning to worry her. She was beginning to have doubts. Were people making a fuss of her work because she was a prisoner and, as such, a novelty? The women tried to assure her that they certainly didn't think so. But it was plain the pressure was getting to Kerry.

There was tension building in Judy's cell too. She hadn't felt well enough to attend the wedding but she'd decorated a pot plant and was putting the final touches to it as a gift to Doreen. Sharon watched jealously, then on a pretext of admiring the plant, took it from Judy and with a swift movement sent it crashing to the floor. For a second, Judy looked down at the shattered pot and the spilt earth and broken plant. Then her hand flew up and she hit Sharon hard across the face.

'You hit me!'

'I should have done it a long time ago.'

Holding a hand to her burning cheek, Sharon turned and stamped angrily out of the cell. Judy watched her go, sad because she no longer felt regret, anger, sorrow – nothing.

The gloom and doom feeling trickled over into the next day until Kerry broke the news to them that she'd come up with a bright idea and the Governor had given the go ahead. Painting lessons! The reaction was not wildly enthusiastic. Kerry took Bea aside. 'Didn't she want to spend a little time with Ken Pearce?' Bea looked suspicious. Kerry laughed. Ken was a mate, had been a great help, but she wasn't his type or he hers. So would Bea like to hear the plan? Bea nodded; she might get as lucky as Marilyn and Eddie.

Kerry looked a question. Eddie had been an electrician who came to fix Marilyn's 'wiring'. 'Course he had free run of the prison. Well, things got so hot between them they finally pushed through the manhole into the attic and they went at it hammer and tongs till the wiring job ran out. And just as well for Eddie that it did. Marilyn had damned near worn him out by that time! Kerry was amused. They mightn't be able to manage quite as much as that, but it was worth a try. And she had a terrific plan. Lizzie had told her about the costumes in the store room that had been used long ago when the prisoners had attempted to put on an Ali

Baba show. A little co-operation from one or two of the women, and it could be a goer.

Bea was surprised the Governor had agreed after all the hoo-hah about Kerry's painting. But that was the point. Davo had invited a reporter to sit in. After the blackmail article that had caused all the trouble, it was important that Wentworth get some good publicity for a change. If this reporter saw Kerry being allowed to instruct the prisoners in a relaxed, informal setting, it would kill the bad publicity and set the record straight.

Bea looked at Kerry in a new light. Not just a bloody great artist, but smart! Kerry chuckled. When Bea knew the rest of the plan, she'd be even more impressed. And then it would be up to Bea to spread the word and get absolute co-operation from the other women. Bea casually flexed her fist and, grinning, assured Kerry that would be no problem at all!

But when the plan was mooted to Lizzie she was strangely distracted. Concerned, Doreen asked her what was wrong. Lizzie was glad to pour out her dilemma to her mate.

That nice Salvo bloke, Mr Barton, had gone ahead and made inquiries about Lizzie's daughter, Marcia. He wanted the go-ahead to try and trace her.

Doreen's reaction was that it was great news. But Lizzie wasn't so sure. All the old guilt feelings had surfaced and she didn't reckon Marcia would want to know her after all these years. In Doreen's opinion, that was up to her. Lizzie sighed. Maybe. She'd have to give it a bit more thought.

Lizzie moved off along the corridor and Doreen paused for a moment to admire her beloved teddy bear, still resplendent in the white wedding bow he'd worn for the big occasion. She didn't hear a sound so that, when she turned and saw Jock Stewart standing in the doorway, it gave her a terrific fright. He kept his voice very low. 'About time you saw sense isn't it?' She looked at him, confused. 'How do you mean?' He hastily shut the door and pushed Doreen up against the wall. 'I'm interested in where you're going to finish up, Anderson.' She looked scared but puzzled. 'In me own house with Kev, that's where.' His grip tightened. 'No it isn't. You're going to reconsider for your own sake.'

Doreen stared at him almost disbelieving this was happening. 'You can't tell me what to do. I'll go to Mrs Davidson.' As suddenly he released her, nodded and turned as if to go. But just as Doreen was thinking of trying to dart past him, he turned and dealt her a stinging blow across the face. Doreen recoiled in shock, her gaze fearful now. He was no longer smiling. She was seeing the real Jock Stewart – a ruthless man who had a price for anything.

What could she do now? If she told anyone, God knows what he'd do to her. And her word against his, no proof. She'd just have to steer clear and maybe before too long she'd find out what it all meant. She wished Kev was there. But he wasn't, and after the wedding there'd be no visiting allowed for a while. Still trembling, she made her way towards the recreation room. Safety in numbers maybe.

Ken and Kerry had already set things up, and distributed paper, pencils and erasers to the women who were seated and who appeared to be in a very receptive frame of mind.

Bea was studiously keeping her distance from Ken,

very aware that Vera and Jock at the doorway were only too anxious for something to happen that would give them reason to stop the class. And Doreen was aware that Jock's gaze was fastened all too often on her.

Sharon was moving about sulkily. Since Bea's return and now her split with Judy the other women had made it very plain that she was no longer of interest. And her spitefulness to both Kerry and Judy (especially the saga of the broken wedding present, so painstakingly prepared by Judy) had set the seal on the general feeling. She was as close to Coventry as they could be bothered with, and knowing that Bea, for all her casual moving about the room, continually kept a close eye on her fuelled the feeling of anger and resentment inside her. Just give her the chance and she'd get these bitches!

At an almost imperceptible nod from Kerry, Phyllis and Mouse moved closer to the doorway, obviously ready to make a prepared speech. 'Wish Judy was here. But she's feeling too tired.' Mouse nodded. 'Yeah, guess she'll be a while getting used to that pacemaker.'

As if at a given signal, Kerry knocked the jar of spare pencils to the floor and as she bent down to pick them up and Ken hastily moved in to help, she was able to pass the word.

'There's going to be trouble. When it happens, go to the store room, fast as you can.' Ken registered concern; what kind of trouble?

'Don't argue.' Kerry fairly spat out the words. 'Bea'll explain later.' His eyes flew across to Bea, sharpening one of the pencils for Margot who'd already managed to get things in a mess. He registered her brief nod and the message in her eyes. 'Trust me.'

Before he could protest further, the action started, Phyllis accusing Lizzie of pinching her pencil, Mouse shouting at the top of her voice that Phyllis was a bloody big bully, and Margot butting in, yelling at them to keep their hands off her mate Mouse or she'd bag the bloody lot of them.

In a moment they were a pushing, shoving melee and with a curt shout to behave themselves from Vera, both she and Jock Stewart were engulfed in the uproar. Kerry almost pushed Ken towards the store room door while the heaving bevy of women blocked the line of vision from the officers.

'All right, that's it!' The women calmed as Jock's voice echoed through the Recreation Room.

Bea stepped forward. 'It was just a touch of high spirits, Miss Bennett.' Vera gave her a cold glance and it was obvious she was about to put paid to the whole scheme when Erica appeared, a young man sporting notepad and pen, obviously a reporter, beside her.

'Attention please, ladies. We have an observer from the newspapers who will be sitting in and taking notes. I trust you will remember you have a guest amongst you.' There was a hint of warning in the words. 'Would you care to sit down?'

The reporter, looking just a little awed, took his place as Erica nodded and left the room.

Vera's sharp eyes swept the room. 'Where is Mr Pearce?' Kerry was ready for her. 'He had to get a few more supplies, Miss Bennett.'

There was the faintest suspicion in Vera's eyes but she let it ride. He couldn't get far with both herself

125

and Stewart on duty. Kerry looked across at Bea. 'Would you get ready now please, Bea?' 'Right.' Cool as a cucumber Bea headed for the store room, opened the door and stepped inside.

'Bea is going to model for us. I thought you'd find something a little out of the ordinary more fun than just ordinary civvies.'

'Thought these models always posed in the nuddy?'

Vera and Jock exchanged a look of distaste at this sally from Phyllis. At that moment they heard Bea calling from the store room. 'Ready for me?' Kerry smiled and crossed to the door. And on cue big Margot walked up to Jock and Vera, obscuring their vision, and demanded to go to the toilet.

Jock reluctantly assented and by the time he'd led Margot out the figure in the flowing Arabian gown and elaborate head dress was seated on the stool, her back to the women and the only thing visible the eyes.

'I've asked Bea to face away from you at first, so you can concentrate on the garment. It's very important you get the line right.' Doreen nudged Lizzie and whispered softly 'Reckon they're at it yet?'

Inside the store room Bea and Ken sat across from each other on old wooden crates. The overhead light was off and only a dim torch lit their faces in the gloom.

'Pretty good scam to get Judy to take your place.'

Bea nodded and chuckled. 'Kerry's bright idea.' She paused, then said with her typical forthrightness. 'I was wrong about her. She's OK.'

After that, there was a long pause. The strange awkwardness of something they had both wanted so much,

126

and now – what to say, where to begin? It was Bea who broke the silence.

'I feel such an idiot.'

Ken's voice was gentle. 'Why?'

'Because I'm a woman of forty and I'm hiding in a cupboard so I can grab a few moments alone with a fella.'

'Any fella?' It sounded casual but she knew from his eyes the answer was important.

'No.' Bea searched for the words. 'I guess I've forgotten how to make small talk.'

'That makes two of us.'

The silence wasn't a worry but there was an urgent need in Bea to communicate with this man.

'I'll probably have to hold on to these few minutes for the next ten years.' She sighed. 'When you're outside, you think you got all the time in the world to tell someone . . . what you're feeling.' The words were coming more easily now. 'After you've been on the inside for a while, you're lucky if you can remember what feeling even means. Or if you do, how do you remember the way to tell someone?'

For a moment Ken didn't reply. He was living all those lonely years in prison, the longing to speak, to have someone understand. And he knew that what he said now was so important for Bea, and for himself.

'You know what I feel about you, Bea Smith?' He kept his eyes on her face, as though he were memorizing it for a future time. 'You're a mixture of anger, fury and a lot of strengths. A survivor. But you've managed to keep so much warmth and honesty and softness.' He shook his head. 'A woman like you's never going to know what it's like *not* to feel.' And the next words were right from the heart. 'I reckon I'm a lucky man to've even met you.'

He saw the tear sliding slowly down Bea's cheek and, gently, he wiped it away with his finger.

'When you did that, the other day,' Bea groped for the right words, 'it made me feel alive again, most of all, a woman.'

He reached for her hands and for a moment they just sat there, touching, feeling through their finger tips, a kind of caressing that was caring at its uttermost.

After a moment, Bea freed her hands and slowly, softly she explored the contours of his face. So good to touch, after all this time. Dear God, the sense of loss when this moment was over. How would she ever live through it?

As though he read her thoughts, he drew her face close to his and slowly, softly, he pressed his lips to hers – a kind of sweet reverence that was almost beyond the physical.

Kerry would wonder afterwards how she managed to keep talking for so long about so little. It was obvious the women, for all their good intentions to Bea, were getting bored and restless. And dear God, most of them had less idea of sketching than a kindergarten beginner.

Vera, too, felt the class had gone on quite long enough. She said as much to Jock Stewart and he heartily agreed, though he was secretly enjoying the discomfort he was causing Doreen, just by being there.

'I can imagine what the standard of art is like.'

Vera gave Jock a cynical smile and moved towards the women, glancing over their shoulders and discovering how very right she had been. Their efforts were appalling! As Kerry continued to coax and explain, Vera came to a halt behind Sharon's chair. She glanced down casually at the girl's drawing and drew a quick breath. Printed across the rough sketch were the words 'CHECK STORE ROOM. SMITH AND PEARCE THERE.'

Vera kept her cool and cursed herself for not checking up properly on Ken Pearce. Never mind, this was even better, to catch him and that belligerent Smith creature first hand. She strolled casually towards the reporter. His notepad was closed and he was obviously getting pretty fed up with proceedings.

'I daresay you've seen enough. And we'll have to terminate class for tonight. The Officer at the Security Gate will see you out.' He nodded and with a brief word of thanks hurried out of the room, plainly glad to have finished a pretty dreary assignment.

'We've been conned, Mr Stewart.'

Jock was instantly alert, hurrying to Vera's side, as she marched to the store room and flung wide the door. A quick flick and the room was flooded with light. Bea and Ken, sitting side by side on the crate, holding hands, were momentarily dazzled by the sudden glare, then all too quickly aware of Vera glaring triumphantly at them.

'Get out of there.'

A swift, regretful glance between them and then they walked quietly out of the room. The women were quiet, shocked, and saddened that somehow they'd let Bea down. Only Sharon felt a quick rush of pleasure as she hastily crumpled her sketch and held it tightly in her palm.

'I can explain, Miss Bennett.' Ken eyed her quite calmly.

'Save it for the Governor, Mr Pearce.' She turned to Jock and he stepped forward, laying a heavy hand on Ken's arms.

Ken had had too much of that kind of treatment over the years. He shook the hand off abruptly and walked to the door, with Jock Stewart close behind him. Once there, he turned – a quick, intimate smile for Bea – and he was gone.

Vera moved to the 'model' and looked directly into the big brown eyes that could only belong to Judy Bryant. She ripped the head dress off with one deft movement.

'Looks like all sorts of people are in all sorts of trouble.' But she wasn't looking at Judy or Bea, but at Kerry . . . revenge was going to be so sweet!

Sharon saw this as her chance to get rid of her sketch. She was making a furtive move towards the wastepaper basket when Doreen latched on to what was happening. With a quick lunge, Doreen grabbed Sharon's wrist, and in a moment had wrenched the crumpled drawing from her. As Sharon made a grab for it, Doreen darted behind Mouse and Phyllis as she read the damning words.

'She lagged on you, Bea.'

'Give me that.' Sharon made a dive for her but the women were quick to position themselves between her and Doreen. And the hatred in their faces stopped Sharon in her tracks. She had committed the unforgiveable sin – shopped a fellow prisoner.

'Get to your cell, Gilmour. And you Bryant. I'll deal with you two later.'

130

Sharon needed no second invitation. She'd acted out of spite and now she was really scared. They'd be out to get her and she didn't even have Judy to turn to.

Judy gave Bea a small, wistful smile. 'Sorry, hon.'

Bea nodded – they'd all stuck their necks out for her. She wouldn't forget that. As for Gilmour – that'd be the first thing she'd take care of!

Vera glanced around the room with disdain. 'I'd have thought a woman of your age would have a bit more dignity, Smith.'

Bea pressed her lips tightly together. Mustn't let Vera get at her . . . hang on to that precious little time you had, don't let her or anyone else spoil it for you.

But if the truth be known, Vera's wisecrack at Bea was just routine, what the women would expect. The real joy was to come as her cold, grey eyes focused on Kerry.

'Get this mess cleaned up.' She savoured her words. 'Then go to your cell, Vincent.' The ugly smile was on her lips.

'I'd say this little fiasco has just cost you the privilege of being able to pursue your precious painting.'

The women turned sympathetic eyes towards Kerry. They knew how much her work meant to her, and like them, she'd stuck her neck out for Bea. 'Show a bit of heart, Miss Bennett.'

It was Lizzie, voicing what they all felt as they registered the devastated expression on Kerry's face. For answer, Vera turned and walked out without another word.

'You've gotta *have* a heart first, Lizzie.' Bea's voice was quiet, and there was compassion in her eyes as she watched Kerry slowly packing up her gear.

*

No one was too surprised at the outcome: Ken Pearce banned from Wentworth, Doreen taken off the gardening duties she enjoyed so much, Sharon moved to a single cell for her own protection (Erica knew all too well how the prisoners treated someone who lagged) and switched to kitchen duties, out of Bea Smith's reach. Erica made it clear that if anything happened to Gilmour, Smith would be the first to be suspected. But the best news of all for Vera was that Kerry's art materials were to be confiscated, immediately!

Vera undertook that personally, of course, and Kerry could only stand by helplessly. She'd pleaded with Vera to at least let her have her sketching pad and charcoal but even this was denied. Vera made as if to snatch the finished painting standing on the easel. 'Please! At least wait until it's dry.' Vera paid no heed and reached for the canvas. In a flash, Kerry had grabbed the painting and bashed it against the cell wall, in a frenzy of anger and frustration. Vera gave her a tight smile, as she picked up the easel. 'Better watch that temper, Vincent. That's what got you inside in the first place.'

A moment later, the rage had passed and as Kerry looked around the cell, empty of her work now except for the broken canvas, an all-enveloping sense of loss swept over her. She threw herself face down on the hard bunk and the sobs that wracked her were from deep down inside, the anguished sounds of a woman who's heart and spirit had finally been broken.

Sharon's bunk was stripped and her things packed. She was putting on a bravado she didn't feel and Judy was well aware of it.

'You realize what you've done, don't you?'

She met Judy's eyes defiantly. 'Bea Smith had it coming to her.'

Judy's lips tightened. 'You've got a lot of people into a lot of trouble. Doesn't that bother you at all?' Sharon shrugged. 'The screws'll be looking after me.'

'They'll want to.' Judy eyed her with mounting hostility. 'As far as I'm concerned, you just ran out of your last friend.'

'So?' She moved towards the doorway. 'Funny, isn't it? You got yourself put inside so you could be near me. Now you're telling me to get lost.' She gave a tight, spiteful smile. 'Well you've got a year left to serve, for nothing. Reckon that's pretty stupid.'

Judy was on her feet, anger flooding through her, and perhaps for the first time ever Sharon was afraid of her. Without another word she quickly grabbed her things and scurried out of the cell. And on Judy's face there was an expression of implacable hardness. Maybe it was time someone really did teach that kid a lesson – one she'd never forget.

Sharon was moving along the corridor when she heard the sound of a man's voice coming from the direction of Bea Smith's cell. But Bea wasn't in there – it was Doreen's scared voice she could hear. And the man was Jock Stewart! Sharon checked . . . no one around. If she crept just a couple of feet closer she could hear what he was saying. Her eyes widened in surprise. He was threatening Doreen about selling her house!

'You wait till I tell Kev.' Doreen's voice was shaky, scared.

'Kev's not here. But I am.' His voice was full of menace. 'And this is just a sample of what's going to happen if you don't do as you're told.' An anguished cry from Doreen as he punched her hard in the stomach.

'I'll be back in five minutes for another "chat". Think it over.' Sharon slowly resumed walking, towards Doreen's cell.

Jock reacted sharply as he stepped out and saw her.

'Just moving my things.'

He eyed her sharply. How much had she heard?

Sharon played her cards carefully. 'Smith and her lot are out to get me. I need protection.' She gave him a sly glance. 'Maybe you and me could be of use to each other.'

Not for a moment did he betray any sign of suspicion.

'In what way, Gilmour?'

'You set me up with a few comforts and extra protection – I won't let on about what I just heard.'

Jock paused, and favoured her with one of his friendliest smiles. 'Looks like you and me are going to get on just fine, Gilmour.' Sharon breathed a deep sigh of relief. She'd be safe with Jock Stewart around.

Bea was looking rather anxiously at Doreen. 'I know you'd rather work in the garden than the laundry, Dor, but it's not the end of the world.'

Doreen was trying desperately to hide how frightened she was and how sick she'd been feeling since Stewart had punched her so violently in the stomach.

'It's OK. Gets a bit lonely in the garden, anyway.'

Bea frowned. 'Sure there's nothing else worrying you?' It was a relief to be able to show genuine concern.

'Was wondering whether they'll still let Kev visit me.'

Bea sighed. 'It's all my bloody fault. How about you have a word with Davo? You weren't to blame.'

'No.' Doreen was panicked at the thought. Gawd knows what Stewart might do if he thought she'd been talking to the Governor. 'Let's wait and see what happens.' Doreen forced that ghost of a smile.

'OK.' Bea decided to let it go, for now. But she was bloody sure there was something going on with Dor and she'd make it her business to find out. That bitch, Vera, they'd have to nail her somehow before she drove every woman in the prison to breaking point.

Vera was indeed feeling very pleased with herself as she carried Kerry's art gear along the corridor leading to the stores. She was so preoccupied with her own thoughts that she jumped when Jock spoke to her.

'Can I give you a hand, Miss Bennett?'

He smiled and relieved her of the cumbersome load.

'I'd no idea Kerry Vincent had managed to accumulate so much stuff.'

They were almost past the staircase when Vera casually glanced up and then stopped in her tracks.

'What's that?'

He followed her gaze to the landing platform. A figure bending over something. They took the stairs two at a time then stopped aghast as Judy Bryant straightened and turned to face them, her eyes wide, her face chalky white.

Slowly Vera let her eyes travel to the platform. Sharon Gilmour was lying there, an arm crumpled under her as if she'd fallen from a great height. Her eyes were wide and staring. It was obvious before Vera even knelt to check the pulse that the girl was dead.

Eleven

There was a sense almost of unreality amongst the women when the news of Sharon's death got out. She'd hardly been the most popular person in Wentworth, but no one wanted to end up the way she had. As Bea had put it, 'The question is, did she fall or was she pushed?'

In her first moments of remorse and anguish Judy had screamed at Bea, accusing her of murdering Sharon.

But after questioning, Detective Teagan soon put paid to that. Meg Jackson had been with Bea and Doreen at the time the tragedy had occurred. Kerry's alibi was rock solid (she was naturally a suspect with her background and record of mental instability).

The finger at first pointed straight at Judy. She'd been the first at the scene of the crime – if indeed it was that. Accidental death was a strong possibility, even though it didn't tie in too well with forensic findings.

But the blatant hostility and lust for vengeance from Judy was hardly the reaction likely if she'd killed Sharon Gilmour. And as Erica delicately pointed out, Judy had had a very special friendship with the girl. Teagan reminded her that Bryant had herself said the relationship had ended two weeks ago. Erica felt that simply underlined the fact that this was most certainly not a crime of passion on Bryant's part.

Kevin was terribly shocked when Doreen, enjoying his visit in the prison garden, passed on the news. God, nothing like that could happen to her, could it? Doreen, mindful of the watchful eye of Jock Stewart, tried to make light of it. She was more concerned that Kev had been, as he'd confided, heavied by some guy over the house. He made light in turn. They weren't going to be bullied into selling, no way! Doreen demurred as much as she dared but Kevin was adamant. Not for twice the cash offered. It was Dor's house, she was to keep it and he'd provide for his wife, and old Lizzie if need be.

All too soon their time was up. Meg Jackson had come out to say hello to Kevin and when he spontaneously went to put his arms around Doreen for a farewell hug, Meg smiled and nodded.

Jock Stewart took her to task – the rule was no physical contact. Meg accused him of being a killjoy. Those two had just got married, surely a quick hug in the garden under the eyes of two officers wasn't going to start a riot?

Jock said no more but his expression was very thoughtful. Meantime, in the interview room, Lizzie Birdsworth was listening intently to Officer Lloyd Barton of the Salvation Army. He'd been spending time trying to trace her children. It seemed Lizzie's two sons had been fostered out relatively early. It would take a long time to trace them through various records and Jigsaw. And of course they might not wish to be contacted. Lizzie looked a bit downhearted at that. The old sense of guilt about her kids came crowding back, but Lloyd Barton's next words sent a flicker of hope through her.

'We've had a bit more luck with your daughter Marcia.' He referred briefly to his notes. 'Seems she was in the home till she was sixteen. And she kept in touch for eight years or more.'

'Where is she now?' Lizzie's voice was eager.

'The last they knew of her, she was married, living in Melbourne. Of course that was twenty years ago.'

Lizzie's heart sank. Twenty years! How'd they ever find her now? 'So,' Barton smiled kindly at her, 'I took the liberty of advertising, and I got an answer.'

'And?' Lizzie was fairly hopping out of her chair.

'The lady says she is, or was, Marcia Birdsworth.'

'What do we do now?'

Lizzie's thoughts were in a whirl. Wonderful news, and yet – her daughter mightn't want to catch up with an old gaol bird, not even one who'd been wrongfully imprisoned all those years.

'We arrange a visit. If you'd like that?'

He watched the thin, sharp face that mirrored the long years of prison and tough survival. Life had been hard for Lizzie Birdsworth. He wanted very much to bring some joy into it.

'Can I think about it?'

He nodded. 'Of course. But you've already waited a very long time for this moment.'

Yes, indeed she had. But Gawd, she looked a wrinkled old skinny fright! And that Marcia, she'd been such a pretty little thing.

He saw the gentleness in her weathered face as she thought about her child. Any doubts as to whether he should have tried to find her daughter were banished, once and for all.

When she returned to the laundry, she found the place in uproar. It seemed Jim Fletcher had come marching in and ordered Doreen to undergo a search. She'd had physical contact with Kevin in the garden and it'd been reported that Kev had slipped her a parcel. Bea was sceptical.

'Dor wouldn't be that stupid. Those visits from Kev mean too much to her.' The women were in agreement. They were stunned subsequently to learn that a miniature of Scotch had been found on Doreen, and Davo, furious at her for abusing privileges (not to mention being allowed to hold the wedding inside), had ordered her to solitary. Bea was worried.

'That kid hasn't been herself for days. This could push her over the edge.'

Lizzie frowned. 'You don't s'pose she got Kev to slip it to her for me? He knows I love a drop.'

Bea shook her head. 'He wouldn't be that dumb, not even for you, you silly old faggot.' She compressed her lips into a tight line. 'Something stinks around here but I'm buggered if I can put my finger on it.'

There was a lot going on that no one seemed able to explain. With no actual evidence – just a sea of suspicions and possibilities – Detective Teagan had no other choice but to presume Sharon Gilmour's death was accidental.

Judy reacted so violently, made such wild threats about Bea, that the Governor decided to move her to Isolation till she'd cooled off. Whether Judy really did think Bea had killed Sharon (in spite of a watertight alibi) wasn't clear. Maybe it was just someone to blame, anything to ease the pain of guilt, grief and remorse that was wracking her.

There was, however, someone who could have enlightened both Judy and Detective Teagan. As Jock Stewart shoved Doreen roughly into solitary, the words he hissed in her ear were the most terrifying she had ever heard. 'Sell that house or you'll go the same way Sharon did.'

The door slammed, the silence seemed deafening. She put her hands over her ears – her head was full of silent screams – and threw herself sobbing on to the hard, cold bunk. When she woke in the morning, the screams were still there, but this time they were for real, coming from her own throat as she fought her way out of the hideous nightmare to blurred consciousness.

She ran, screaming, sobbing, to the door and banged hard on the peephole. As it slowly opened, and the hated face of Jock Stewart was revealed, an evil smile playing about his lips, she choked back the sobs. 'I want to make a phone call.'

His smile broadened. 'I thought you might.' The smile faded. 'But it's against the rules. The Governor would never allow it.'

She looked at him pitifully. 'I wanna ring that lawyer, tell him I'll sell.'

He glanced swiftly over his shoulder then turned back to her. 'In that case, I think we can bend the rules just this once.' Again the smile. 'I'll dial the number and stay with you, just to make sure.' She nodded. Let them have the house. God, she couldn't live through another night like that!

It took only a moment to make the call. Why hadn't

she just done it in the first place and saved herself this horror stretch. Kev would be disappointed in her, but he'd understand, he'd have to.

Kevin was standing at that very moment, staring at his van. It had been done over good and proper with a message scratched into the paint work to assure him he could expect more of the same. That did it. A half an hour later he was standing outside Doreen's mother's house. So that was it. The house on either side had already been bulldozed. A sign spelt out what kind and how many units were about to be erected on the sight of the three houses. And there was a SOLD sign on Dor's. He might have known some shonky, stinkin' developer was behind the whole thing.

He was dismayed when Meg told him he couldn't see Doreen because she was in solitary. They couldn't do that to his Dor. Meg explained briefly and she knew from his reaction that he was telling the truth. No way had he slipped anything to Doreen.

He turned away, shattered, then a thought struck him. 'Could I see Bea Smith?'

Meg was pleased to follow through for him and in a few minutes he was facing Bea across the table in the interview room with Meg keeping a watchful but sympathetic eye on them. Bea was taken aback. 'But the house can't have been sold.'

'Got a sold sign on it. You see, that's why they upped the cash, 'cos only Dor's house is stopping the units being built.'

'Bloody creeps.' Bea grinned at Meg. 'Sorry, Mrs J.'

Kevin looked at Bea searchingly. 'Why? She was as determined as me to keep it. Why did she change her mind and sell?'

It was a question that bugged Bea for the rest of the day. She was lying on her bunk, deep in thought, when a voice hailed her from the doorway.

'How's tricks, Queenie?'

Bea knew that voice. Helen Smart, the unsmart prostitute who kept getting herself nabbed. Good looker though, and a good sort. 'Come in for a rest did ya?' Bea grinned at her.

'Gawd no.' Helen propped herself against the cell door. 'A lot easier to just lay back and think of England than pushing this bloody tea trolley 'round in here.'

'You just missed your mate Kerry Vincent. Got paroled yesterday, though how the hell she wangled it I'll never know.'

'Easy.' Helen offered Bea a fag and lit up herself. 'That smart-arse agent of hers got the press all excited about the kid that was murdered. Practically had the big wigs in the Department begging old Davo to get Kerry out faster than a speeding bullet so the reporters'd get off their backs and stop asking awkward questions about Wentworth.'

'I still don't reckon it was accidental.'

'The word is Judy Bryant swears you did it.'

'I hated Gilmour's guts but I'm not that stupid.' Bea chuckled. 'When I go into action, I like a little finesse. You ought to know that.'

Helen laughed. 'So – what's the real story?'

'Dunno, yet.' Bea eyed Helen speculatively for a moment.

'Tea lady, eh? Reckon you could get a message to Doreen in solitary?' Helen wiggled her shapely form seductively.

'With my brains and my gorgeous tits, the sky's the limit, kiddo.'

'How will you do it?'

'Just give me the note.' Helen dropped her cigarette and ground it out. 'I don't give away trade secrets.'

Bea would have been impressed with how easily Helen did manage to get the note to Doreen. Officer Barfield admitted her with the loaded food tray and just as she was about to put it down, Helen caught her footing, stumbled and sent food flying everywhere.

While Barfield bawled her out for making such a mess, Helen quickly slipped her lipstick to Doreen. She answered the question in Doreen's eyes with a quick wink, as she scrabbled about picking up the cutlery and china.

When she was finally alone again, Doreen hastily extracted the flimsy piece of paper from the lipstick case. 'WHY DID YOU SELL? K.' Doreen's hand shook as she pushed up the bright red lipstick and quickly wrote her reply. Another moment, and the slip of paper was safely back in the lipstick case.

She was literally holding her breath when Officer Barry opened the door to admit Helen with the evening meal. And it was a simple thing to slip the lipstick back to Helen who had little trouble in distracting the good natured Joan Barry's attention for a moment. Thank God Stewart hadn't been on duty! There'd have been no way he wouldn't have seen the exchange.

Bea didn't get a chance to see Helen before she was discharged next day. Smart was OK, but she wasn't the most reliable girl on the block! Bea was a bit doubtful whether she'd remembered her promise, let alone pulled it off. But she' have been proud of Helen as she made a show of touching up her lipstick while Jim Fletcher searched her bag and belongings before she took a frivolous leave of the other officers in reception.

Lizzie was mulling over her own problems when Bea expressed her doubts to her old mate. She didn't get much joy out of Lizzie and things weren't a lot brighter when she strolled into the recreation room a little later. The mystery that still hung over Sharon's death had unnerved the women. Added to that, several of the women were beginning to have grave doubts about jovial Jock Stewart. He could turn pretty nasty when things didn't go his way.

Phyllis put in her two bob's worth. 'Helen reckons he gets his sex jollies out of bashing up the ladies.'

'He wouldn't be the first.' But it was giving Bea food for thought.

She tensed as big Judy Bryant walked into the room. Jude had been pretty ugly – a side of her Bea hadn't seen before – and she was on the alert, ready to lash out first if need be.

But Judy was low key, moving off to a corner, obviously too miserable to stay in her own cell, but in no mood for company either. It was Mouse who enlightened them. 'She wanted to go to Sharon's funeral. They knocked her back.'

Phyllis looked sympathetic. 'That's a bit bloody rough. Why not?'

'Said she wasn't family.'

Bea shrugged. 'Strikes me she was a lot closer to Sharon than anyone else. Who ever visited the kid?'

Margot leered. 'They was close all right.'

Lizzie had come quietly in in time to hear Mouse's

145

explanation and she turned sharply on Margot. 'Bit of respect for the dead wouldn't go amiss.'

'Gawd, you've really gone holier than thou since you got mixed up with them bloody Salvos.' Margot gave Lizzie a prod and took herself off to the television. For once Lizzie didn't even attempt to hit back and Bea noticed.

'What the hell is wrong with you, Birdsworth?'

Lizzie sighed. 'Just can't make up me mind whether to see Marcia or not. What if she takes one look and runs a mile?'

'Her loss.' Bea gave her old friend an affectionate pat on the shoulder. 'Go for it! She might have turned out a real good sort, like her mother.'

Lizzie chuckled and her face brightened. 'Yeah. Why not?'

The Governor had hardly got herself settled in her office the next day when Meg Jackson brought Kevin Burns in to see her. Helen had been as good as her word. Kevin explained that he'd received a note. Erica frowned. Did he realize he and Doreen were violating prison regulations?

Meg looked sympathetically at him; alas, rules were rules. But when Erica saw the note he proferred her expression became very serious. In bold red lipstick were the words 'HE WOULD HAVE KILLED ME.'

'To whom is Doreen referring?'

'I don't know.'

It was a very honest, straightforward face that Erica was looking into.

'Whoever he is, he was putting pressure on Doreen

to sell. I checked. The lawyer got a phone call from her yesterday morning.'

'Impossible. She was in solitary.'

'It was her all right.' Kevin managed a smile. 'She said her name was Anderson, then apologized and said she forgot she got married and her name's Burns.'

Meg couldn't hide a small chuckle. 'That's Doreen all right.' Erica looked again at the note.

'Leave this with me, Mr Burns. I assure you I will get to the bottom of it.'

'Does she have to stay in solitary? I mean if there is someone . . .' He looked appealingly at Erica.

'You can rest assured I'll attend to that too.'

After he'd gone, the Governor turned a worried face to Meg. 'This could be very serious indeed, Meg.'

'Yes.'

Erica sighed. 'We're in enough trouble with the Department now!' She shook her head as if to clear it and take one hurdle at a time. 'See that Doreen's released will you? And I'll call an emergency meeting of the male officers.'

When Vera came on duty she was all questions as Meg drank a quick coffee in the staff room.

'Has someone made a direct accusation against a male officer?' Meg shook her head. 'Just a suspicion at this stage, no actual proof.' But Vera noticed the particularly thoughtful expression on Meg's face. 'What else?'

Meg shrugged. 'I was just wondering who was on duty in solitary when Doreen was allowed to make a phone call?'

Vera's eyebrows shot up alarmingly. 'Make a phone call!'

147

Meg nodded. 'I've checked it out for the Governor.'

Vera thought for a moment.

'Jock Stewart. I was on the same shift.'

'Curiouser and curiouser.' Meg drained her cup and stood up.

'I wouldn't mind being a fly on the wall at that meeting.'

Unfortunately, Erica achieved very little. The men mainly reacted with hostility, apart from Jock Stewart who felt it was only reasonable that Erica should investigate an accusation of any kind.

But when Doreen was brought in to verify the note, to the Governor's surprise, she denied categorically that she had written it or indeed knew anything about it.

After the men had gone, however, Erica sat thinking for some time. There was no denying that Doreen had been nervous, very nervous. If there was even a shadow of a doubt . . . But until she had more evidence she could do nothing.

A shaken Doreen sought out Judy Bryant in the garden. She had decided it was high time Judy stopped displaying aggro towards Bea when she could now be told the truth of what had happened.

Doreen looked about her nervously as she told Judy to listen carefully. Jock Stewart had killed Sharon, he had as good as told Doreen when he was threatening her about the house. Judy's reaction of anger and outrage had to be quickly jumped on. Didn't Jude see that the only way they'd get anyone to believe them was to somehow make him trip himself up? No good a prisoner's word against an officer, they all knew that.

It was a long moment before Judy was calm enough to think clearly. 'But why would he do it?'

Doreen shook her head. 'Dunno, less she latched on to what he was doing to me and he thought he'd better shut her up.' 'We've got to get proof.' They put their heads together. Judy would have to goad Jock at every opportunity. Doreen would spread the word that the women must stick around at all times that he and Judy were together, for her safety, and for witnesses.

'What if it doesn't work?'

Doreen's face hardened. 'It has to. I'm going to get that bastard if it's the last thing I do!'

There were plenty of women to back up their plan, but in spite of every attempt on Judy's part, Jock Stewart was keeping his cool, playing it safe. Even when Judy blatantly accused him, he was impassive, unruffled, laughing in their faces. But Vera had noticed. Why was he letting the women speak to him in that way, and without so much as a reprimand? When she tackled him he laughed it off, talking about their hysteria, probably a mass case of PMT.

Puzzled, Vera was almost ready to dismiss the whole thing. No one could be as relaxed and pleasant as Jock was if there was any sort of threat hanging over them. And then she saw it. He'd offered her a lift; she'd declined and walked to her usual bus stop. She never knew why she looked back but she was glad now that she had. She'd recognized the man who had walked up to Jock Stewart and handed him a packet. That awful creature, Harry Bone, who had visited Anderson about the house sale. Vera never forgot a face, and seldom a name. What was in that packet?

Stewart might have been friendly to her and, indeed, involved her socially! But for all her stringent behaviour to the women, Vera had her principles when it came to corrupt officers.

Being Vera, she tackled him, albeit in private, head on. He assumed a rather woebegone expression. The pay was so bad, he'd run up a few debts. It was nothing to do with the prison or the inmates – just a private deal and all above board.

He'd rather it didn't get out. He'd been named in one Royal Commission, didn't want another black mark on his record. And then he made his big mistake by inferring he'd be happy to see Vera 'right' if they could keep it between them.

Vera kept her cool but in fact she was outraged at this obvious attempt at bribery. She laid the whole matter before the Governor. The phone call, his peculiar reactions to Bryant when she accused him of murder, and, finally, the bribe from Harry Bone, and the offer to herself.

Doreen was brought before the Governor once again. She was willing to admit that she'd been pressured by Harry Bone, and she'd got word that Kevin's van had been just about wrecked. But she wouldn't come forward about Sharon. For her part, she just wanted to forget it all, sell the house and make sure Kev was safe.

But for Erica, Vera's findings were enough. She called Jock Stewart in, accused him of being a party to extortion and informed him she would request an immediate transfer. And of course she would contact Detective Teagan.

He took it remarkably calmly and Erica began to

150

realize that under the affable exterior there was quite another person and perhaps someone capable of being guilty of Sharon Gilmour's death. But like Judy she was baffled as to a motive.

It was desperately frustrating for Bea and Judy and the others to learn that even under close examination Detective Teagan was unable to come up with anything concrete in the way of evidence. It was all circumstantial, not enough to put a man behind bars.

Doreen felt nothing but relief to know Jock Stewart was being immediately transferred. And Kev was right, it was all over now and they had decided not to sell. She still hadn't signed and the Governor had assured her she'd see to it that there was no further trouble. The developer and his whole entourage were under investigation.

Judy took little comfort. This man was walking away, scot free. She was working in the garden, near reception, when Jock Stewart exited the main building for the last time.

He checked, and to all appearances and intentions, he was simply saying a pleasant farewell to a prisoner. But Judy would never forget the sadistic smile on his face as he hissed those final words at her.

'No justice is there? They've suspended me but you wanted more didn't you? You'll never get it now.' He gave a mirthless laugh. 'Silly little bitch was trying to blackmail me. Well she pushed me too hard . . . So I "pushed" her. Never cried out when she hit the platform, just a dull thud.' He straightened, so that anyone watching would think he was chatting normally. 'I walk away and you do your time. Them's the breaks, Bryant.' And he was gone.

She wanted to scream, to lash out! She knew it was all futile. 'One day, Sharon,' it was a heartfelt vow, 'I'll catch up with him, and I'll prove he murdered you. I promise!'

Twelve

Bea could understand Judy's anger and frustration. Indeed, now the truth had filtered through to the women about what really happened to Sharon, feeling was running very high. Even those who'd actively disliked the girl were burning with the injustice of it all, and Jock Stewart getting off so lightly. But what could they do?

Bea had quickly squashed Judy's suggestion that she would go on a hunger strike. She knew from experience that they'd simply get locked in their cells and starved out. The women would never be on for it and it was madness to plan any kind of action without proper preparation. If they were going to strike – and Bea was more than willing for a bit of action – then they'd have to prepare for a long siege.

It was obvious both Lizzie and Doreen were anxious to steer clear of trouble. The Governor had told Doreen that if she behaved herself she would ask the Classification Committee to consider a day pass so she could spend time outside of the prison with Kevin. And Lizzie, nervous and still not quite sure, was bracing herself for the meeting with her daughter Marcia whom she hadn't seen for thirty years.

As it turned out, the meeting went very well. It was a pity old Vinegar Tits had to be the duty officer but at least they'd been allowed to meet in the garden; she was glad of that. She could tell right off that Marcia was nervous, probably – thank God – never been near a prison in her life.

After the first rather stilted exchanges, they fell to talking about old times, and if Lizzie had at any time thought her visitor just might be an imposter, her fears seemed groundless. Marcia was only too happy to reminisce. But Lizzie was disappointed not to see her granddaughter, Josie. Marcia, a bit embarrassed, explained that she was worried the surroundings might upset the child. But now that she'd realized they could meet in this pleasant garden, she'd be sure and bring Josie along on the next visit allowed. After all, it was very important the three of them make up for lost time. In fact, it was Marcia's hope that when Lizzie was released, the three of them could get together, find a little place and start a whole new life. Marcia was now alone, and Josie would be thrilled to get to know her 'new' grandmother.

Lizzie agreed, with just a little reserve. P'raps she'd gone past living with a thirteen-year-old? Marcia smiled; she'd find Josie a lovely girl; affectionate, well-behaved. There was no time for further planning: Vera brought the meeting to an abrupt halt and after a quick, affectionate kiss from Marcia, Lizzie was led back inside the prison, her thoughts in something of a whirl.

As she confided to Doreen later, it was bound to feel pretty strange after all those years. You couldn't just bridge the gap in one short meeting. Doreen gave her a slightly concerned glance. But was this woman Lizzie's daughter, Marcia? Lizzie's reply was almost sharp. Of course! She wasn't that senile she didn't know her own flesh and blood!

And after Lizzie had met her granddaughter Josie, she confided to Lloyd Barton of the Salvo that she'd realized for the first time in her life how much she'd missed her kids and how wonderful it was to have a family again. She wished she could get her hands on her compo right now so she could set Marcia and Josie up – it was plain they didn't have a feather to fly with. Not that they said or asked for a thing. Marcia didn't even want to hear about the compo.

Doreen had the perfect solution. How about Marcia and the kid move into her house till they both got out? Not good to have it sitting there empty, and Kev didn't want to move in till they did it proper, like a real married couple. Lizzie jumped at the idea and it was obviously a Godsend for her daughter.

With typical kindness, Kevin had arranged to drive Marcia and Josie to Echuca to get the rest of their stuff. Marcia thanked him profusely and it was only after he'd gone that she quietly told Josie to be careful what she said in front of her 'grandmother' and this nice man Kevin Burns. Josie nodded eagerly, but the truth was she was so excited about the trip she really didn't pay much heed. Doreen, on cloud nine because the Governor had told her her day release was going to be allowed, confided to Lizzie that Kev really was one in a million. Lizzie agreed, but in fact, at that moment, Kevin was sitting opposite Josie, enjoying a cup of tea after the packing, and looking a bit puzzled.

Josie had been rattling on about one thing after another and in the course of it had talked about her policeman uncle – Sergeant Morgan – who was stationed at Sale. Kevin had listened with interest. That's where he came from himself. So what relation was Sgt. Morgan? Mum's brother, had been the reply. And that didn't quite add up.

According to Josie this uncle and her mum had both been left at the orphanage and kept there for years. Kevin didn't press the child for any further details. Maybe this Morgan guy had changed his name by deed poll. But the faintest seed of doubt had been sown in his mind and he determined to talk to Dor about it later.

Back at Wentworth another name was being bandied about. A new arrival, Leanne Burke, had just been introduced to the women in the recreation room. Lizzie frowned, the name was so familiar. Bea fronted the tough looking eighteen-year-old and there was no mistaking the the chill in her voice.

'Noelene Burke's daughter, aren't you?'

The same set of the jaw, small, sharp brown eyes and, while she wasn't built on the generous lines of her mother, she surely looked as if she could take care of herself.

'Yeah, who are you?'

Bea gave her a small, cynical smile. 'Thought your mum would have talked about me. Bea Smith – ask her when you see her. Believe me, she'll remember.'

Leanne shrugged. Bugger Bea Smith, she could take care of herself. But for all that she was aware of the hostility around her. It was pretty plain her mother hadn't made too many friends during her 'stay' at Wentworth.

She was even more uneasy when she found she'd been put in a single cell. She complained bitterly to

Vera Bennett. Vera listened with a slight smile playing around her mouth. She put it to Jim Fletcher. 'Why dirty up another cell? Burke could go in with Bryant.'

Jim squashed this quick smart. This girl wasn't going in with that bloody great dyke. Vera shrugged; Burke might as well find out the score, might even teach her a lesson and persuade her not to come back for more. But Jim was adamant. The girl was in for petty larceny, two months – throwing her to the wolves wouldn't do much to mend her ways. Vera doubted anything would. In and out of remand homes, a short stretch in Fairlea, and as for her mother . . . enough said!

But Jim had his way and the cell door clanged behind a nervous Leanne. She managed to keep her cool, removing her nail polish till the lights went out. She tried calling out, trying to find someone to at least talk to, but she was greeted with a barrage of abuse and orders to shut her trap.

She lit a cigarette, stared thoughtfully at her lighter for a moment, then at the bottle of polish remover. Quickly she sprinkled the liquid onto her bedding; the next moment she'd set it alight and as soon as the flames had begun to take hold, she rushed for the door screaming 'fire' at the top of her lungs.

A cacophony of sound broke out, more alarmed shouts of 'fire' as the women smelt the smoke. Jim Fletcher came running at the double with the fire extinguisher and Vera Bennett, jangling keys, quickly opened the door.

As Jim doused the flames, Vera hurried her into the corridor. Leanne was all apologies, she'd dropped the bottle, then the lighted cigarette. Neither Jim nor Vera were convinced, but it was obvious the girl had

157

achieved her aim. There was no way she could sleep in that cell now.

Vera gave a small triumphant smile. 'Looks like it's share with Bryant or spend the night in the corridor. The stores are locked, so's the infirmary.' Jim didn't approve but he had no choice, till the morning, then he'd have a word with the Governor.

In Judy's depressed state of mind, she really didn't care one way or the other if she was alone or sharing. But when she learned that Leanne had deliberately set fire to the bed because she was scared, she warmed to the kid. Naturally, Judy didn't know Leanne's mother, so she accepted without question the girl's confidence that at last her mother had gone straight. She was working as a tea lady for a very respectable firm nowadays.

Judy let the kid rattle on for a while. She was still talking when Jim Fletcher unlocked the door and handed over a supply of fresh sheets and blankets. He was looking at Judy, not Leanne, when he ordered her to make up her bunk and, if she had any sense, sleep in it, alone. After he'd gone the girl looked questioningly at Judy. Judy gave a wry grin. 'I'm a lesbian. He just wanted to make quite sure you knew that.' Leanne shrugged, not in the least fazed. 'It's not my bag, but if you like it that way, why not?' Judy watched, amused, as the girl went cheerfully about the business of making up her bunk. Could be she'd be OK as a cell mate. At least it would temporarily assuage the awful emptiness she still felt over Sharon.

But when, next day, Leanne was told she could work in the garden but she would not continue to share Judy's cell, Judy was philosophical about it. 'We've got a plan going, kid. You're best out of it.' Why embroil her when she hadn't even known Sharon or Jock Stewart? She wasn't to know that this only served to make the girl feel more isolated, and stirred up a quick resentment in her.

But Bea agreed with Judy. She'd already got the wheels in motion. Bernadette, on kitchen duty, was to pinch anything that wasn't nailed down, then, on trolley duty, distribute food, bit by bit, to the different cells. The more they spread it, the longer they'd be able to hold out when they called the strike.

Doreen, for one, was glad to know nothing was going to happen before she had her day out with Kevin. She'd made all kinds of plans. She'd go to the bank and draw out some cash and buy her husband a real beaut present. Maybe something for herself too. Then she wanted to go and see her mum's house. And of course she'd promised Lizzie she'd catch up with Marcia and Josie for her.

But at ten o'clock next morning when Kevin, smart as paint and beaming, called to pick her up, she found out he had very different plans. He'd have loved to have taken her for a really great candlelit dinner but since she had to report back by 6 p.m., he'd found a nice dim restaurant where they could have a romantic lunch, hold hands and then remind each other that they were a married couple who had every right to do what married couples do! Doreen giggled a bit when he told her, then after lunch – and that was extra good – they went back to Kev's flat.

She was touched by how gentle and thoughtful he was. Some blokes would have been at it like a bull at a gate, waiting all that time. But for Doreen, this was a new experience. A sense of loving and caring she'd never known before. And as she confided to Bea afterwards, 'The sex was bloody good too.'

And that wasn't all she had to tell the others. Judy was holding forth about going to see the Governor and demanding a fair and independent inquiry into Sharon's death. But Doreen could tell her she was wasting her time. Kev had heard the news that morning. The inquest was over! Accidental death, case closed.

Judy looked at Bea. Bea nodded. Bernadette had probably got as much stuff out as she could from the kitchen.

The bell rang for the end of recreation. Time for the women to be hustled back to their cells. Bea looked around the room. A nod from Margot, Phyllis, Mouse and the rest.

Jim Fletcher and Vera Bennett appeared in the doorway.

'On your feet, ladies.' Jim, pleasant, just thought them a bit slow to respond to the bell. But no one moved. Vera stepped forward. 'You heard. On your feet.' Nothing.

Bea glanced across at Judy who nodded briefly. 'We're on strike until Bryant can speak to the Governor.'

Judy stood up and eyed Vera squarely. 'We want a new and independent inquest. We don't budge until it's been discussed.'

Vera's expression was contemptuous. 'I attended personally. It was all perfectly in order. And the finding is definite.'

'The Governor, Miss Bennett.' Judy's voice had a new ring of authority.

'I'll alert the Governor and Security.' Jim turned and walked out quickly.

Vera turned her gaze on to Bea. 'You never learn, do you? Your past riots have been disastrous. What makes you think this will be any different?'

Bea's voice was super cool. 'This isn't a riot, Vera. It's a peaceful sit-in until we talk to Mrs Davidson.'

Phyllis chipped in smartly. 'You screws got what you wanted when you went on strike.'

'Watch your tongue, Hunt.' Vera was tense now, ready for any sign of real trouble, but she couldn't resist the jibe. 'That's the difference between officers and prisoners . . . we have rights, you have none.'

Big Margot and some of the women were getting restless and things could have got heavy for Vera had not Jim and Erica entered at that moment.

'What was it you wanted to say to me, Bryant?'

Judy kept her voice as calm and reasonable as possible. 'We know what happened at the inquest.'

Doreen hung her head as she felt Erica's eyes turn to her, the obvious informant.

'We don't accept that verdict. We want another inquest, or at least a Departmental enquiry.'

There was an assenting murmur from the women. Erica secretly sympathized but there was nothing she could do.

'I'm sorry, but the matter has been decided.'

'I wasn't called to give evidence.' There was a trace of anger in Judy's voice now.

'I'm sure you realize that it would have been pointless. Your word against an officer simply would not stand up in court.'

Bea rose slowly to her feet. 'There's a bit more to it, Mrs Davidson.' She glanced around the room and she could feel the women solidly behind her. 'The way it is, we're at the mercy of someone like Jock Stewart, no redress, no protection. And we're staying here till someone does something about that.'

'If that's the way you see it. But I'm afraid you'll soon get tired of being cooped up in here. And I must warn you that any destruction of prison property can only result in your loss. It simply will not be replaced.'

Erica turned and walked from the room, followed by Jim Fletcher and Vera Bennett. The women could hear the clash of the security gates, and for all their chorus of insults and abuse at the backs of the departing officers, Bea had a shrewd suspicion that their minor victory had a hollow ring to it.

Her fears were soon to be confirmed. Big Margot checked, yep, there was an officer at the gates and obviously there'd be someone there all night. And, Bea reminded them, the food they'd pinched was still stored in the cells and they couldn't get at it. They'd jumped the gun and now they were up the creek without a paddle.

Lizzie tried to cheer things up a bit. They still had the telly and they could play a bit of poker. Mouse piped up quickly. 'And we want a blow by blow description of what went on with you and Kevin, Dor.'

Doreen blushed. 'It was a bonzer day, real terrific and that's all I'm saying.'

There was a general chorus of laughter from Mouse and the others. 'Come on.' It was Phyllis. 'We can

162

watch the late and the late late and the late late late movies!'

'Yeah!' Mouse hurried towards the TV. And at that moment the lights went out.

'Oh shit!' It was Margot. 'Bloody screws have fixed the fuse box.'

Judy's voice came out of the darkness, trying to strike an encouraging note. 'As long as we stick together, we can make something happen.'

There was a moment of sulky silence, then . . . 'Hey, I want that chair.' 'Get lost!' The thump of someone getting a rough deal from Margot.

'I'm hungry.'

'You'll be a bloody sight hungrier by the morning.'

'Hey Leanne. Are you one of them like Jude? How about a little kiss and cuddle in the dark?'

'Go play with yourself.' But Leanne was alert, scared too.

Bea listened to the dissenting voices around her and sighed. She knew from long experience that loyalty to the cause would mean very little by the morning. What was that old saying, an army marches on its stomach? Well this bloody army was stuffed after its first manoeuvre!

Thirteen

Bea looked wearily around the recreation room as the early morning light filtered in. Women were slumped in chairs, on the floor, wherever they could find a place to try and get some semblance of rest. Only Lizzie, mouth wide open, was snoring her head off contentedly.

Jude was slumped in an easy chair, her eyes open, her mind going over and over the recent events. Big Margot was grumbling about a wasted bloody night, Bernadette was whining about having the cramps and Doreen confided that she needed to go to the loo. Bea told her to hang on and tried to divert her problem by asking about her day out with Kevin.

Doreen was only too ready to rhapsodize but in the middle of it, she frowned. She'd just remembered. Something Kev had said about Lizzie and her daughter. That was it! Was this Marcia really her daughter? He reckoned she might be having Lizzie on, planning a rip-off. Bea looked across at the sleeping Lizzie. The old girl was so happy, forever talking about Marcia and the kid. They'd keep an eye on things, but let her enjoy it while she could.

The rising bell rang shrilly through the room and

Bernadette, cramps forgotten, rushed to the security gates demanding an urgent trip to the toilet.

Jim Fletcher and Joan Barry were on guard. They opened the gates quick smart, but as Bernadette moved through they grabbed her. That's the way they'd get the women, one at a time. And sooner or later they'd all have to answer nature's call.

Bea sized up the situation and moved over to Judy.

'It's your bunfight, Jude. But if you'll take my advice we go to Davo and tell her it's off.'

Judy looked grim. 'So they just bloody get away with it.'

Bea lowered her voice. 'For the moment. We didn't think it through.' Judy nodded. OK, they'd let the Governor and the screws think they were beaten. But there was no way she'd sodding well give up.

Erica received Bea and Judy quite calmly. She didn't for a moment think Bryant was going to let go – she was out for retribution. Vera shared the view. Still, for the present, best that they appear to accept Bryant's story.

But when Bea and Judy had left the Governor's office Erica instructed Vera and the other officers to keep the security doors locked at all times. Any more bad publicity and the Department would be asking a lot of very pointed questions and she had enough headaches without that.

A slow sense of excitement was building as the women worked in the laundry. Under the guise of carrying out their routine duties they were already hard at work. Sheets were ripped up to make banners. They'd need to pinch a few things from the workshop – Margot could organize that. Paint for the banners, a hammer and nails if they could manage it – Phyllis could make out the list and slip it to Margot at lunch.

Bea slammed the steam press down hard to get their attention. 'Keep nit Phyllis. We don't want old Vinegar Tits sneaking up on us'. She gestured to the women to stop what they were doing and listen.

'We need something to get the journos excited. A demo in the garden probably. We've got the food stashed in our cells in case we get stuck out there for a while.'

Doreen looked troubled. 'But the screws'd herd us back inside in no time flat.'

Bea shook her head. 'The mob in the workshop can set up barricades to keep them in the main building. And just to make sure someone notices us, we'll need a good sized bonfire.'

'Good.' Phyllis grinned at them. 'I always used to love Guy Fawkes.' Bea's smile was cynical.

'With a bit of luck we might stir up as much publicity as he did.'

Judy was working in the garden when Big Margot, on a pretext of dumping rubbish from the workshop, slipped the word to her of the action being planned.

Leanne was all ears and excited at the idea of something so dramatic. Judy pointed out that it wasn't Leanne's fight and she was only in for a couple of months; better to keep her nose clean.

The girl was obviously hurt and disappointed, but when Margot explained the problem of getting word out to the press, she saw her opportunity. Her mother would be visiting her today – she could slip the word to her, no worries. Judy was still a bit reluctant for her to be involved but as long as that was as far as it went, OK, that'd be great.

Margot sidled off to give Bea the info and Judy went back to her raking. Leanne was looking thoughtfully at the wooden handle of the fork she was using. She jiggled it and took a closer look at the screws – only just holding the steel pronged base in place. A bit more judicious wiggling and fiddling and she had the base free.

'What are you doing?' Judy didn't like the idea of weapons, specially something as ugly looking as the steel pronged fork. Leanne stuck the wooden handle in the ground – no one would tumble that she'd whipped the base off. She hid the pronged base in her uniform. Better to be prepared. Judy voiced her disapproval but the truth was she was more preoccupied as to whether Noelene would get the message out.

'Listen.' Leanne's face was a study in innocence. 'Mum's going straight, I told you. She hates the screws every bit as much as you do . . . course she'll do it.'

But when Bea had the news relayed to her she was furious. 'That bloody Noelene! She'd just as soon dob us in, let alone help us.'

Doreen didn't think Noelene would go that far.

Bea was busy pouring sewing machine oil into a container, the best thing she could find so far to start the fire. 'She hates my guts for starters. And she's just about the greatest bloody ratbag you could ever set eyes on.'

Mouse agreed. 'She plays rough, all right. And as for her being reformed, that bitch couldn't lie straight in bed!'

'Well, the fat's in the fire now.' Bea's mind was

working overtime. 'We've got to get rid of the evidence in case she shops us and the screws start searching. But how the hell do we get the food out of the cells?'

Lizzie smiled angelically, coughed, held her chest and turned to Bea. 'Reckon I can handle it.'

They would all have been a lot more concerned if they'd heard the conversation going on between Leanne Burke and her mother Noelene. It was quite clear, even though they were watching their words in front of Officer Knox, that Noelene was no ordinary tea lady. Amazing how careless people were about leaving their bags and their spare cash lying about! She winked at Leanne.

'Can't wait for you to come out and start doing an honest day's work with me, girl.'

As arranged, Judy called out to Officer Knox, diverting her attention, and Leanne quickly moved close to her mother. 'They want you to get word to the press – get 'em here at four o'clock; there's going to be fireworks.'

Noelene's reaction was instant. 'Who's idea – that Bea Smith bitch?'

Leanne nodded and indicated Judy. 'And Judy Bryant. She's my friend.'

Noelene sneered. 'You don't make friends in stir, remember that. And I don't like the look of that big faggot. You keep your nose clean. I need your help outside of here.'

Leanne, aware that Knox was back and observing them closely, nodded. 'It'll be good to be able to help each other, won't it?'

Noelene would have liked to have said a lot more

168

but she nodded and by the time her visit finished, Leanne confidently told Judy that her mother was going to get word to the media for sure.

Officer Barry rather doubted Lizzie's wheezing turn but she took her back to her cell to rest, anyway. Trouble was you couldn't take any chances with Birdsworth. She was forever crying wolf, but she did have a dickie ticker, and the one time you disbelieved her, that'd be the day she really was having a heart attack.

Lizzie assured her she'd be all right if she could rest. And with a firm reassurance that she'd take Birdsworth to the nurse later, when she came on duty, she left Lizzie to rest on her bunk.

The moment Joan Barry's footsteps died away, Lizzie was on her feet and on the job. She'd grab the food from the other cells, and try to get it all into the dorm she shared with Bea and Doreen. She'd have to work fast if she was going to move it all before the screws came poking round.

She would need to be fast indeed! Noelene Burke, a malicious sneer on her lips, had just imparted enough information to Vera to set that lady hot on the trail. She hadn't said in so many words that a demo had been planned. Oh no, much more subtle. The garden was looking lovely and yet, such a tempting place to stage a riot wasn't it? And had Vera noticed, there seemed to be an awful lot of nudging and whispering going on between the woman she'd seen working in the garden. Not that it was any concern of hers. Her eyes met Vera's for a brief moment – message given, message received.

It was enough for Vera. Lizzie was scurrying out of Judy's cell with an armful of goodies when she heard the voices of Vera and Officer Barfield, obviously about to round the corner.

She dived into her own cell, stashed the stuff quickly under the blanket where she'd already assembled quite a heap, and threw herself on to her bed, delicately nibbling a biscuit (which she'd snaffled along the way – after all, the more she could eat, the less to hide; well, that was her story!).

Lizzie could hear Barfield poking about in the opposite cell. She'd got the stuff out of there, thank Gawd! Vera kept darting suspicious glances at her, as she pushed and pried and opened and shut cupboards.

'Looking for anything special, Miss Bennett?' asked Lizzie, all innocence.

For an answer Vera slammed a cupboard shut and headed for the door.

'You'll make yourself sick eating biscuits right on lunchtime, Birdsworth.'

Lizzie smiled. 'Probably won't bother with lunch. Just fancied something light.'

Vera looked a touch sceptical but at that moment the lunch bell was heard ringing through the corridors and she turned and marched towards the dining room. Lizzie breathed a sigh of relief. She hopped off her bunk, straightened the covers over the food stash and, after a moment's hesitation, helped herself to another biscuit before she headed for the dining room.

The officers were forced to admit to the Governor that the search had been fruitless. Erica was not overly surprised. Noelene Burke had proved a vicious prisoner and made few friends either among the prisoners or the staff.

Nevertheless she instructed the officers to keep the

security gates locked between the blocks. The intermediary gates could remain open but there'd be no garden recreation that afternoon.

This was greeted with fury by the women, and Bea in particular. Doreen dismally commented that that was the end of their plans. But Bea, tightlipped, assured her not only would the demonstration go through, she had worked out a way whereby the Governor could help them!

As the women began to file out of the dining room, Lizzie moved up to Meg Jackson. 'I'm feeling a bit off, Mrs J. You reckon I could give the laundry a miss this arvo and do the tea trolley?'

'I noticed how little you ate at lunch, Lizzie. All right, but if you feel any worse, let me know and I'll take you off to Nurse.'

'Thanks Mrs J.' Lizzie trotted happily off to the kitchen – her part in the demo was working, anyway.

Judy and Margot were not so lucky.

Leanne and Judy were carrying the big bin of kitchen scraps along the corridor, part of their duty to collect the food scraps and take them outside.

As prearranged, Margot started to bait Judy, and between them they managed to tip the entire contents of the muck bin all over the corridor floor. So far so good. Judy and Margot needed to get themselves on the mat in front of the Governor, the only way to snatch the prison keys.

Vera had no idea of their plans but inadvertently interfered with them. Instead of berating Judy, Vera chose to blame Margot and Leanne and said she was not bothering with a report to the Governor. They could spend the afternoon scrubbing this corridor and all the others in the block. That might teach them to be a little more careful.

Judy tried to hide her dismay. Now what? And Bea looked thunderous. Now that little Burke bitch was in the thick of things and that was the last thing Bea wanted – wouldn't trust her as far as she could spit!

Once Bea reached the laundry, the place became a hive of activity. Blankets and sheets were separated, banners whipped out of driers, Bea making sure the blanket she'd soaked in the flammable machine oil was safely in her keeping. But how the hell was Judy going to get to the Governor?

Judy was thinking fast as she emptied a load of rubbish into the tip. Jim Fletcher was on guard nearby. She took a deep breath and walked up to him.

'I need to see the Governor, Mr Fletcher.'

Jim eyed her a bit coldly. 'We've been through all that.'

Judy shook her head. 'Not that. The thing is, Noelene Burke wasn't giving Miss Bennett a line. There is going to be a demo.'

Jim's interest was caught and held. There was no doubting the sincerity in Bryant's voice, and maybe with that pacemaker she didn't want to find herself in the middle of what could turn out to be a violent scene.

Outside the Governor's office, Margot and Leanne were vigorously applying themselves to their cleaning duties. Inside, Lizzie was pouring Erica's tea and trying not to let her nervousness show as she automatically answered Erica's questions about Marcia and Josie.

She made her escape as soon as she could and moved back to her trolley. It was a simple thing to send a handful of teaspoons clattering to the floor. Meg, on guard, asked Margot to wipe up the small amount of mess as Lizzie wasn't feeling too well. Margot, happy to oblige, hissed at Lizzie 'Where the hell is Judy?' In two seconds flat the action would start.

They quickly masked their surprise as Jim Fletcher walked into view with Judy beside him.

'Bryant wants to see the Governor. And I think it's important.'

Meg nodded but before she could step forward and usher Judy into the office, Joan Barry came running along the corridor.

'All hell's broken out in D block. The women are trying to get out into the garden.'

'Right.' Jim was off and running with Officer Barry. Meg cast a cursory glance at Margot and Leanne but both were busy with their cleaning. She moved to the door of Erica's office unaware, as she leaned forward to open it, that Margot and Leanne had silently leapt up behind her – Margot armed with the mop and Leanne hastily digging into the bucket of cleaning water and coming up with the steel pronged fork.

As Meg opened the door, still unconscious of the danger behind her, Margot tripped her expertly with the mop and Meg tumbled head first into the room. In a second, Judy and Leanne were through the doorway and into the office.

Erica's hand was already on the phone. Judy's hand closed over it, wrenching the phone from her grasp.

'Don't be a fool, Bryant.' Erica's voice was calm, no sign of nerves. There was little Meg could do. She lay where she had fallen and, while she showed no outward fear, the fact that Leanne was standing over her menacingly, the pronged fork base in her hand, was enough to

173

give pause for thought. Rash action now would achieve nothing and probably result in both herself and Erica being attacked, possibly killed.

But there was no way Judy was going to listen to reason at this moment. Her mouth was set in a grim line as she talked on the phone to a startled reporter and told him of the impending riot, and the reason for it.

It was obvious that her statement was being received with a lot of scepticism. In her heart, she had no desire to threaten Erica Davidson, but if she didn't act now, it would all have been in vain.

She pushed the phone close to Erica's face. 'Tell them it's the Governor and that you're being held in your office.'

Erica glanced at Leanne holding the vicious steel prongs close to Meg's throat. Without hesitation she assured the reporter that there was indeed trouble at the prison, and yes, she and another officer, Meg Jackson, were being held and threatened.

'Satisfied?' Erica kept her eyes on Judy's face.

'For the moment.' She turned and frowned, as she saw Margot up-end a decanter of spirits and take a long, hard swig.

'That's not why we're here, Margot.'

Margot rubbed a fist across her wet lips. 'I do it my way, Bryant. And if I want a bloody drink I'll have one.'

Judy knew better than to waste time arguing. She'd just have to hope Big Margot didn't get out of control and do something crazy. She moved swiftly across the room and deftly unhooked the prison keys from Meg's belt.

174

'Don't do this, Judy.' In spite of the personal danger, Meg could still care. 'You don't belong in this kind of mess.'

Judy avoided meeting Meg's eyes. She had a purpose and that was all she could think about right now.

'Margot, take over from Leanne.'

Margot needed no urging. She'd enjoy sticking that fork into some bloody officer's throat, even Meg Jackson. They were all bastards when the chips were down.

'Leanne,' Judy held out the keys to her, 'find Bea, tell her I'll be right there. And unlock all the gates. Spread the word that this is going to be a full-scale riot.'

'Gotcha.' Leanne had grabbed the keys and rushed excitedly out of the office. She was in the thick of it now and the adrenalin was pumping hard.

Judy turned back to Erica. 'Now you phone the Department and demand an enquiry into Sharon Gilmour's death.'

Erica sat very still, tense but determined. 'No.'

Judy glared back into the cool, blue eyes.

'We're running out of time. Don't make me do something we'd both regret.' Her gaze travelled to Margot bent threateningly over Meg.

'Bryant, you know I've done everything in my power on the Gilmour issue. And believe me, this kind of action won't cut any ice with the Department. The most you'll achieve is my dismissal and a longer sentence for yourself.'

Erica's eyes never left Judy's face. And too late did Judy realize that while the Governor maintained her steady gaze and spoke so rationally, she had disconnected the external telephone.

Judy flung the phone aside. 'I've got to get to Bea.'
She strode across the office and flung the door wide.
'Lizzie, we need you in here.'

Lizzie came in hesitantly. She'd hoped it wouldn't
get to this. The Governor had been pretty nice about
the Marcia business. She was shocked to see Margot
holding the fork at Meg Jackson's throat. Judy registered her reluctance.

'You don't have to do anything. Just help Margot to
keep these two in here. Right?'

Lizzie looked sheepishly at Meg. Surely Mrs Jackson'd understand later that there wasn't no choice?

'Are you going to jeopardize your future with your
daughter, Lizzie? What was Sharon Gilmour to you?
You're being used.'

She knew the Guv was talking sense, but Bea and
Dor were her mates and they were in it up to their
necks.

Margot was quick to read Lizzie's jumbled thoughts.
'Help yourself to a drop of the good stuff, Lizzie. Why
should we leave it for these bastards to guzzle while
we're swilling down that muck they call food?'

Lizzie eyed the decanters and their tempting contents. P'raps just one to settle her down, clear her
thoughts.

'Your friend Lloyd Barton wouldn't approve.' Meg
said it softly, hoping not to inflame Big Margot into
doing something rash, but desperate to reach Lizzie.

'Well he's not here, is he?' Big Margot leered at Meg
then flicked a glance at Lizzie. 'Go on, coupla belts
won't touch the side, eh Lizzie?'

The temptation was too great. With trembling hands
Lizzie poured herself a tumbler of scotch and put it

greedily to her lips. She wouldn't let Margot do nothing bad. But as the familiar warm glow spread through Lizzie's skinny body, Erica saw, with a sinking heart, the look of sheer bliss that spread over the weather-beaten face. Not much good pinning any hopes on Birdsworth. The truth was, regardless of circumstances, the booze would always win with her.

At the end of the corridor leading to the laundry the officers were face to face through the bars with a mob of screaming, shouting women. Jim Fletcher had tried everything he knew to reason with them but they yelled him down, chanting, showing their banners, screeching to be let out into the garden.

An agitated Vera turned to Jim. 'What the hell is keeping the Governor? And where's Meg Jackson?'

Jim shook his head. 'You'd better find out. They can't break out into the garden from here.'

'Right.' Vera took off at speed along the corridor leading to the laundry. She was almost past the door when the sound of excited voices stopped her. She paused to glance in, and in a moment, rough hands had grabbed her and yanked her into the room.

'Got too curious for your own good, did you Vera?'

She looked into the hard eyes of Bea Smith and knew she was in trouble, but she tried to brave it out.

'I don't know what you think you're up to, Smith, but we've already quelled your supposed riot before it started.'

'That's not the way we read it.' A smile that promised trouble lit Bea's face. 'OK, Vera, strip off.'

'Are you raving mad?' Vera tried to back off but she was held fast. Bea was already taking off her prison uniform.

177

'Might be a bit of a tight fit but I reckon I can just about wriggle into your uniform.'

Greedy hands tore at Vera's clothes and she would long remember the awful humiliation as she stood there, stripped to her bra and knickers, amid a chorus of ribald, insulting remarks.

Bea tossed her prison uniform across to her. 'Better put it on. Wouldn't want those Vinegar Tits to get any colder now, would we?'

The smile was quickly wiped off Bea's face as Leanne came running into the room, jangling the keys in front of her.

'Jude got these off Ma Jackson. Said to go ahead, she'd be right with us.'

'You were told to stay out of this, Burke.' Leanne shrugged. 'Yeah, well I'm in, aren't I, and I've got the keys.'

Bea knew better than to waste time on the kid now. She turned quickly to Doreen and the others, nodding in Vera's direction.

'Tie her up and as soon as you've done it, take off. You know where we're meeting Jude.' Bea hurried to the door, Doreen at her heels. She couldn't resist one last look.

'How about that! Officer bloody Bennett looks just like one of us now, doesn't she?'

A few moments later Jim Fletcher stared hard at the sight of an officer leading half a dozen women towards the security gates near the stairs. He tried to call out above the hubbub of the shouting women facing him but either he couldn't make himself heard or the officer was ignoring him. Something bloody strange was going on!

178

With a quick word to Joan Barry to take over, he was off and running in the direction of the laundry. Where the hell had Vera Bennett disappeared to?

A few moments later he found out. Vera cut a pathetic figure, dressed in Bea's prison uniform and roped firmly against the big steam press. He quickly released her while she poured out her story.

'Get back to the gates. I'm going to check out the Governor's office.'

Jim raced off. Vera's lips were a hard, thin line as she looked down at the bedraggled prison uniform. Someone would pay for this, and dearly!

Jim had already realized the Governor must be under some kind of threat and the one thing that might go in his favour would be the element of surprise. He wrenched the door open then stopped short at the sight of Margot standing over Meg.

'Come any closer and she gets it.' Big Margot's expression told it like it was. But she'd been drinking, he could hear it in the voice. He turned his gaze to Lizzie. The old girl had certainly been imbibing; reflexes would be slower with both of them. His thoughts raced furiously.

'I didn't know there was trouble. Lizzie's daughter is here to see her.' It was a desperate gamble but it paid off.

Lizzie's face lit up. 'Where is she? In the garden?'

Jim drew a deep breath. 'Interview room.'

Lizzie nodded, obviously trying to pull herself together.

'OK, Mr Fletcher, let's go.'

'Not till Margot puts down the fork.'

'It's a bloody trick.' Big Margot moved in so that

the prongs were touching Meg's throat. 'You stay where you are, Lizzie.'

It was just what he'd hoped for.

'I'm going to see Marcia and just you bloody try and stop me.'

Lizzie swung a wild punch in Margot's general direction. It was enough. As Margot's attention was momentarily diverted, Jim lunged and grabbed her, as Meg wrenched the fork from her hand and quickly flung it out of harm's way.

'Bastards!' Margot's face was contorted with fury but there was no way she could break out of Jim's grip.

'Get them both back to their cells and lock them in.'

As Meg led a protesting Lizzie out, and Jim forced a struggling Margot through the doorway, Erica was already ringing the alarm bell, switching back the phone and dialling the police. No good trying to contain things now, they'd need the police and the fire brigade and every officer they could muster.

It was certainly beginning to look that way. From the garden, the officers could see the women on the roof, flying their banners, shouting and gesturing towards the gate where they'd spotted the TV van and press cars arriving . . . the alarm bell ringing as if perfectly timed.

Judy was the last to clamber up the iron stairs through the hatch and on to the roof. It was the signal they'd been waiting for. The blankets were already piled into a heap and under Bea's supervision Mouse and Leanne were adding the oil-soaked blanket while Doreen poured on an extra supply of machine oil from the container Bea had filled.

At a nod from Bea, Leanne lit the match and flung it on to the heap.

From the garden, Erica stood with her officers, watching as the thin spiral of black smoke began to climb. Thank God the officers had managed to round up Hunt and her cohorts before they could get to the roof. But Bryant and Smith were up there and with the latter's long-learned expertise and Judy's current obsession for revenge, there was no knowing to what lengths they might go.

On the roof, Bea and Judy watched the black smoke thickening – not much flame but the smoke would draw the attention they wanted. The police had already arrived, sirens screaming, and the brigade would be along any minute. They'd make the TV news tonight!

Leanne was dancing about excitedly. This was real action, stuff to brag about to her mates when she got outside again! Her mum'd realize she was a chip off the old block all right! She picked up the container and threw the last of the oil on to the smoking blankets. The thick black smoke whooshed right into her face, searing her eyeballs, sending her spluttering, backing away from the fumes, rubbing her eyes.

Doreen peered through the smoke, and saw Leanne reeling backwards.

'Hey! Leanne. Don't step back.'

The piercing scream was something they'd never forget as Leanne took one more fatal step backwards and toppled over the edge of the roof. No one could survive that fall.

Fourteen

The first weeks after Leanne's death were difficult for both staff and prisoners. Judy's continuing feelings of guilt and remorse cast a gloom over them all. Erica had fobbed the press off as best she could but there'd been some very searching questions asked by the Department. She knew she was treading a very fine line; more trouble and, they'd made it clear, her capabilities as Governor would be seriously investigated.

Thanks to the riot all the women had lost remission. Strict security had been reinforced, Buy-up cancelled for everyone involved, leisure and recreation time curtailed and work duties substantially increased. It depressed them but they knew in their hearts they'd got off lightly. It could have been solitary all round.

Vera had pushed hard for it. But it was Erica's opinion that the guilt felt over Leanne's death was a punishment in itself, and one the women would have to bear for the rest of their lives. Her attitude did little to assuage Vera's anger and continuing humiliation. Well, she would just have to bide her time. But one day, Bea Smith would pay dearly for that. There was no rush. Smith still had ten years to serve and meantime, Vera wasn't going anywhere. Wentworth was her life. She'd be there till the day they forced her to retire.

Lizzie was the most apprehensive. Would Davo put an end to her visits from Marcia and Josie? But Erica, in spite of her disappointment at Lizzie's participation during the riot, clung hard to her principles and her hopes for Lizzie's eventual rehabilitation. If she had a daughter and granddaughter waiting for her when her release came through, surely she would grasp the opportunity to spend her remaining years in some kind of domestic harmony rather than in the sterile surrounds of Wentworth?

But as Marcia continued to visit and Lizzie eulogized over her new found granddaughter, Bea and Doreen began to have grave doubts. Kevin's original suspicions had not been forgotten and when Bea fired some pretty relevant questions at the old girl, it was clear she was hedging, unwilling to let so much as a thread of doubt cross her mind.

She'd be collecting her $40,000 compensation pretty soon now, and she was determined to use the money to see that Marcia and little Josie had some kind of decent life from now on.

Bea had confided her concern to Meg and she'd promised to chat to the social worker and find out just how many facts did tally. Secretly Meg hoped and prayed Marcia was the genuine article – the happiness her visits inspired in old Lizzie were a joy to behold. Meg would check it out as promised, but she had a problem of her own right now that was worrying her. She'd decided a change of scene was in order and was thrilled at how quickly she'd found just the sort of flat she wanted. She'd invited Vera and Jim and a few of the other officers over for a house-warming and, because she'd done a stint on night shift, she'd hardly been aware of her next-door neighbours.

It was a different story now! Gail and Tim Summers had three children and the youngest, little Stevie, seemed to be in a permanent state of screaming. Gail, whom Meg sized up as a nice friendly young woman (obviously lonely and frustrated as a housebound wife and mother), had assured Meg that the doctor could find nothing wrong with the little boy.

And at eighteen months he certainly looked and seemed healthy enough. Five-year-old Katrina was already at school but Jason – Meg wondered about him. At three years old he was a nervous, clinging little boy, with an expression that seemed to be continually apologizing for being in existence.

She'd soon learned that Katrina and Jason were the children of Gail's first marriage, and Gail, seemingly thrilled to have some female company and a sympathetic ear in close proximity, soon poured out the whole story.

Tim was forever drinking with the boys, late home for meals, impatient with the kids. And she was going crazy locked up with a screaming baby and Jason who was always falling over his own feet and so accident prone she almost felt like one of the staff at the local hospital.

Meg confided to Vera that she hadn't been too impressed in her couple of brief meetings with Tim and she was beginning to find the whole situation rather worrying. Was Jason 'accident prone' or was there a more sinister explanation?

Vera's advice was to steer clear of the neighbours,

and their problems. They had enough of them at Wentworth! For starters, it was her opinion that Erica must be going round the twist to even contemplate the work release programme she'd mooted. Either that or she'd fallen head over heels for that Andrew Reynolds person, and Vera had strong suspicions about the latter reason.

Meg couldn't agree. After the privations of the last few weeks she could only feel that some kind of incentive would help the women. And at least putting in a few hours a day outside of the prison, in Reynolds clothing factory, would be a change from the daily drudgery and monotony of their usual routine. And in spite of the recent events at the prison, the Classification Committee did back Erica and vote in favour of the women taking on the work. True, they'd only be working on Government contracts, making uniforms, but as long as they were strictly supervised, then some contact with the outside world must be beneficial.

Lizzie was disappointed not to be selected but she had her visits from Josie and Marcia to look forward to, and anyway, she was used to the routine in the laundry and she didn't exactly have to work her guts out there, with good old Bea in charge.

Judy was surprised to be selected. But as Doreen pointed out, you had to give the Guv credit. She'd have to notice how bad Jude had felt since Leanne's death, real depressed and that. Judy looked thoughtful; maybe this was the way out? Doreen was immediately apprehensive. Gawd, they hadn't started yet and Jude was already thinking of maybe escaping! That'd bugger it up for the other five on the job, not to mention that

Bea had warned them they'd be in big trouble if any of them stuffed up the work release.

Judy nodded, but Doreen knew she hadn't convinced her by a long chalk. Jude had been really off the air since the riot and there was no way of knowing which way she'd jump.

Big Margot was tickled pink to be selected. Boy, she should be able to clean up a packet on the geegees, must be plenty of women in that factory who'd want to have a flutter on the horses. Mouse and Jean were looking forward to it; even getting a drive to the factory would be something! Bernadette was mainly concerned with the extra cash they'd get credited to them, but, as she confided to Doreen, you never knew – might be a bit of slap and tickle going on the side if they were lucky. Doreen had looked very prim – she'd just had another beaut letter from Kev and there was no way she'd be playing around with any joker now that she was a respectable, married woman!

But she was uneasily aware in the first few days of work at the factory that the overseer, Vince Talbot, was paying her more attention than the work warranted. The woman, Kay White, seemed OK. She was bustling about, getting extra rolls of material for the women, helping them to get the hang of the machines and generally making them feel really welcome on the job. And to Margot's delight, Kay was a keen punter – laying out a bit heavily, but in Margot's book a pigeon ripe for the plucking, with more enthusiasm than real racing know-how. And with Kay on their side, Vera had no authority to stop them listening to the races if Kay was betting.

It was just another thorn in Vera's side. She was

against the whole project from the start. And now, to have to sit with Officer Barfield, cooped up in the stuffy little tea room, supervising the women, and being forced to condone the radio being turned on at Madam White's pleasure, was stretching Vera's patience to the limit. Barfield was only too happy to relax with a magazine and nurse the factory cat – a moth-eaten old bag of bones which offended Vera even further.

Vera had never confided to anyone that the little dog she'd taken to so fondly had been rudely snatched away from her. They'd been out for their regular after-work walk together and of all the unbelievable things to happen, she'd walked slap into the dog's owner. No doubting it – the dog had made it quite clear she recognized her former master. Well, there wouldn't be any more pets! Just get yourself attached to the wretched things, and they trot happily off and leave you for dead. She looked disdainfully at the cat – serve Barfield right if the stinking thing was covered in fleas.

Judy, meanwhile, had sized Kay up as someone to be trusted and after the first few days of work it had been pretty simple to direct the conversation around to the other kind of work being done in the factory. Kay had confided that the women in the garment area were resentful of the prisoners, seeing them as a possible threat to their employment. If the firm could get cheap labour form Wentworth, what was to stop them gradually employing all prison labour?

Judy could see their point but assured Kay there was no such plan afoot. However, it could make Kay look good in management's eyes if the prisoners exceeded their uniform quota each day – and they'd do it for a little extra incentive. Like a dress to wear for when they were released? Judy was short term, but being pretty generously built wouldn't find it easy to get something cheap, in her size, when the time came.

If Kay had any suspicions about Judy wanting a dress to wear outside of prison, she didn't let them bother her. If Jude could guarantee the women would work hard and not cause any trouble, especially with the other women working in the factory, then a dress should be no problem. Judy smiled to herself. Step number one in her escape plan. And it was more than a plan or an idea now. Wentworth with its tragic memories had become unbearable.

The 'garment workers' took a lot of ribbing when they returned at night to the prison. All sorts of lewd suggestions as to how they'd spent the day were put forward, but as Meg confided to Erica, it was all quite good natured.

In fact, it wasn't only the women on release work who were more cheerful. Their contact with the outside world seemed to be rubbing off on their fellow prisoners and for the moment there was a degree of quiet harmony that hadn't been felt in Wentworth for a very long time. From Erica's point of view, the whole scheme appeared to be a great success. And when Meg laughingly accused Erica of particularly enjoying her contact at management level with Andrew Reynolds, there was no denial.

The Governor had found herself attracted to Andrew from the very beginning. She'd tried hard to keep the association at arm's length – both for the sake of the enterprise and for her own protection. She'd been proven vulnerable before in affairs of the heart. Why set herself up for another disappointment?

188

But for all her good intentions, she'd succumbed to Andrew's charm and let him blatantly use their mutual work plan as a springboard to several intimate dinners and a delightful day at the races.

Vera commented in scathing terms to Meg that the Governor was making a fool of herself; the women would soon latch on and realize they were being used to promote a romance for their 'keeper'. Meg wryly remarked that the women were too interested in the wages being credited to them and would undoubtedly apply their usual rule – get it while it's going, mate!

But for all her lighthearted replies to Vera, Meg was more than concerned about her new neighbours. The nightly arguments were escalating, Jason had been taken to hospital yet again and Meg wondered just how closely his latest 'accident' was related to the loud thumping she'd heard, the ensuing screams, and worst of all – the almost palpable silence that came after-wards. She couldn't go on ignoring it. Next time . . . But would that be too late even then?

She was preoccupied with these thoughts as she checked on the laundry where Bea was keeping the women firmly in line and Lizzie, as usual, was doing as little as possible without actually 'retiring' from active service.

Bea gave a quick jerk of her head in Lizzie's direction and lowered her voice as she spoke to Meg. 'Had a chance to chat to the social worker, Mrs J.?'

Lizzie was preoccupied, reading a letter which, from its many creases, she had obviously read and re-read.

'Yes.' Meg glanced in the old girl's direction.

'I can understand your concern. She certainly never had a son called Robert Morgan.'

Bea looked grim. 'Reckon this Marcia woman's setting her up?'

Meg shrugged. 'Paul Reid's making further inquiries. It seems Lizzie's determined to set the woman and her child up, with her compo cash, so he certainly wants to make sure she's not being ripped off.'

Bea nodded. 'Poor old bugger. She's getting such a buzz out of that kid Josie, but I'm not going to stand by and see some vulture take her for all she's got.'

'I'll let you know if there's more news on it.' Meg reached into her pocket and her eyes twinkled as she handed over a letter to Bea. 'This came, special delivery. It had to go through the usual censoring but I promise I've forgotten every word I read.'

As Meg moved off, Bea quickly tore the envelope open. She wasn't disappointed. It was from Ken Pearce. Thank God old Vinegar Tits hadn't been the censor. She'd have been full of snide remarks and innuendo which would have spoilt the moment.

As her eyes travelled over the closely written pages, there was a softening of the mouth and something very close to happiness in Bea's eyes.

So that fleeting time they'd had in the store room really had meant something to him! What was he saying . . . 'That feeling of one-ness is still with me.' That would be something to think about tonight when she lay in her hard prison bunk with the lights out and all those empty years stretching ahead of her.

She was snapped out of her reverie by Lizzie's raucous laugh.

'You should see your face!' Lizzie turned to Phyllis and the others. 'Looks like a lovesick calf.'

'Shut up, Lizzie.' But Bea was smiling.

'Letter from that Pearce joker, I reckon.' Lizzie's old face was full of curiosity.

'Yep.' Bea put the letter in her pocket. 'Any news in yours?'

'It was me granddaughter, Josie.' Lizzie fingered the pages gently. 'Got her fourteenth birthday coming up.'

A spark of suspicion ran through Bea. 'Letting you know so you can spend big on a present, eh?'

The old girl was indignant. 'Doesn't want one. Just telling me she and her mum are going to make a cake and bring it here to share with me, so there!'

Bea silently swore that she'd personally tear that Marcia bitch apart, bit by bit, if she was conning Lizzie, but she kept her thoughts to herself. No point in upsetting her till they had the proof.

'I heard a bit of gossip.' Bea knew how to divert Lizzie: the old girl was immediately all ears. 'Remember Kerry?'

'Yea, she give Dor that beaut painting for a wedding present.' Lizzie suddenly laughed. 'And she set you up for a bit of slap and tickle with that Pearce bloke.'

'Yea, I haven't forgotten that. I owe her. Anyway,' – Bea checked to see that Phyllis wasn't listening – tell her and you told the bloody world. 'Seems that agent bloke double-crossed her and she tried to do him in. Bashed him over the head with an ashtray, just like the time she murdered that bloke.'

'Gawd!' Lizzie shook her head. 'Looked like butter wouldn't melt in her mouth, too.'

'Well, this time she didn't hit hard enough. Pity, strikes me that Austin bloke was a real bastard.'

'They sending her back here or something?'

Bea shook her head. 'Judge reckoned she needed

special treatment. She's been sent to some kind of sanatorium or other.'

'Will they let her paint there?'

'Hope so. She's got a real talent, that one. The painting she gave Dor'll probably end up being worth a fortune.'

Doreen's mind was a long way away from those kinds of thoughts. In the last couple of days at the factory Vince Talbot had been sending out some pretty clear signals in Doreen's direction. Bernadette and Jean had teased her good naturedly about it at morning tea. Kay had managed to infer that it was no skin off her nose if Doreen wanted to grab a bit of action while it was going – as long as it didn't affect the work.

It had all seemed harmless enough at first and anyhow, Vince would run a mile when he knew she was a married woman who didn't play around. But during the afternoon, Kay was dead keen to hear a particular race and anxious to get Vince out of the way – he was a moody bugger and, like as not, he'd turn off the transistor in the middle of the race if he thought it would annoy her.

Kay pressed him to bring an extra supply of materials from the store and he'd need to take one of the women along to help. Margot nudged Doreen, and backed by Kay and the other women she had little choice but to follow Vince to the store room.

Everything seemed normal enough at first. He quickly picked out the rolls of material needed and handed them over to Doreen. She stood there, waiting for him to open the door but instead he'd moved up very close.

'Anything you fancy for yourself, sweetheart?'

Doreen's heart started to race, but she tried to keep her cool. 'No thanks.' She took a couple of steps towards the door. 'I'll just go ahead with this lot, shall I?'

But he was too quick. In a moment, he'd turned, locked the door and pocketed the key.

'What are you doing?' There was panic in Doreen's voice now.

'You'd better be nice to me if you want to keep your job.'

'You touch me and I'll tell your boss, and the Governor.'

Vince gave a nasty little laugh. 'Reckon they'd take the word of a prisoner against a trusted employee? They all know you women are sex-starved and they've all seen the way you've been giving me the eye.'

Doreen's face was pitiful. 'Kev and me are married. I don't want no one till I get out and we start living together prop'ly.'

'You reckon he's not playing around? 'Course he is.'

Doreen shook her head, her eyes pleading now. 'Please don't do anything. I'm not like that. I – just want to keep meself for Kev.'

Vince's face was vicious as he clapped one hand hard over her mouth and with the other sent the rolls of material flying. She struggled but she was no match for him. He was bending her back over the bench, tearing at her clothes, pushing himself against her and then brutally forcing himself on her.

She never knew afterwards which hurt her more. The hot, searing pain in her body as he raped her, or the sharp scream of pain in her head that cried out in shame and humiliation at this vile invasion of her body.

She couldn't believe, when she trailed back into the workroom with her arms full of rolls of material, that every woman in the room couldn't see at a glance what had happened to her. But they were finishing up work for the day, with Margot bragging about her good day's takings, Vinegar Tits marshalling them like a herd of sheep and Kay strangely sullen and angry after a big loss to Margot.

Vince never so much as glanced in her direction as she miserably followed Officer Barfield out of the room to the waiting bus outside. She was aching to get back to the prison, to get under the shower and try to wash away the hideous, dirty feeling that enveloped her.

Jude chided her lightheartedly – cat got your tongue? Somehow Doreen managed to answer. She could never speak of it. And he was right. She was a prisoner. She had no rights. They wouldn't believe her. And what would the women do if she tried it on? They'd lose their work release and their extra cash and they'd beat the hell out of her if she was to blame. And probably half of them wouldn't believe her either.

She was in no mood for Lizzie's chatter but the old girl was full of talk . . . another visit from Marcia and poor Josie needed this operation on her leg. It'd cost an arm and a leg but the dear little thing had had pain for years and now this specialist could fix it, and of course Lizzie was going to see that it was done, nothing but the best for her little granddaughter.

She was piqued at Doreen's lack of interest but Bea was taking in every word and when the old girl finally took herself off to the showers, Bea confided to Doreen that they couldn't afford to wait for the bloody social workers to fart arse around. They'd have to do something about this Marcia person themselves.

Doreen wasn't really taking much in, but she nodded and, before lights out, Bea had written a letter to Marcia Huntly letting her know in no uncertain terms that they were friends of Lizzie's and they were on to her. If she didn't want to find herself behind bars, she'd better go back where she came from quick smart – and find another patsy to cough up the cash!

There was an even bigger drama being enacted in the Governor's office. A distraught Meg was explaining to the Governor just how Gail Summers had ended up in Wentworth.

Meg had finally been unable to live with her conscience and after a particularly violent eruption in her neighbour's household she'd called the police. How could she let it go on and on, knowing a child was being beaten by a brutal and drunken stepfather?

She was still reeling from the revelation that had taken place when the police arrived. Hysterical and screaming, Gail had confessed that it was she who was abusing her son, Jason. She'd been going around the bend with Stevie always crying, Katrina whining, Jason clinging to her twenty-four hours a day and a husband who offered no support and spent his few hours at home yelling obscenities at her or smashing the place up in a drunken rage.

Erica sympathized. It would be difficult for Meg having Gail in her care, but she had still done the right thing. The girl was obviously in need of psychiatric help but for the moment she had been remanded to Wentworth and they were stuck with it.

The important thing, as Erica had stressed to Summers, was to lie about the charge. If the other women knew she was in for child abuse, she'd be given hell. They'd seen it all before. Summers was to say she'd been caught shoplifting; a small lie for her own protection.

There was no such sympathetic reaction from Jim or Vera. Jim, still bereft over the death of his two sons, agreed with Vera that anyone accused of child abuse was the scum of the earth and deserved to be treated accordingly.

Vera, pleased for once to find a sympathetic ear, took the opportunity of expressing her dissatisfaction with the work release plan. The controls were far too loose, she had keen suspicions that Gaffney was running a book and, frankly, she strongly suspected the Governor's enthusiasm sprang from an increasing personal involvement with Reynolds himself.

Jim was not going to be drawn on that subject although personally he wasn't particularly in favour of the outside work – the temptation to escape could only be heightened once outside the confines of the prison.

Vera would have been intrigued to know just how far Erica's relationship with Andrew Reynolds had developed. She had suggested dinner at her place and she had been somewhat startled at the intensity of her own reactions. And when Andrew had made it very clear he would like to spend the night with her she'd realized she wanted the involvement just as much as him.

The next morning, it had seemed the most natural thing in the world to be sitting across the table from him, sharing breakfast, making small talk, but knowing something very special had happened between them. It had been a long time since she had felt that kind of happiness and fulfilment.

She could sense Vera's disapproval without her ever putting it into words, but then Vera would probably never allow herself to lay her feelings bare, risking humiliation for the chance of loving and being loved. She was sorry for the Summers girl. Meg had relayed the news that the husband had made a prison visit but only to inform his wife that he intended divorcing her. Heaven knows, Gail needed support not rejection. With this thought in mind, Erica was furious to learn that the word had leaked out that Summers was in for child abuse. She'd summoned Bea Smith to her office and threatened dire consequences if anything happened as a result of the leak.

Bea knew better than to challenge the Governor in that mood. She spread the word that Summers was to be ignored, sent to Coventry to at least let her know that, convicted prisoners or no, the women didn't want to mix with the likes of her.

What Erica did not know was that Gail herself, intimidated and upset, had found a friend in Lizzie and had confided the truth to her. Lizzie had been around long enough to realize the dreadful remorse the girl felt and it was only out of sympathy that she had passed the word around, hoping to make things easier for the girl.

When Bea took Lizzie to task over it – Bea didn't appreciate being put on the mat in front of the Governor – Lizzie was ready to hit back. She'd just heard from Mr Reid, the social worker. Marcia and Josie had fallen through thanks to a threatening letter someone had got smuggled out to them. Bea met her head on. The woman was a bloody faker. To Bea's astonishment, tears replaced the anger in Lizzie's eyes.

'You think I didn't know that, from the start?' Lizzie's voice was shaking. 'What did I care? I'd found meself a family, a girl I'd be proud to call daughter and a dear little girl to love and live for when I got out of this hole.'

Bea could only stare at her. 'You knew?'

'Yes.' Lizzie fairly spat the word at her. 'And now you've put your bib in and mucked it up and I'll never see them again.'

Bea felt deeply sorry for the old girl but Gawd, she had to face the truth. 'They were only going to hang around till you handed over the cash. Then you'd have had no one and no bloody money.'

For answer Lizzie turned her back on Bea and, a small, bent figure, plodded miserably back in the direction of her cell. Bea sighed. Pretty hard to help some people, sometimes.

Well, she wasn't going to catch up with Lizzie for a while, let her cool down a bit. And as for Dor, who knew what the hell had got into her. She'd done everything to get herself taken off the work release – cheeking Vera, missing roll call, stirring up shit at meal times with anyone who'd take her on. And Bea couldn't get a word out of her. Maybe Jude would be able to throw a bit of light on things.

But Judy was engrossed in her own thoughts. She indicated the letter from America lying beside her on the bunk. It was to tell her that her father was dying.

Bea picked her words carefully. 'I thought you didn't

have any contact with them after the way they treated you.'

Judy nodded. 'That's right. But Pop was the only one who gave me a fair shake, went on believing in me.' She glanced at the letter. 'They wrote to say it's his dying wish to see me.'

Bea wanted to say something comforting, but what? Judy was stuck in Wentworth and there was no way around that.

It was as if Judy had read her thoughts. 'Looks like you'll have to solve all the problems round here, Bea.'

Bea frowned. 'What do you mean?'

Judy looked her straight in the eye. 'I'm going to see my Pop.'

Bea shrugged. 'I understand how you feel. But getting out of here's tough enough! Let alone finding your way to the States.'

'I'll find a way,' Bea had never seen Judy look so determined, 'and God help any bastard who tries to stop me!'

Fifteen

Erica stared unseeingly at the report in front of her but Andrew's words were still ringing in her ears. 'There's something I should have told you before this started between us.'

They'd been sitting on the couch, things warm and intimate between them, an unspoken understanding that Andrew would stay over. 'I'm married.'

Why hadn't she questioned it before? She should have known it was too good to be true. The instant attraction between them, the mutual chemistry, the remarkable *simpatico* even when they just sat comfortably, silently, together.

Perhaps she hadn't wanted to know. Well, it was over. He'd tried to talk about it, assure her his marriage was literally a formality but she'd been too hurt and angry to listen.

Had Vera been right all along with her snide hints that Andrew Reynolds was just using her? Getting cheap labour for his factory and keeping her happy in bed to make sure the contract continued? Her thoughts were rudely interrupted by Meg's hurried entrance.

'Sorry to barge in. There's been an accident in the laundry.'

Erica was instantly alert. 'What kind of accident?'

'Bryant.' Meg looked a bit puzzled. 'I'm not quite sure how it happened but she fell heavily against one of the driers. The electrical current seems to have reacted pretty seriously on her pacemaker.'

'Has she been taken to the infirmary?' Erica was all Governor again, thoughts of Andrew hastily pushed to the back of her mind.

Meg nodded. 'Yes, and the ambulance is on its way.' Meg managed a wry smile. 'Vera's got some outrageous idea that it's a deliberate escape attempt.'

'What did Nurse say?'

'The sooner the ambulance gets here the better.'

Erica looked thoughtful. 'We'll need a replacement for the factory work. How do you feel about Bea Smith?'

Meg smiled broadly. 'Vera will hit the roof, but I agree. She'll keep the women in order and the less she sees of Gail Summers, the better.'

Erica hesitated a moment. 'I simply can't understand Doreen Anderson . . . Burns, I should say. She seems to be doing everything in her power to be taken off the work release.'

'I know.' Meg shook her head. 'It's very puzzling. You'd think she'd be glad of the extra money let alone the chance to get out of here for a while.'

'Keep your ear to the ground, Meg.'

Bea had decided to take it a step further. She was fed up with the cold shoulder she was getting from Lizzie over the Marcia business, and Doreen was worrying her considerably. So far, Bea hadn't been able to get a word out of her.

It was at the lunch break that the chance came.

For no apparent reason Doreen started baiting Gail Summers, calling her a baby-basher and doing everything in her power to make the girl lash out and start a bunfight.

Gail didn't oblige. She ran from the room, tears streaming down her face, and Bea was forced to admit to herself that maybe there had been extenuating circumstances in the girl's case. She did seem to love her kids. But as far as Dor was concerned, enough was enough!

'You were told to ignore Summers. Why the hell are you trying to pick a fight?' Doreen's lips set in a stubborn line.

Bea thought fast. 'I think I'd better give Kev a ring, see if he can sort you out.'

'No!' The reply was so vehement that Bea's eyebrows shot up in surprise.

'Why not?'

Doreen was looking quite tearful now. Bea got up from the table.

'Come on. We don't want to talk here with these loud mouths hanging on our every word.'

Together they left the dining room and made their way along the corridor and slowly the story came out.

Bea was beside herself with rage. That rotten bastard! But why hadn't Doreen at least had a word with Davo? She'd have got a fair hearing. Doreen shook her head.

'Everyone knows she's on with that Reynolds joker. She don't want nothing rocking the boat. Anyway, no one'd back me up. I mean, at first, I thought it was just a bit of fun and I joked round with him like the others done and they'd all just say I was asking for it.'

Bea frowned. 'What about that woman you talk about, Kay White?'

Doreen shrugged. 'She's only really interested in winning a packet on the races. Already owes Margot a bundle, though. Anyhow, she wouldn't stick her neck out for me.'

The solution was easier than Bea would ever have hoped for. The Governor was giving her the chance to replace Judy Bryant. Bea let Erica know that she appreciated the chance and, as she confided to Dor later, the Guv didn't know just how nicely she'd set things up for Bea to give Vince bloody Talbot a lesson.

Doreen was a bit fearful about it. They'd get hell if they mucked up the work scheme. But Bea assured her they'd do no such thing; just teach that prick-happy bastard a lesson he wouldn't forget!

Vera went through the roof when she learned Smith was to go out on work release. Talk about asking for trouble! Besides, Bryant would probably be fit to work in a couple of days.

At the hospital, the doctor examining Judy was inclined to agree. The tests he'd conducted had shown no signs of irregularity in the pacemaker. However, he would hook her up to the monitor again and they'd see what showed up.

Judy was apparently quite relaxed, submitting to the hospital routine with every sign of acquiescence. But she was sharply aware of the heavily built policewoman on guard outside the door. And she'd taken careful note of her surroundings when they'd wheeled her down to the cardiac ward.

If she could just get this guy to leave her alone for

a few minutes! It was no problem. The doctor's beeper sounded and with a quick apology he hurried out to the phone in the hospital corridor.

It took only a moment to free herself from the monitor. Then she quickly slid off the bed and grabbed the full carafe of water from the locker and positioned herself behind the door. She didn't want to hurt anyone, but she had to get out.

She leant across and hit the steel locker hard with the carafe. As she'd hoped, the policewoman stepped inside to check the noise, and Judy, from behind the door, brought the heavy water carafe down on the back of her head. When the doctor returned a short time afterwards, he was confronted by an empty bed, the disconnected monitor and the unconscious body of the policewoman lying on the ward floor, minus her uniform.

When news of the escape filtered through to Wentworth, Vera was positively jubilant. Perhaps Erica Davidson would realize now that none of the scum could be trusted! Look at the likes of Birdsworth, joining in the riot after all the privileges she'd been allowed. Well, it seemed like that precious daughter of hers had been a fake and serve the old clown right if she had been taken for every penny she possessed.

But Vera was doomed to disappointment on that score. To her amazement and Lizzie's delight, the old girl was informed that Marcia and Josie had come to see her and the visit was being allowed.

Lizzie sensed the constraint in Marcia when they met in the garden. Josie was her usual affectionate self but the old girl realized that the first overture must come from Marcia.

'I wasn't sure you'd see us.'

Lizzie smiled. 'Miss out on a visit? Not likely.'

Josie took Lizzie's gnarled hand in her firm young one. 'I didn't want to go away without seeing you, Grandma.'

Marcia looked embarrassed. 'Josie, I explained. Lizzie isn't really our . . .' She broke off, looking distressed, then the words came rushing out. 'My real name is Ellen Morgan. I was in the orphanage with Marcia. She was my best friend. We used to talk for hours on end when we were kids. We ended up knowing all there was to know about each other.'

Lizzie nodded. So that's how it had been so easy.

'Marcia died in an accident just a few months before her twenty-fifth birthday. We'd always kept in touch up till then. I'm sorry.' Ellen's troubled eyes were begging forgiveness.

Lizzie clung tight to Josie's hand and a slow, gentle smile lit the wrinkled face. 'I knew all along.'

Ellen was dumbstruck. Could this be true?

'But I wanted a family so much. And I liked you, right off.'

Ellen's voice was trembling. 'I don't deserve that.'

'Listen.' Lizzie put her hand on the young woman's shoulder and gave her a reassuring pat. 'You saw the ad., and a chance to help your kiddie. That's not such a dreadful thing to do.'

Ellen shook her head. 'I think the court would call it extortion.'

'Well, I don't and no one else's going to either. I want you to go right on being my daughter. And as for this dear little soul, she's going to have her operation and get that leg better. And when I come out, she's going to be the granddaughter I always wanted. And I reckon I could never have got one I'd love more.'

Josie's answer was a warm, loving hug.

There were tears in Ellen's eyes. 'I don't deserve this.'

Lizzie's eyes twinkled. 'I'll be the judge of that. Anyway, all's well that ends well.' She chuckled and looked down at Josie. 'See, I know me Shakespeare. I'm not as stupid as I look.'

'I think you're the best grandma in all the world.' Josie's eyes were shining and the sweetness of her smile touched Lizzie to the heart.

'We'll get you moved back into Dor's house then you can make arrangements with the doctor and all that.' Lizzie's face clouded for a moment. 'They *can* fix Josie's leg, can't they?'

'Yes.' Ellen hesitated. 'But it is going to cost a lot of money.'

'Then we haven't got a problem.'

Lizzie glanced towards the main building and saw Officer Barfield coming towards them. 'I'll have to be getting back inside. You'll keep in touch, won't you?'

Josie gave her an affectionate hug and kiss. 'I'll write every day, Gran.'

Lizzie laughed. 'You don't have to go quite that far, lovie.'

Marcia hesitated for a moment, then she put her arms around the frail old body and kissed Lizzie tenderly on the cheek. 'How can I ever thank you?'

Lizzie looked a little wistful. 'You could call me Mum.'

Barfield knew full well she shouldn't be allowing this physical contact, but poor old Birdsworth had been so down in the dumps when her family stopped coming to see her. And you didn't see too many scenes as happy as this one at Wentworth.

She waited patiently with Lizzie at the main entrance while the old girl waved to Marcia and Josie till they were past the guard and outside the fence.

'That's a nice little granddaughter you've got, Lizzie.'

Lizzie put her chin up proudly. 'Pretty nice daughter too.'

Wait till she told Bea! Silly bugger would probably go bananas, but to hell with that.

Bea had bigger fish to fry. Her first morning at the factory was proving more than interesting. This Kay White would need watching. She'd already heard Margot trying to get this woman to pay up – she'd had a couple of really hefty flutters but there'd been no cash forthcoming. A lot of piffle about cash flow and needing to get to the bank. And Bea had distinctly overheard Kay tell Margot, in a pretty nasty tone of voice, that there wasn't a blind thing Margot could do about it.

Vince Talbot? Bea had sized him up quick smart, bloody great bully and a chauvinist pig from way back. She gave Doreen an encouraging wink. She had his number and a nice little plan developing.

She'd had a gander at Andrew Reynolds too. Not her type but she could understand Davo going for him. He'd looked pretty worried, something about doing an early stock take. That had seemed to upset Madame White more than somewhat.

All in all, Bea was enjoying herself. Lots of room

for action round this joint! And there were plenty of wisecracks from the women when the news leaked out that Jude had not only given the hospital the slip, but had taken off in the lady copper's uniform! What a bewdy!

The policewoman's uniform wasn't a particularly good fit and Judy had felt pretty self-conscious as she'd hurried to a phone box to contact her friend Pauline Curtis. She knew she could count on her. They'd been lovers ten years ago, just a whirlwind affair of a few months, but they'd remained good friends even after Pauline married. And when Judy had formed her plan to get into Wentworth she'd left her passport and a few valuables with Pauline, and thank God, enough clothing to see her through now.

Pauline explained, as she picked Judy up from the phone box in her car, that there were no problems for the moment about her staying. Husband Peter was away for a couple of days. Of course, when he came back . . . She left the sentence unfinished.

Judy understood. Peter knew nothing about what had once been between them. And there was no way she'd rock the boat for Paulo. She needed just enough time to get her hands on some cash for a forged passport and the air fare out of the country. She explained her plans as she thankfully struggled out of the uniform and back into her own civvies. There was money in the account she and Sharon had shared but Pauline couldn't try and draw on that. She'd really have to be careful. Unfortunately she and Pete had just laid out most of their spare cash doing up the house. She was working part time but not earning much. But at least she could supply a bed and some tucker.

But when Judy explained that the letter from her father, which Pauline had sent on to her, had decided her on getting to the States to see him, Pauline looked doubtful. A pretty big project. Judy didn't say anything at that stage but she eyed the police uniform thoughtfully. She wouldn't get rid of it just yet. It could come in handy.

The idea forming in her head took even firmer shape after she'd called on the contact she'd learned about in Wentworth. They called him 'The Weasel' and he had the doubtful honour of being the best forger in the country. Off the top of her head, the only name Judy had been able to come up with was Debbie Raye – well, Dor wouldn't mind and she didn't need that alias any more. But $500! And there was no haggling with The Weasel. How the hell was she going to come up with that amount?

There was nothing for it but to put her earlier idea into action. Back in the policewoman's uniform – she'd done her best to smarten it up a bit – she realized how simple it could be. The first two prostitutes she saw scooted off like startled rabbits. Then she spied the thin, vulgarly dressed girl waiting in the doorway. What with Judy's imposing physical build and the uniform, extortion was simple. Only forty dollars, but it was like taking candy from a baby. There'd be plenty more who'd pay up rather than face even a brief stay in stir.

In spite of the danger of the situation and little pleasure in what she'd just done, Judy couldn't resist a chuckle. God, Bea would get a buzz out of seeing this bit of action.

*

Bea was in fact enjoying herself hugely at the factory. Barry and Knox were chatting away happily in the tea room – there was only the one entrance to the place so there wasn't much point in standing around like the Gestapo. The women had nowhere to go but the inside toilet. And by the look of them, they didn't have any intentions of causing any kind of trouble.

With Vince Talbot called to Andrew's office it was easy for Kay White to lodge another bet with Margot. The latter would like to have turned her down but she knew she had no choice and at least this time Kay had coughed up twenty dollars in cash.

It was at this point that Jean, who was so thin she had to just about walk past twice to cast a shadow, made her little joke.

'Pity I'm so skinny. Reckon if you could stuff a couple of those bolts of material up your jumper you could get a good thing going, raise a bit of cash.'

Bernadette cackled. 'Bet you're not the first one who's thought of that little racket.'

'You keep your trap shut!' Kay White had turned on Bernadette in an instant, in blind fury. And for a moment the women thought she was really going to go berserk. Her hand had clenched around the wrench which Talbot kept for machine repairs. It was a heavy, ugly looking thing and Bernadette had been scared shitless.

But the woman had seemed to recall herself to her senses as quickly as she'd flown into a rage. She took a deep breath and tried to keep her voice normal. 'Sorry; but that's the kind of talk that gives people ideas. And you lot would cop it sweet if anything did go missing.'

Bea looked at her shrewdly. Was she giving them a message? Or maybe already up to something and confident that if anything went wrong the first finger to be pointed would be at the Wentworth workers.

She was mulling this over when the answer was literally dropped into her lap. Andrew Reynolds had made a point of seeking her out, supposedly welcoming a new worker and one he believed was the 'boss lady' at Wentworth.

She was aware that he'd looked a bit furtively in the direction of the tea room, obviously checking that the officers weren't taking too much interest. And then he'd quietly put the proposition to her. If the women would consider making some non-Governmental garments he's slip them an extra ten dollars a week. Things were pretty difficult in the garment trade at the moment, wages exorbitant and the outside women worked nowhere near as hard as the Wentworth women.

Bea appeared to be thinking about it. She knew the women would jump at it. And best of all, if anything did go wrong, if the White woman happened to pass the buck, Bea and the others would have something on the management.

She nodded. 'I reckon that'd be OK.'

With a quick promise to sort out the details next day, he was on his way. A small cynical smile played around Bea's lips. What would the Guv say to her fancy boy bribing the prisoners, and using slave labour to get the cash to spend on her?

Things were really starting to get interesting around this joint, but first, she must attend to the little matter of Vince Talbot!

It was a simple thing to turn off the machine and bend the worn flex until the bare wire was exposed. She tucked it back then, arms folded, sat back, waiting. Officer Knox was quickly over. Why wasn't she working? Bea explained the problem and Knox called Vince Talbot.

Bea fabricated a nice little story about the stitches jumping and Vince moved in to take a closer look at the problem. He'd just begun to dismantle the machine when Bea 'accidentally' flicked the power switch on. The electric shock sent him crashing to the floor. Bea glanced down at the unconscious form and looked meaningly across at Doreen. 'One for you, Dor girl.' Doreen allowed herself a small, tight smile.

Later, when he'd been revived, Bea was very apologetic but she knew from the wary look in his eyes that he'd twigged it had been no accident. Well, that should put paid to that prick's standover tactics!

Judy had reluctantly moved into more standover herself. She'd confided to her friend Paulo that her police lady impersonation had just about raked in the five hundred. And Paulo, obviously nervous that her husband might return sooner than expected, offered to find the cash for the ticket. Call it a loan, a gift, whatever. Judy understood and gratefully accepted.

But when she'd called back to The Weasel he'd found out her real identity and doubled the price for the passport – danger money involved with a crim on the run.

She was all too aware that time was running out. And there was no way she'd make trouble for Pauline. But there was a last resort.

Many a time her taxi had taken eager gamblers to the Fan Tan Club where big money changed hands regularly and everyone in the know was aware that the club, and many like it, paid out generously in cash for the cops to leave them alone.

Pauline looked very nervous when she confided her plan. Judy shrugged. She'd come this far, too late to turn back and she had to have that passport. They exchanged an affectionate hug – it was unlikely they would ever meet again. Pauline made a last ditch plea to Judy to give herself up. It was a rotten life on the run and what about that heart condition? Judy knew the advice was well meant, even made a lot of sense, but after all that had happened in the last months, Sharon, Leanne, and then the news about her father – the die was cast. She had to go all the way.

Back in the uniform it was a breeze getting past the lookout and into the club. Of course, the money had all been removed from the tables – so the officer hadn't really witnessed anything. But the payout was ready and, from the size of it, generous.

Judy strolled out and down the stairs, firmly clutching the reassuring package. She was almost across the street when she saw the two burly officers bearing down on her. How the hell had they spotted her?

It was a bitter Judy who stood sullenly listening to Vera Bennett read out the charges against her. To have been so close . . .

Pauline was staring at the television with unseeing eyes. Would Judy ever understand why her old friend Paulo had shopped her to the police? It was for her own good, surely she'd understand that? Jude wasn't a criminal. She had to stop before she did something worse. So why didn't she feel better about it?

Meg looked sympathetically after Judy as she was led away. Things would be even worse for her tomorrow. A letter had been forwarded to the prison that day. Meg had censored it. Judy's father had died. It had all been in vain.

Sixteen

'I'd like to request factory duty.'

Erica looked at Vera Bennett in surprise. 'I understood you found it desperately boring.'

Vera gave a small, slightly apologetic smile. 'I did say that. But I've done three double shifts in the last fortnight and to be honest, I'd appreciate a couple of days' light work.'

Erica was thoughtful for a moment. Andrew had already been on the phone concerning the Vince Talbot incident. He was of the opinion that it was quite definitely an accident, some of the machines were a bit prehistoric, but he couldn't afford to replace them all at once.

It was a bit of a coincidence, though, that it'd happened as soon as Bea was put on the work release scheme. But Andrew had spoken highly of her, said she seemed a good influence on the other women and was certainly a good worker herself.

She tried not to think too much about the rest of their conversation. He'd been so pressing about seeing her again, just to explain the way things really were, that in the end she'd agreed and now she wasn't sure it had been such a good idea. But she granted Vera's request. She over-reached herself at times, but there was no denying her commitment to the job and her willingness to work extra hours. And there were all too few officers with that attitude.

Meg was glad to swop duties. Summers' trial was imminent and she was terrified. Meg had had several indepth talks with Gail and done her best to give the girl some kind of hope for the future. She'd even pointed out that Chrissie Latham had her baby in maternity, and in spite of a murder charge was proving to be a very good mother indeed.

That had seemed to cheer Gail but she was dreading being fingered in public for child abuse and sure the judge would despise her even more than her fellow prisoners did. Old Lizzie Birdsworth had made her feel a bit better, telling her what had happened to her kids and how she was going to make up for the past mistakes by taking care of Marcia and Josie. Never too late to make amends and start again.

Lizzie had less luck trying to cheer Doreen. Certainly Doreen felt a deep satisfaction that Bea had arranged Talbot's little 'accident' but the memory of that awful experience wouldn't go away. And each time she got a letter from Kevin, she'd feel a wave of despair at the thought of him maybe one day finding out and turning away from her. Bea told her she was nuts, look at the way he'd already stood by her, but she wasn't convinced.

She wasn't too happy about what was going on at the factory either. It was OK to get another ten dollars a week but it was Doreen's opinion that if the outside women workers found out the prisoners were making civvie garments there'd be hell to pay. Bea's attitude was that the work release wouldn't last forever anyway, so get it while they could, and the other women were in full agreement with her.

Kay White was voicing much the same thoughts to Andrew Reynolds. They'd have a strike on their hands if they weren't careful. And Vera, anti the project from the start, was smugly observing what was going on. She gave off not a hint that she thought anything untoward was happening but she was fine tuned to every nuance in the place.

What was happening now was a lot more important than a bit of betting on the side. That would be wiped out the moment Vera blew the whistle to the Department, anyway. Vera looked across at Officer Joan Barry who was sharing the factory duty with her. She wouldn't pick up something like this if a house fell on her! Well, it would be Vera who got the kudos from the Department. And just wait till the whole story came out – the Governor consorting with the factory manager and giving her seal of approval to the whole shonky business! She'd be in really big trouble.

At that moment, Erica's thoughts were very different. She'd settled with Meg that Bryant remain in Isolation for a few days. She seemed morose and sullen since her return. The news of her father had naturally upset her, but something had happened to the woman since those two fateful accidents. And now she'd ended up with a criminal record like the rest of them and apparently little interest in trying to rehabilitate herself.

She was happy with the way the social worker, Paul Reid, had settled the Birdsworth business. Dared she hope Lizzie would now stay out of trouble? But she was even happier with the dozen red roses which had been delivered half an hour earlier. Jim Fletcher had teased her lightly when he'd brought them in to her.

Poor man, life was very empty for him since the loss of his family. And that regrettable Simpson affair. Thank goodness the Department hadn't seen fit to pursue it. He was a good Deputy Governor and perhaps, in time, he'd find someone he wanted to share his life with.

Did she want to share hers with Andrew Reynolds? Well, they would talk. But this time, she must weigh things a little more carefully, not let her heart rule her head. Always that nagging doubt came back. Was he using her?

Vera was sure of it as she watched Andrew surreptitiously removing the civvie garments and hurriedly taking them through to the other section of the factory. She'd been aware once or twice that Bea Smith was looking at her rather questioningly. Smith knew that she didn't miss too many tricks. Well, she'd just bide her time.

But she didn't have to. As the end of the work siren sounded and the women moved towards the exit, with Joan Barry leading the way, Vera found herself confronting an extremely militant looking woman. She quickly made it known that she was the Union Rep., Hazel Crowe.

'I'm Officer Bennett.' Vera allowed herself a small smile; this was almost too good to be true.

Hazel Crowe spelt it out fast. Did Officer Bennett know these women were working against Union Rules? Making civilian garments as well as Government uniforms? Usurping the jobs of the permanent factory workers?

Vera assumed a remarkably innocent expression. 'Does Mr Andrews know this is going on?' The woman gave her a pitying look. 'He's the boss, isn't he? He calls the shots.'

'Well,' the woman smacked her lips in satisfaction, 'we'll be calling a strike if the matter isn't rectified immediately.'

Vera could hardly wait for the bus to pull in to the prison grounds. She went with almost unseemly haste to Erica's office only to find she'd just missed her. It was desperately frustrating.

But then another thought occurred to her and she smiled grimly. It was very likely that the Governor was spending the evening with the factory manager! It would be even more satisfying to deliver this broadside in the morning! And meantime, she'd write her report for the Department. There'd be no need to spell out Erica's personal involvement. That would come out soon enough when the whole work release fiasco was investigated.

Erica's thoughts were very much otherwise engaged. It was so good to be with Andrew again. And wasn't it time she told him the truth. She'd let him pour out his story, two children, a son twenty-four, a daughter twenty. And his wife Julie, sadly, as in so many cases, someone who shared the house with him and presented a united family front to the world in general. In truth, two strangers under the same roof, nothing in common now that the children had moved out; no animosity – both in limbo and willing to let go if either found someone to really care for.

'I wasn't completely honest with you either, Andrew.' Erica glanced down at the long, cool drink in front of her. 'Michael and I haven't lived together for a long time. But we're not divorced.'

He put his hand over hers briefly. 'In our own way we're both free. Couldn't we go on seeing each other? It would mean nothing to my wife Julie. And your case isn't all that different.'

Erica gave a small, forlorn smile. 'I was going to be so strong. But when I'm with you . . .' The words trailed off.

'I feel the same way.'

Erica sighed. 'There's always so much gossip in a prison.' She managed a small laugh. 'And no doubt the women on work release are watching you like hawks and making all sorts of assumptions.'

'This has nothing to do with your job or mine.' He smiled reassuringly across at her. Surely he couldn't look and sound so convincing unless the words were sincere? Right now, sitting so close in the intimate atmosphere of the discreet little restaurant, she wanted to believe him with all her heart. And she would – for tonight, at least.

Meg commented lightly on Erica's happy go lucky mood the next morning. She had no doubt it was connected with the dozen red roses. Erica smilingly admitted that it was. But the glow was short-lived.

Vera was inside the door with indecent haste, her neatly typed report in her hand. She pushed it rather unceremoniously in front of Erica. It would appear Mr Reynolds had been taking advantage of the prisoners. They'd been making garments not stipulated in the contract. He'd made some kind of cash deal with them no doubt.

Erica felt her heart sink. So her worst fears were to

be realized? Vera saw the expression on her face and felt a warm glow of satisfaction. 'Of course, my report need not go to the Department? At this stage, only you and I know the situation.' The words hung in the air, heavy with innuendo. She was placing the full onus on Erica. Let her be the one to dob her fancy boy in to the Department.

Erica eyed her coldly. She must not let Vera Bennett get the upper hand. 'You do have proof of this.'

'Oh yes.' Vera's smile was tight. She wasn't going to tip the Governor off about the strike. That would force her to act. No, let her grapple with her conscience and decide whether her boyfriend mattered more to her than her job!

Erica knew she had to tackle it head on. And it was with a heavy heart that she listened to Andrew confirming that he had indeed allowed the women to do work outside the contract. He was sorry, it would stop immediately, he had massive problems with the factory. The auditors had that morning discovered discrepancies in the stock returns. He'd simply been trying to save the firm, the women's jobs, the work release scheme.

She chose her words carefully. She was never going to let him know the extent of the hurt he'd inflicted. The work release plan would cease immediately.

He tried desperately to arrange a meeting outside of work, to tell her exactly what had happened and why, but she explained as calmly as she could that she had a heavy work load and, later, a meeting.

She didn't know as she put the phone down gently on its cradle that Andrew was receiving the final body blow. The story had somehow been leaked to the press.

A full police investigation would follow concerning pilfering of stock which had been going on for months.

He found it hard, as he looked across his desk at Kay White, to believe this woman he'd trusted so implicitly had been robbing him blind. Vince had tipped him off that she was a heavy gambler but he hadn't paid much heed to that. But this morning it had all been confirmed on a big scale. In order to pay her huge gambling debts Kay White had stolen the weekly pay roll from the factory safe. 'I can pay you back,' she'd screamed at him across the office, brandishing her bulging handbag. 'I borrowed it. I had to make a big plunge to get myself clear.'

She threw the heavy handbag across the room at him. 'You're just as big a cheat, using prison labour, lying to the workers. Well, you won't see me again!' But as she turned to flee the room, Vince Talbot had blocked the doorway and taken her in a firm grip. And she'd reacted violently when the police arrived, a side of her he'd never seen.

He'd wanted to keep the place going, didn't mean to use the women from the prison unfairly! But it was all hopeless now. And worst of all, he knew Erica Davidson would never believe that his feelings for her were not all part of the plan. She'd brand him as a user. Maybe he was.

In the end, Vera submitted her report and Erica knew there'd be a full Departmental inquiry. But for the moment, the personal loss was so acute, she couldn't even bring herself to contemplate what the outcome might be. And she went about the business of the next few days in a state of near numbness.

*

There was little hope of forgetting the 'incident'. A few weeks later Kay White had been brought into Wentworth, a reminder of the whole fatal episode, and she would mean trouble. The women were angry that the work had been cancelled. And unbeknown to the Governor, Big Margot was eager to get her hands on White and force her to pay back the money she owed.

The bonus was that Judy was brought out of Isolation. Kay was to take her place, word having been discreetly circulated to Meg via Bea that letting White loose could mean all sorts of problems. The women had read the full story of the factory fiasco in the paper and, as one, blamed White for losing their jobs and the extra money.

Erica ordered extra protection for White, so Jim and Meg were suitably stunned when they checked the Isolation ward and found Big Margot Gaffney lying on the floor, with Kay bending over forcing food into her mouth in a particularly vicious fashion.

They jumped her quickly, but although it was obvious Kay had somehow managed to floor Margot, the big woman stuck to her story that she'd slipped. And the force feeding was a joke. Kay had made a crack about the food being poisoned and wanted someone to taste it for her.

Jim and Meg both knew it was a load of rubbish but they couldn't do a thing about it while neither prisoner would press charges or tell the truth. At least it made them wary. It took a very strong person indeed to KO Gaffney. Kay White had better be treated with caution.

But as Margot confided to Bea, she wasn't fazed. White had taken her by surprise and yeah, she was a hell of a lot stronger than she looked. More ways to skin a cat, though! What they needed to do was get Kay invited to the barbecue the Guv was letting them have – then they'd see.

Bea nodded grimly. No love lost on that bitch for buggering up the factory project. But she was a bit puzzled the Guv had kept mum to the women about the work release – not a word of condemnation for taking on the outside work. But letting them have the barbecue? Bea grinned to herself. Guilty conscience, Davo?

Doreen showed no enthusiasm whatever about the treat in store. Bea told her to forget the bloody diet, Kevin liked her the way she was.

Lizzie was a bit preoccupied about little Josie and the coming op., but she reckoned – if her teeth held up – a few bangers and dead horse would be a nice change from the usual kitchen mush.

And no one would have felt the least suspicion, seeing big Margot drop a glass in the kitchen and meticulously clean up the mess, that she had an extra little surprise planned for the barbecue.

Jim was dead set against the White woman being allowed to mingle, and on this occasion Meg backed him up. But Erica had already talked to Paul Reid. He'd advised that confining a woman of Kay White's temperament could be even more dangerous. It wasn't just the gambling obsession that had to be dealt with. There was an innate violence, and bottling that up indefinitely could only lead to an emotional explosion.

Vera was disparaging about the whole enterprise. The rotten scum had abused their work release opportunity, and the Governor was apparently rewarding them for it. Well, her detailed report was in and it was only a matter of time before the balloon went up. And if Bea Smith and her lot were out to get White, it might just be the opportunity Vera had been waiting for. Let Smith at her, and then that boss lady bitch would get the stretch in solitary she deserved; give her time to rethink any future idea of stripping an officer of her uniform!

Judy was a lone voice in trying to defend Kay White. She hadn't forgotten that the woman had managed to get her a dress made, for her escape. OK, as it happened, she hadn't collected it, she'd changed plans, but she still owed Kay.

Bea wouldn't have a bar of it and she was sounding off in no uncertain terms to Dor and Lizzie as they tidied themselves up for the barbecue. Lizzie made affirmative noises but she hadn't been on the project so what would she know, and anyhow, she was more concerned with Dor: looking real peaky and hardly eating a bloody thing the last couple of days.

But when Bea started another lecture aimed at Doreen and her damned stupid fads and diets, they could see something was really wrong. Slow tears trickled down Dor's cheeks as she looked first at Bea, then at Lizzie.

'S'pose you've got to know sometime.'

Bea frowned. 'You're not sick are you?'

Doreen shook her head and gulped. 'I'm pregnant.'

Lizzie's face was wreathed in smiles.

'Dor, that's bloody wonderful.'

'No, it's not. It's bloody terrible.'

Bea frowned. 'What are you talking about?'

The anguish in Doreen's voice was heart stopping. 'It isn't Kev's.'

Her eyes were wide and frightened as they met Bea's steady blue ones. They both knew what that meant!

Seventeen

'It was lunacy to let White mingle with the work release prisoners.' Jim's face was tight and angry. God, he was getting sick of Wentworth. Sometimes he felt smothered by the femaleness of the place. A male prison was tough and sometimes violent but he was becoming sickened by the vicious bitchiness that prevailed here twenty-four hours a day.

His thoughts went briefly back to Caroline Simpson. Thank heaven he'd managed to help her get out. He was still deeply saddened at the way things had ended for them. But after what had happened to his two boys, they'd had no future, and indeed, he doubted if he would ever be capable of feeling deeply again.

Across the table from him in the staff room, Meg glanced at him compassionately. From the expressions that flitted across his face she could almost read his thoughts.

'White asked to attend the barbecue Jim. And both the social workers and the solicitor have confirmed that Isolation is the last thing she needs.'

'She didn't need a lump of glass stuffed into her hamburger either.'

Meg sighed. Certainly Erica's little 'compensation treat' for the work release prisoners had gone awry.

The women had seemed passive enough. If she'd but known it, Bea had told them to lay off – they'd find a way to make White cut her own throat and cop a bloody tough sentence. No point in them getting fingered and White being put back under wraps.

But Big Margot, still determined to get the money Kay owed her, and smarting from the attack in Isolation, had made her own plans. She'd made peaceful overtures, even told Kay she'd wipe the slate clean. And then she'd given her the hamburger. It wasn't a big lump of glass, but it was sharp enough to cut White's lip. The blood had gushed out, given her one hell of a fright, and everyone else for that matter.

The cut wasn't serious but Erica was enraged that the women had shown such disregard for her magnanimity. It would be a long time before she considered any sort of extra privileges for them.

Meg moved to the sink to rinse her coffee cup.

'I hear they're looking for a new Governor at Barnshurst.'

'Yes.'

She looked at him, a small smile playing about her lips. 'You'd still be knee-deep in knickers and bras. It's just another women's prison.'

He nodded. 'But I'd be Governor and I could do things my way.'

Meg chuckled. 'You sound like Vera.'

But there was no answering laugh in his eyes.

'I've got a lot of time for Erica, you know that. But the way things have been going lately, well,' he gave a shrug, 'I'd like to have been making a few of the decisions.' He hesitated for a moment and spoke a little more quietly. 'She had plenty to say about my getting personally involved. Strikes me she was up to her neck with this Reynolds bloke and I'm not dying to be around when the shit hits the fan from the Department.'

Meg could see his point of view. But she'd spent last evening at Erica's and she was probably the only one who knew how badly the Governor had been hurt; and how depressed she was that, not only had the release plan failed, but the women had abused the privilege into the bargain. She'd miss Jim if he got the job at Barnshurst but staff came and went in this sort of job; and it was understandable; she often wondered how she'd stuck it out this long herself.

She was still in the same thoughtful state of mind when Doreen tackled her in the corridor asking to see the Governor.

Bea, Lizzie and Doreen had talked long into the night. Bea's advice had been to get rid of the baby – who'd want a rapist's kid? Lizzie thought Dor should keep the baby at all costs. In the end, they'd decided on a different plan. Doreen should get an overnight pass to be with Kevin. That way, she could pass the kid off as his and he need never know about bloody Vince Talbot.

Doreen didn't like the idea of deceiving Kev but it would be her baby, and she did love Kev and she could make it up to him in lots of other ways.

Meg promised to approach the Governor, but in the end, Erica, busy and certainly in a less sympathetic frame of mind than usual, decided it was the social worker's job to hear Doreen's problem. And a fat lot of use that was. With Paul Reid on leave – they reckoned he prob'ly wouldn't come back which was bad news – she had to see the new geezer, Agnes Forster, a dopey old bitch who only listened to half you said and forgot it five minutes later anyway.

Lizzie heard Dor out but she was full of her own news. They'd let her visit little Josie in hospital and the dear little thing was having a rough time but standing up to all the tests and that OK. And after, Ellen had taken her for afternoon tea and they'd talked like a real mother and daughter and it'd been just beaut.

Bea listened sympathetically but she was a bit preoccupied. Margot had buggered things up, planting that glass in White's hamburger. The Guv had spelt it out loud and clear to them, Bea in particular (always got the bloody blame for everything!), that any violence towards Kay White would land the culprits in solitary and it wouldn't be an overnight stay.

Well, she'd been in Wentworth long enough to know when old Davo was in a shitty mood. And this last little romance had obviously back-fired with a bang. While the Guv was licking her emotional wounds, it wouldn't do to get her back up.

It was Margot who came up with the best idea. She'd done her darndest to coax Kay to bet on the geegees again, but so far no go. The bigwigs had spelt it out to White that if she wanted a sympathetic hearing in court, she'd have to lay off the betting altogether. If she was caught once more, her solicitor would wipe his hands of her and no doubt the court wouldn't take too kindly to the evidence either. But a friendly game of cards? No cash at first – maybe that was the way to get her hooked again?

As Bea pointed out to the others, the best way they

could get back at White was to see she got the heavy sentence she deserved. So, let her cook her own goose.

The first part of the plan worked like a charm. Doreen didn't want to play but Lizzie persuaded her, it'd take her mind off things for a bit. Judy didn't want any part of it – she had no axe to grind with Kay White.

As Kay won hand after hand, it wasn't hard to persuade her to risk a few dollars as the play went on. They could sense the gambler's excitement as Kay went on winning and by lights out she'd totted up a tidy sum. Bea would pay her in the morning.

It was Margot who handed over the cash next morning and, after a little subtle needling, suggested a sure thing in the fifth that day. There was an almost feverish gleam in White's eyes as she looked at the money in her hand and tried not to make the bet. But the habit was too strong. She handed over most of her winnings and as Margot turned away there was a satisfied smirk on her face. Bea was right, this was the way to trap the bitch!

By chance, Judy was passing Kay's cell while the race was being broadcast. She paused, frowning. So much for all Kay's talk about reforming! A look of frustrated fury came over the woman's face as she clicked off the transistor. Some bloody certainty! Judy watched her, concerned.

'You'd better not let the screws know you're gambling again.'

Kay looked up quickly.

'Mind your own bloody business.'

Judy was a bit surprised at the vehemence. She'd never done anything to upset the woman and she personally didn't approve of Bea's plan. 'It's just that it'd go badly for you in court, hon.'

Kay leapt up from the bed, grabbed the hard wooden chair from against the cell wall, and brandished it above her head. 'Get out before I knock you out.'

Judy didn't need any second telling. Shit, the woman really was on a knife edge. Gambling surely wasn't her only problem! Did Bea realize just how dangerous this Kay White could be?

Bea heard her out but she wasn't too fazed. She'd dealt with tougher customers. Anyway she'd think about White later. It was Doreen they had to concentrate on for the moment.

Judy nodded. She'd heard Dor had had a visit from Kevin. How did it go?

Bea shook her head. 'No good.'

The way Doreen had told it, she'd broached the subject of a family to him but he'd been adamant. No kids till she got out and he'd had a chance to build up the work and be sure they had security. There was no moving him. And Dor still hadn't heard a thing about an overnight from the bloody old social geezer.

Judy frowned. 'Looks to me like that's the only way.'

'Now now.' Bea sighed. 'Even if she spends the night with him he's made it very clear, he doesn't want kids until a lot later.'

'Then she'll just have to make a mistake.' Judy shrugged. 'Once he knows she's pregnant, he'll change his mind.'

Bea grinned at her. 'You dykes know it all, don't you?'

'I know he loves her.'

'Yeah. But,' Bea looked dubious, 'it could backfire.

232

I've seen it happen plenty of times.' She sighed. 'It's rotten but I reckon abortion's the only way.'

When they talked to Doreen later she'd obviously done a lot of thinking since Kev's visit and she was in agreement. She'd decided to talk to the social worker – she ought to be able to get something as simple as this through her thick head. Anyway, if she didn't, Dor would go to the Governor. The sooner it got fixed up the better.

Lizzie was depressed about the decision but after all she did have her own 'family' now and she looked forward to the day when she'd get out and she and Ellen and Josie could all be together. She'd heard that day that the op had taken place and so far things seemed to have gone well.

The same couldn't be said for Bea's plan to get Kay White. They'd repeated the card scam, letting her win a decent amount of cash. Then she'd tricked Margot into outrageous odds on a nag that had come in. Margot was ropable but on second thoughts decided she'd deduct the cash owed to her from Kay's bets at the factory. That left Kay broke again, and fighting mad.

For all her protestations to the Governor, the social worker and her solicitor about wanting to kick the gambling habit, locked up in prison with little else to think about, the compulsion was stronger than ever.

When Big Margot started taunting her in the recreation room that night, talking about all the good betting she was missing and letting her know loud and clear she'd get no credit, Kay reached breaking point. As her rage mounted, she seemed oblivious that Vera Bennett was standing in the doorway on Rec. duty, and that she was surrounded by a small sea of unfriendly faces. She hurled herself across the room like some demented creature and sent Big Margot cra-shing to the floor, with a show of strength that literally stunned the women looking on.

Vera had collared her in a minute and marched her off.

'Reckon that takes care of that.' Bea grinned around at her mates. 'Solitary I'd say, and for quite a while.'

But Bea was reckoning without the current state of Erica's mind. When Vera pushed White into the Governor's office with a terse explanation of what had happened, Erica was still smarting from a very belit-tling call from the Department. It seemed Vera's report had finally surfaced and the initial reactions were far from good for the Governor.

At another time she might have been less amenable to Kay's version of what had taken place. She was simply protecting herself. The Governor knew she'd been under threat since she'd been put into Went-worth. She also knew the Gaffney woman had put the glass in her food. Naturally, no one else had come to her defence; she'd had to take care of herself as best she could.

Vera was listening open-mouthed, hardly able to believe her ears. 'White did the attacking, Mrs Dav-idson.'

Erica turned a cold eye in her direction. Her feelings towards Vera at this moment were anything but friendly. And for heaven's sake, Kay White might be guilty of embezzlement and larceny, but the woman had been a secretary-cum-manageress! She was half the size of Gaffney and looking at her standing quietly on the other side of the desk, Erica could sense no trace of physical violence in her demeanour.

'Do you wish to be transferred back to Isolation?'

Vera stared in astonishment. Was this all the action Erica was going to take? And White was so plausible!

'I'd prefer to stay where I am, Mrs Davidson.' She managed what seemed to be a rather timid smile. 'I think I've learned a valuable lesson from what happened. I won't lay myself open to that type of incident again. And I'd like to say on Gaffney's behalf, that it was simply a misunderstanding.'

Erica was impressed. Both the solicitor and the psychiatrist who had interviewed Kay earlier had been convinced of her intentions to reform. And even if that were not so, if the worst happened to White and she received a hefty sentence, she'd be coming back to Wentworth and the sooner she learned to handle herself the better.

After she'd dismissed her and Vera had found an officer to return her to her cell, Erica had slight misgivings. Gaffney was certainly a troublemaker, but was she, Erica, having her judgement coloured by what Vera had done to her with that report? Her emotions were currently in such turmoil that she couldn't be sure. God, if only she'd never met Andrew Reynolds. Now their relationship was over she had nothing but her work. And how much longer was she going to have that?

Her problem would have seemed minor to Doreen who was on her bunk, sobbing, when Bea and Lizzie and Judy came looking for her next day, to ask how her visit from Kevin had gone.

235

It was a sorry tale, indeed. It seemed he had indeed been contacted by old Agnes in welfare, but when he'd hurried to the prison to find out what was what, she'd really blown it: asked him straight out if he approved of his wife having an abortion!

Poor Kev had been staggered, didn't even know there was a baby on the way. But then, as he told Dor later, he thought about the way she'd been talking, kind of sounding him out, and he'd realized right off that she'd been scared to tell him she was preggers in case he wasn't happy about it.

Worse was to come. The more he thought about it the more over the moon he was. He'd work harder, start making things, a cradle and that sort of stuff, and gee! Did she reckon it would be a girl or a boy? Dor had tried to get a word in, but he was that excited. And then he'd sort of stopped, sudden, and said well, why was she talking about an abortion?

'I started howling and I called out to Mrs Jackson to take me back inside 'cos I knew I'd make a mess of it, talking about it then.' Doreen was gulping back the sobs as she talked. 'But he kept on and started saying things like "please don't kill my kid", and that, and I just couldn't take any more and I – I told him it wasn't his.'

For a moment, the three women just sat there. Poor little bugger. 'He – he asked me a lot of questions after that.' The tears were running down her pale cheeks and Lizzie slipped a comforting arm around her shoulders. 'You know, who done it and was it really rape and – all that.'

Bea could feel the anger rising in her but she tried

to keep her voice casual. 'He believed you, didn't he, Dor?'

Her face was pitiful as she looked up at them. 'I – I think so. I mean, he said he did, only I don't reckon he's real sure 'cos he made me promise I'd talk to the police.'

She was sobbing again now, and Lizzie held her close. Bea and Judy exchanged a glance – bloody men. Had Doreen been asking for a report on his sexual activities while she'd been locked up inside? And if he loved her and she said it was rape, then he ought to damned well believe her – where was the stinking trust?

They didn't put their thoughts into words. They said what they could to comfort Doreen, but Bea had plenty to say when she talked later to a sympathetic Meg Jackson.

'You know what Dor's like, Mrs J. She'll crack up under a police interview.'

Meg nodded sympathetically but explained that things were a lot different nowadays. The women police were much more understanding, Doreen would get a good hearing. The Governor would have to know of course. Bea nodded.

'Bloody work release scheme poured shit on all of us, though.'

Meg didn't relish telling Erica. She knew how much she was hurting inside and how anxious she was about the Department's reaction to Vera's report, let alone the newspaper publicity at the time.

'Poor Doreen.' Erica was genuinely upset. 'One likes to think things like that don't happen any more.' She glanced appealingly at Meg. 'I would never have condoned the scheme in the first place if I'd had any

237

idea it could have this sort of repercussion. Where was Andrew? Did it happen with other women in the factory? And why is that vile creature walking around, just waiting for his opportunity, no doubt, to rape some other helpless female.'

There was a brief silence between them, then Erica took a deep breath and met Meg's gaze very directly. 'There is no doubt in your mind that she is telling the truth?'

'None.' Meg met the look very candidly. 'I saw Vince Talbot when I was on factory duty. Nothing like this crossed my mind at the time but now that it has, I have to admit I'm not too surprised. I'd say he was quite capable of that sort of behaviour.'

Erica was very understanding when a tearful Doreen was brought before her later. She made it clear to her, and later to Kevin Burns when she spoke with him, that they believed Doreen.

The memory had come back to Erica of how reluctant Doreen had been to continue the work. If only she'd confided in her then. But the truth was that Doreen wasn't very bright and her reasoning on so many occasions had turned simple situations into unnecessarily difficult ones.

'I want you to be present at the interview, Meg. the last thing we need is Vera being militant and officious and frightening Burns out of her wits.'

Doreen was very grateful. She was desperately nervous and if it hadn't been for Meg's gentle encouragement she'd have turned tail and hiked it back to her cell the minute the woman police officer came into the room.

She was nice enough, pretty sympathetic really, but

she had to do it by the book. And such a lot of questions. As Doreen confided later, she knew right from the start that not talking about it till nearly eight weeks later would sound pretty queer. She'd had to admit they'd all joked around with Vince when they first started the work. And she'd known he had his eye on her. And then, no witnesses, that was pretty bad news.

Bea and Lizzie listened to her in silence. The poor kid had obviously got herself in one hell of a tizzy and even Meg Jackson would have found it hard to unravel Dor's muddled explanation once she got wound up.

'Anyhow,' there was more relief in Doreen's eyes than disappointment. 'She was real nice about it but she said it's no go.' She gave a shaky laugh. 'Told me what to do next time it happens, though.'

Meg gave Erica the official version. Owing to the time lapse there was no forensic evidence and that, coupled with the lack of witnesses and time taken to report the rape, there was no chance. It would never get past the committal stage.

'Kevin Burns seemed a good type of young man. Do you think he'll stick by her?'

Meg hesitated. 'At the risk of sounding cynical, I'm far from confident. Whatever happens, we must keep an eye on her. If he doesn't support her, she's going to be in a very depressed state.'

After she'd talked to Kevin the following day she was indeed depressed. He took the police report really bad, and as she confided to Bea, he seemed to need some sort of official proof that Dor really had been raped. Bea would like to have called him all the bastards this side of the Black Stump, but she held her

239

peace. The kid was putting up a good front, but she was obviously broken-hearted.

Bea confided to Lizzie that Dor wasn't up to the scam they'd planned for White, but they'd have to go through with it if they were going to nail her before her hearing. Judy had had second thoughts about Kay White. She'd seen for herself the violence in the woman, and she couldn't help pointing out to Bea that if they set Kay up and she got sentenced, undoubtedly she'd get sent back to Wentworth. Is that what they wanted?

Bea saw it differently. She'd buggered the work release, all those other women lost their jobs because of her; Margot wasn't the only one she'd bashed and they knew for a fact she'd lagged more than once. Margot, Phyllis and the others were a hundred per cent on side. But Lizzie would have to give a good performance to get the screws in.

Lizzie did. It was no trouble to talk Meg into letting her do the trolley for the staff room. No one apart from Vera liked to see her doing heavy work in the laundry or kitchen.

She was a bit taken aback to find Vinegar Tits in for afternoon tea, as well as Meg Jackson and Jim Fletcher. Still, if she could convince *her*, it would really be on! Lizzie dolled out the teas cheerfully, all the time keeping her eye on Meg's bag which she'd already taken from the locker so she could pay Vera back a small sum she owed her.

The moment they were sipping their tea, Lizzie turned furtively towards the bench, and, making sure she wasn't too expert, she flipped a twenty dollar note out and clumsily tried to stash it in the pocket of her uniform.

'Lizzie!' Meg couldn't believe her eyes. 'You took money out of my bag.'

Lizzie looked suitably crestfallen at being nabbed. 'I'll pay you back Mrs J.'

She favoured Meg with her most pathetic expression. Vera and Jim exchanged surprised glances. Had Birdsworth flipped, pinching money from an officer's bag in front of the three of them?

'Put it back at once.'

Meg didn't want trouble. But Vera was outraged.

'Is that all you're going to say, Mrs Jackson?'

But Jim was looking thoughtful. The old girl must be desperate to pinch from the staff room. And gradually he got the story out of her. She'd been losing heavily at cards. there'd been a poker school all that week. They knew she couldn't resist a game, but Kay had kept pushing the ante up and Lizzie'd got in so deep before she knew it, and she had to pay back tonight – they'd seen what White could do to someone Margot's size. Gawd, she'd make mince meat out of Lizzie.

The lids were down over the shrewd old eyes, but she knew she had taken them in, hook, line and sinker.

Meanwhile, Bea was playing her part. She took Phyllis Mouse along to make things look genuine and fronted Kay in her cell.

'Listen, we've got a proposition.'

Kay looked up, her eyes suspicious and wary.

'Like what?'

Bea eased herself inside the doorway. 'Word's got

241

out you did the right thing by Margot. Didn't lag and put in a good word with the Guv.'

Kay shrugged. 'That's history.'

'Yeah, well, takes a while for the word to get out. We reckon we've leaned a bit hard on you.'

'I can look after myself.'

Bea nodded. 'Fair enough. We just wanted you to know that we're going to lay off, help you keep your nose clean till your trial.'

Kay eyed her warily. She sounded genuine enough but you couldn't be sure in this place.

But it was Lizzie who clinched the deal. She came hurrying down the corridor, flashing her twenty dollar note.

'Come on Bea, let's get the game going. I'm loaded.'

In spite of herself, Kay's eyes lit up. Bea noticed but to all intents and purposes she was only interested in Lizzie and her cash.

'I'll take that off you in the first hand.'

'Playing poker?' Kay couldn't help herself. She eased up from her bunk.

'Yeah.' Bea started moving off. 'You can sit in for a couple of hands if you want to.'

Bea walked casually away, Lizzie and Phyllis jabbering excitedly about the coming game and Mouse speaking loudly enough for Kay to hear that she too would be splashing out good cash on the game.

They were settling themselves at the card table when Kay came in, just a bit hesitant. What if the screws caught them?

Bea smiled. 'Watch this.' She gave an almost imperceptible nod. In a flash, the women had swept cards, money, all traces of evidence off the table.

Kay was impressed. She drew up a chair and from the moment the cards were dealt, Bea knew they had her. The feverish look was back in her eye, and as she won the first hand and stacked the cash in front of her, her hands were shaking with the excitement of the game.

Lizzie was trying to give the impression of someone desperate to win, and when Doreen wandered in she paid her scant attention. They'd talk later. Doreen said it didn't matter, she'd been thinking and was just wondering, if she and Kev didn't get back together would Lizzie be OK? Lizzie rather impatiently said of course she would and let her get on with the game.

Doreen hovered by Bea's chair for a moment. Bea had been pretty tough on her along the line, but she'd been a real good friend when the chips were down. She touched Bea's shoulder fleetingly. Bea looked up and smiled.

'Is that for good luck, kid?'

Doreen managed a smile. 'Yeah. All the luck in the world.'

She kept the smile intact till she'd left the room and made her way quietly to the toilets. She'd worked things out a while ago, nice and quiet, and she knew just what she was going to do. It was all over with Kev. And she wasn't going to have Vince Talbot's baby.

She'd sneaked in earlier and broken the mirror. Somone'd disturbed her so she'd stashed the broken pieces till she could get at them later. Lizzie'd be OK, she had a family now. Kev'd find someone else and really, apart from Bea and maybe Jude, who'd miss her? She rummaged around in the bin where she'd hidden the sharp fragments. They were gone.

The women, blissfully unaware of Doreen's intentions, were locked into the game. Kay was at fever pitch, hands trembling as she dealt. And then, once more, the almost imperceptible nod from Bea. Kay saw it but there was no need for panic after the way the women cleared the decks before.

But this time was different. At Bea's signal only Lizzie and Margot stayed at the table. No one made a move to hide anything. The other women hurried to the TV, grabbed up books, and the prearranged dialogue started as Jim Fletcher and Meg Jackson burst into the room.

'Told you not to play a pro, Lizzie.' It was Bea, shouting across the room as Lizzie and Margot joined in, berating Kay. For a moment, she seemed turned to stone. Then with a lunge she sent the card table flying, cards and money going everywhere. But Jim Fletcher was too strong for her. He had her in an iron grip. Meg ordered the women to set things to rights as Jim roughly marched Kay White to the door.

A small smile of triumph was on Bea's face. But it was short lived. A white-faced and breathless Vera Bennett came rushing into the room.

'Meg, quickly. The laundry.' Her eyes were wide and shocked. 'Doreen Burns has hung herself.'

Eighteen

'We ought to be bloody ashamed of ourselves.' Bea slammed the steam press down with a thump and glared at the other women working with her in the laundry.

'She's going to be all right, Bea.' But Lizzie looked as miserable as the rest of them.

Old Vinegar Tits had got there in time, cut Dor down, rushed for help and got Dor trundled off to the infirmary quick smart. But the thing was, they'd known how the kid felt. And they'd been so busy trying to nail that stinking Kay White that they hadn't been there for Dor when she needed them.

'She didn't lose the baby, that's something.'

Bea looked hard at Judy. 'I'd call that a bloody mixed blessing.'

Mouse paused in the midst of shoving another load of linen into the big drier.

'The way old Vinegar Tits feels about us, I'm surprised she didn't just let nature take its course.'

'Thank Gawd she didn't.' A small shudder shook Lizzie's thin old body.

'I give Mr Fletcher her teddy bear and he said she was real pleased to have it.'

Bea raised her eyebrows. 'I'm surprised he did it.

245

He's been going around like a bear with a sore head the last coupla days.'

'Didn't get the Barnshurst job.' Lizzie gave a small triumphant grin. 'Heard Vera telling Mrs Jackson. Biggest smile I've seen on her face in a long time!'

Phyllis heaved a load of folded sheets onto the trolley. 'Anyway, we blew the whistle on White. The Guv went through the roof when they told her about the poker game. Let's hope we're rid of her for good. They've stuck her back in Isolation.'

Margot came in at that moment with a load of soiled linen from the kitchen. 'Be nice if she could have a little accident there. Sort of tidy things up permanently.'

'Lay off.' There was no mistaking the authority in Bea's voice. 'The court'll do the rest. Doreen's our priority now. Once she gets out we're going to have to watch her like a hawk. The way she's feeling, she'll try it again first chance she gets.'

Meg shared Bea's opinion and she'd stayed on after her shift was finished to sit with Doreen and try to talk her into a more positive frame of mind.

Cuddling Teddy, propped up on pillows in the hospital bed, Doreen was a pathetic figure. Apart from a sore throat and some bruising, she'd done herself no real physical harm. But mentally she was at rock bottom. As she told Meg Jackson, she couldn't even hang herself without making a mess of it!

In carefully chosen words, Meg pointed out to her that it would have been a very dreadful thing if she had taken her own life. Couldn't she imagine the grief and guilt her friends would feel? And even if things were over between Kevin and herself, that would have been an awful thing to lay on him.

Doreen nodded. She didn't have the words to describe the black despair that had engulfed her when they'd parted. But what was the good of it? There'd be no future for either of them without trust, and he'd never have been able to look on the baby as his.

'Do you remember when Chrissie Latham got her baby back from the hospital and was able to take her to Maternity?'

Doreen nodded, the ghost of a smile on her face. 'Yeah. She was real happy, wasn't she?'

'She still is.' Meg smiled at Doreen. 'She doesn't give a damn about the father. It's her baby. And that's the way it will be for you.'

She could tell her words had reached Doreen. There was a flicker of interest in the eyes that hadn't been there before. But she wouldn't labour the point. Let Doreen think things out for herself.

When Meg rose to go, Doreen gave her the shy smile which, in spite of everything, still made her look like a ten-year-old.

'Thanks Mrs J. You've always been real good to me. I appreciate it.'

Walking away from the prison hospital ward Meg felt a touch of guilt. What if she had given a little of her time to Doreen? She owed somebody after dobbing poor Gail Summers in. Oh, she'd meant well, something had to be done for those kids, but Wentworth had been an ordeal for Gail which she'd never forget. Thank God her trial had gone well (in spite of the damning evidence Meg had been forced to give); a good behaviour bond, constant welfare contact and, down the track, a very good chance of getting her children back and trying again.

The news was not so good for Lizzie. She'd been called out of the laundry and was thrilled to know Ellen had come to visit. But her face crumpled as Ellen unfolded the medical facts. There was a bone marrow problem. Serious? Very, but the really devastating news was that the treatment Josie must have was only available in Chicago.

A tearful Lizzie confided to Bea that it wasn't the money nor nothing, the kiddie was to have everything needed, but would Lizzie still be alive and kicking when Ellen and Josie eventually got back from Chicago?

Bea's heart went out to the old girl but she knew from past experience that the only way to deal with Lizzie was to give her a good swift kick in the bum and turn her thoughts in another direction. She'd better stay alive and kicking! What about Dor? Wasn't she also like family to Lizzie?

'Josie'll be OK. She'll have the best.' Bea gave her a brisk pat on the back. 'What you've got to do in the meantime is get your arse over to the hospital and cheer up our Dor.'

Lizzie did just that and was thrilled to find Doreen almost back to her old self. She'd had a beaut talk with Mrs Jackson and thought things through and Mrs J. was right. It was *her* baby and she was going to keep it. She and Lizzie would look after it together! Lizzie was ecstatic. As she said to Bea later, one door opens and another shuts! Bea explained that she had the quotation arse-up, but she was pleased to see the old girl back on an even keel.

And when Ellen and Josie were allowed a special visit before they flew out, Lizzie handled it very well. Meg watched, a touch misty-eyed, as Lizzie hugged the

248

little girl in the wheel chair and promised to write and to keep well and to be waiting for when Josie was better. Ellen might not be Lizzie's real daughter, but there was no doubting the affection she'd developed for the old girl and the sincerity of her words as she talked about the life the three of them would share when Josie was well and they could all be together.

Erica was relieved when Meg reported on Doreen. She'd grant her request to come out of hospital but she'd have to be closely watched and she wouldn't be expected to work until she was feeling absolutely fit again.

When Meg queried if Erica had had any further word from Mr Douglas of the Department, the Governor reported an ominous silence. And meantime she was not a bit cheered that the new admission had been remanded on a drug charge. Tracey Morris, nineteen years of age and accused of smuggling heroin into the country. Meg could imagine how Bea Smith would react to that! Erica would talk to Smith and warn her off but the officers would have to be very vigilant while the girl was awaiting trial. Meg queried the question of bail and Erica explained that the police had refused it. The girl's father was overseas and so the matter was in abeyance pending his return and any information he could give the police.

Meg made sure it was she who took Tracey Morris through to the dining room, after her induction. She showed her the ropes, helped her to get her meal then, very much aware of Bea Smith's eyes on them, led Tracey to the empty seat at Judy Bryant's table.

'Judy, I'd like you to meet Tracey Morris. And since

she's in on remand, I'm sure I can count on you to make her feel at home.'

Meg's tone of voice and significant expression were not lost on Judy. The word was out on Tracey and the heroin story, it had come over the TV news. And while Judy certainly didn't approve of drugs, one look at this attractive young girl, and her thoughts had flown back to Sharon. She'd let her down, and Leanne; maybe this was her chance to make amends. She smiled at Tracey.

'Hi. Judy Bryant, and yes I'm American, but please don't hold that against me.'

Tracey was desperately nervous but there was something so warm and friendly in this woman's voice and face that she felt a small wave of relief. Meg noticed and with a quick smile to Judy, she turned and walked casually to the table where Bea, Lizzie, Mouse and Margot were finishing their meal.

'How's the food today, ladies?'

Lizzie made a face. 'Can't get me snappers round these chops, Mrs J.'

Quick as a flash, Big Margot speared one of Lizzie's chops and plonked it on her plate. 'Waste not want not, you old faggot.'

Meg chuckled but her eyes were on Bea when she spoke again.

'There seems to be a nice, peaceful atmosphere in here, since White departed.' Her tone was light but the meaning was clear. 'Let's keep it that way, eh?'

Bea watched her leave the dining room, then her eyes travelled to Judy, talking animatedly to the new girl at her table. Slim, blonde, pretty and classy. Bloody dyke probably thought she'd struck gold!

Sharon had been into drugs and she wasn't too proud to shack up with her! Well, the Guv might have warned her off, but just let that Morris kid put one foot wrong and she'd bloody get it, in spades!

The dining room was practically empty when Judy and Tracey finished their meal. Tracey had explained that she'd been put in a single cell for her own protection, and she found that pretty scary on both counts. Judy was as reassuring as she could be; lots of officers always around, and anyhow, Tracey would no doubt be out on bail the minute her dad got back.

Tracey hesitated then looked very directly at Judy. 'You do believe me? I didn't know it was heroin in the case. I truly did think it was gold.'

Judy did believe her. She guessed she knew the truth when she heard it. She could pick Sharon in a second when she was lying. But this one, she was on the level. As they stepped out into the corridor Bea was waiting. Judy felt Tracey tense. The kid might not know who Bea Smith was, but she saw in front of her, barring her way, a very tough lady, hands on hips, blue eyes snapping fire and and the mouth set in a frighteningly grim line.

'Lay off, Bea.'

Judy's voice was calm but her eyes were giving Bea a warning. Hurt this kid and you'll regret it.

'I just want to know the score.' She moved a fraction closer to the girl. 'We don't like pushers around here.'

'I'm not. I didn't know it was heroin. I never touch drugs.'

Bea didn't react the way Judy had. That's what they all bloody well said! 'Tell that to the marines. We saw you cop it sweet, on the telly.'

'Tracey said she was set up and I, for one, believe her.'

Bea returned Judy's steady gaze. 'Taken a fancy to her, have you Jude?'

That was below the belt in front of this scared kid, but Judy kept her cool.

'I'm giving her the benefit of the doubt. That's the way you'd have wanted it for your daughter Debbie, isn't it Bea?'

Bea was caught off guard. The mention of Debbie always stopped her in her tracks, brought the old familiar lump back into her throat. Bea took a deep breath.

'I'm just warning you. Any dope appears on the scene, I'll know where it came from and what to do about it.'

Bea turned abruptly and walked off. Tracey's face was as white as a sheet. Judy patted her arm. 'It's pretty hard to believe, but she can be a damned good friend. It's just, well her daughter died from an overdose while Bea was inside. The very idea of drugs really tips her over the edge.'

Tracey nodded. God, why did she ever agree to bring that case in? And how the hell was she going to survive twenty-four hours in this place let alone maybe years, if they sentenced her.

Judy saw the fear mirrored in the young face. 'Don't panic kid. I'll be around. I'll look after you.' The girl gave her a grateful smile. And for the first time since Sharon's death, Judy experienced an emotion she thought had maybe gone for ever. A tingle of chemistry, a swift warm rush of sympathy, a sensation somewhere between maternal and pitying – perhaps even the first tiny spark of something that could be called love.

There was a very different feeling in the air when Vera Bennett turned up in Tracey's single cell and ordered her to the interview room. Tracey protested that she'd told the police everything she knew, more than once. She didn't want to answer any more questions. She got short shrift from Vera. And there was a nasty edge to Vera's voice when she told the girl that if she was innocent, then she had nothing to fear, did she?

Detective Inspector Grace's attitude was not much friendlier. He reminded Tracey that in her original statement she'd admitted that her trip to Thailand had been financed by a friend, in return for smuggling back a suitcase of gold. She had had no idea there was heroin in the case, yet she had refused to name the 'friend'. Did she wish to add anything to that statement?

A nervous Tracey assured him she had nothing to add. Detective Inspector Grace shrugged. A pity; if she'd be more co-operative the police would allow bail and she could be out of prison immediately. He was watching her closely and he saw how strongly tempted she was. It was obvious she was scared stiff.

'Does your father know the trouble you're in?'

She shook her head. 'No.'

'Well,' Grace leaned back in his chair but his eyes rested sharply on her face. 'That's not too surprising. We've checked things out. Your father's in Hong Kong on business, can't be contacted at his forwarding address.' He leaned suddenly towards her. 'P'raps his trip was financed by the same "friend"?'

There was no mistaking the shock in her face at the suggestion.

'He's always going away on business. And he doesn't know anything about – what I was doing.' Grace was inclined to believe her but the important thing at this stage was to keep her pressured. She'd crack sooner or later.

'Just the same, I think we'll keep an eye out for Mr Morris when he flies in, put him through a routine check at the airport.'

'I told you, he doesn't know a thing about this.' She was upset but she wasn't ready to talk yet.

Grace rose to his feet. 'All the more reason for us to be there to break the good news, eh?'

While Officer Barfield was taking the shaken Tracey back to her cell, Vera Bennett was supervising Detective Inspector Grace signing out from reception.

There was nothing precisely direct in his conversation but Vera got the gist of it very clearly. If she could do anything to help bring new evidence to light, encourage a little confidentiality between herself and Tracey Morris, he'd be very sure she got the credit for it. Vera remarked rather tersely that she'd tried once before with unfortunate consequences. Grace shrugged, just a thought – never hurt to get a gold star from the police; the Department was always impressed.

Vera conveyed the bare bones of Grace's remarks to Meg. The latter stirred her coffee thoughtfully.

'That's their job. I think we cop enough as it is.'

Vera nodded. 'To tell you the truth I sometimes think I've had enough of the prison service.'

Meg glanced up in surprise. 'You've always said it was your life.'

254

'I know.' She hesitated, seeking the right words. 'I know it's a secure job and in some ways I like the set routine. But where do I go from here?'

It was true. Jim's hopes for the job at Barnshurst had been shattered and Erica was definitely a permanent fixture. In her realistic moments, in spite of the report and all the trouble over the work release scheme, Vera didn't really think the Department would axe Erica. Douglas of the Department had always been pro, and there was no question that Erica, through her family connections, had friends in high places.

'You could always transfer?' Meg looked at her questioningly. Vera gazed thoughtfully in front of her. A thought . . . or would it be out of the frying pan . . . ?

Meg was still thinking about their chat and how surprised she'd been to know Vera was even thinking about a change of place, or work. She'd always assumed Vera would be literally carried out. Just the way Lizzie had claimed so many times it would no doubt be her fate.

But it was hard to believe that now. Since Doreen's release from hospital, she and Lizzie had been like a couple of kids, begging Meg for white wool and knitting patterns, talking to the Governor about their cash, and how they should spend it. Erica laughingly told Meg afterwards that neither of them seemed ever to have heard of the word 'invest' but she was determined to do what she could do to cement their financial futures.

They were at it again when Meg took them a new supply of white wool and some leaflets on baby wear she'd picked up for them. Lizzie was very anxious about Josie but she'd had a card from Ellen and so far everything was going all right. Doreen seemed to have managed to push the thought of the father of her child to the farthermost reaches of her mind. She would always be grateful to Meg for her advice. It was *her* baby – yours and mine, Lizzie had chimed in – and she was going to see it had a darned sight better chance than she'd had.

Tracey was forming a very different opinion of the officers at Wentworth. Vera had done a bit more quiet thinking. If she was going to stick to the job she might as well earn herself as much kudos as possible: it could be useful if she did later consider a transfer or applying for the top job elsewhere. She'd ferret around the Morris girl, see if there was anything forthcoming that might interest Grace. But she had never been any good at the confidential approach. Intimidation was more her style and it was plain the Morris girl was already frightened out of her wits. Lean a little, hint a little about some of the tragic 'accidents' that had taken place over the years, and Vera felt pretty sure the kid would panic and start talking. And if she was a pusher, well Vera would let her know she was watching her every inch of the way. One foot wrong . . . She'd talk, just a matter of time – and a little persuasion perhaps.

Alone in the cell after lights out, Tracey was desperately trying to think of some way out. That awful officer, she'd hinted at all sorts of vile things that happened to women in prison, specially anyone suspected of pushing drugs. And her father! He'd be so hurt and humiliated when the police jumped him at the airport. Or would his shock turn to anger, against her? No! He had to stick by her, help get her out of this dreadful place.

It seemed hours before she finally fell into a troubled sleep. And only minutes when she was rudely awakened by a babble of voices and the shaking and hammering of cell doors as the women screamed out for help.

Lizzie and Bea were the most vocal. Poor little Dor. She'd been talking her head off all night about the baby and all the beaut things she was going to do for it. They'd finally convinced her a good night's sleep wouldn't go amiss for the expectant mother, let alone themselves. But she'd been restless and when a dull pain started nagging at her abdomen, she got up to get a glass of water. As an excruciatingly sharp pain racked her body, she'd dropped the glass and let out a scream that had Bea and Lizzie literally falling out of their beds in panic.

Bea didn't like the look of it. The kid was in real pain and where the hell were the bloody officers?

Tracey called from her cell, frightened and confused at the uproar, but no one paid any attention, if they heard her at all.

Then running footsteps as Meg and Officer Barry had come rushing down the corridor. One look and it was all stations go. Lizzie looked fearfully at Bea as they carried Doreen out of the cell on the stretcher. The kid looked so white and she was still in terrible pain.

'What do you reckon?'

Bea shook her head. 'They'll tell us soon enough.'

Lizzie sat down on her bunk, shoulders dropped,

and her heart heavy. She'd seen too many miscarriages in her day not to know what was happening.

Meg, meantime, was with Doreen as the doctor explained. He'd done his best. An injection might have done the trick if they'd had more warning. Doreen was very calm. She understood what he was saying. But Meg found something rather disquieting in the placid way Doreen was accepting the situation. Only a few hours earlier she'd been so happy, so full of plans. It was hard to know what was really going through the girl's mind but she would need watching, for sure.

After the doctor and Meg had gone and Doreen was lying quietly in her hospital bed, just the shadowy outline of the nurse sitting at her desk at the end of the ward, she let herself face what had happened.

She hadn't wanted Talbot's kid, but as the weeks had gone by it had become her baby: hers and Lizzie's. Well, there wasn't any baby now. Probably brought it on herself, with that caper in the laundry.

A slow tear trickled down her pale cheek. Just as well her and Kev had broke up. The doctor hadn't wanted to say but she'd pressed him. Not much hope of ever being able to carry another one. That wouldn't have been fair to Kev. And that was her fault too: had her first kid adopted out, then the two abortions. What ever had made her think she was fit to be a wife and mother?

Meg had hurried back to the cells once she'd signed the doctor out. She knew she was bending the rules but she couldn't leave old Lizzie and Bea to fret and worry all night. She told them quietly what had happened and hinted that Doreen was going to need her mates sticking by her – round the clock!

Bea got the message and quietly passed it on to Judy in the opposite cell. And gradually, a quiet descended over the place as the women dozed off into troubled sleep.

Alone in her cell, Tracey Morris lay rigid on her bunk. What had it meant? The banging, the uproar, that awful scream? She'd strained to hear what they were saying but all she'd managed to work out was that someone had been rushed to hospital.

Tracey shuddered. Was this what Officer Bennett was talking about? Had someone had an 'accident' in the middle of the night? Was there someone out there already planning one for her?

Nineteen

'I want to see my daughter immediately.' Bob Morris was tense and angry as he faced Vera Bennett in reception. He was a fine looking man of middle years, obviously in top physical condition and good looking to boot. But this moment, after being picked up by the police at the airport and unceremoniously searched, he was furious.

Vera eyed him disdainfully. So this was the little pusher's daddy! And who did he think he was, turning up and speaking to an officer in that tone of voice?

In truth, Bob was an extremely courteous man and in no way was his rage directed at Vera or anyone else at Wentworth. It was the reaction to the shock he'd experienced when he learned about his daughter. He was a busy man, highly successful in electronics and often away for four to five months at a time, but he loved Tracey dearly. And the thought of her being in prison had absolutely stunned him.

Meg sensed the tension and stepped in quickly. 'I'll take Mr Morris to the interview room, Vera, while you get Tracey.'

Vera looked a touch belligerent but she turned abruptly and made her way out of reception. She might even enjoy letting Morris know her father was waiting for her – in a towering rage!

Bob Morris had taken a good look at Meg and he liked what he saw. There was compassion in this face, not like that ferret-faced woman who'd gone to get his daughter. He was apologetic about the way he'd spoken. He was still so shocked and confused. Meg understood and apologetically explained that she would have to stand in on the interview between father and daughter – prison regulations.

And she was embarrassed when, the moment Tracey walked into the room, her father jumped to his feet, his anger forgotten at the forlorn sight of her, and went to put his arms around her. 'I'm sorry; no physical contact.' Meg looked an apology and he nodded and quietly sat in the chair opposite the white-faced Tracey.

As he listened to her halting words and saw the fear in her eyes, his heart went out to her. Of course she hadn't known it was heroin. She'd never been into that sort of thing! She'd been set up and the only thing was to tell the police who, how and when, and he'd get her out of this dreadful place.

He reacted to his own words and cast a rueful glance in Meg's direction. She smiled reassuringly.

'It's all right. That's the way most people feel.'

'I've told them all I know, Dad.'

She was a little girl again, asking her daddy to make things all right, pathetic in her innocence.

He leaned forward to pat her hand, remembered the rules, and awkwardly drew back. 'I'll talk to the Inspector. See if we can't arrange bail.' She nodded, cast a nervous look at Meg, and spoke hurriedly.

'I need money, Dad.' Again the timid glance. 'One

of the women told me you can have a lot easier time in here if you can pay for it.'

Meg looked disapproving.

'That's not quite the way the system works, Tracey.'

But Bob was already pulling out his wallet, fingering notes.

'I'm sorry.' Meg moved to the table. 'That's not allowed.'

For a moment Bob Morris looked desperately frustrated, but it was vital he reassure his little girl, so he replaced his wallet and tried to make his smile convincing. 'I'll have a word with the Governor, see what we can work out.'

Tracey smiled lovingly back at him. 'I knew you'd fix things, Dad. You always make everything right.'

Looking back on the interview, Meg found her feelings very mixed. The rapport between father and daughter was real enough, but something niggled. There was a definite feeling that Tracey could wrap her father round her little finger and had probably done so on many occasions. And if she was innocent, why wouldn't she name her 'friend'?

Naturally Erica was unable to condone Bob Morris's offer of money to benefit his daughter. She simply gave him an assurance that everything possible would be done to keep the girl out of trouble until her hearing, or until bail could be arranged.

But someone else had already made plans to see that Tracey was 'looked after'. Kathleen Leach was not a newcomer to Wentworth. She'd been in before for petty crime and it was the same old story again. Vera treated her with the disgust she felt for the habitual petty criminal. And her opinion of the girl was not helped when she'd confided she'd known Tracey Morris at primary school.

Both officers would have taken a much keener interest in Leach if they'd seen her in her cell, casually unrolling her rather elaborate hair do and extracting two crisp fifty dollar notes. It was time she had a word with her old 'school mate'!

Tracey was whiling away the time in her cell talking to Judy, the only person she felt safe with and one person at least who believed in her and was interested in what she had to say. She'd been sympathetic about how lonely Tracey felt with her boyfriend Joe on the outside probably missing her desperately, as she was him. Judy, her feelings for the girl deepening by the moment, wasn't fazed. For the moment she was happy to act as protector and friend; there was time to see if anything more intimate developed.

The bell was ringing to shepherd the women to bed, when Judy left Tracey's cell. Kathleen waited for a moment then quickly stepped inside the doorway. She smiled brightly at Tracey.

'I was telling the officers, you and I are old friends from primary.'

Tracey frowned, trying to find some shred of remembrance.

Kathleen laughed. 'Gee we used to give old Ma Parsons a time, didn't we?'

She was moving closer to Tracey as she spoke and suddenly her voice dropped to a whisper and she slid the two fifty dollar notes into Tracey's hand. 'Joe and the boss will see you right. And I'm here to look after you.'

Tracey was rather scared at first, but suddenly a great

wave of relief swept through her. Joe was worried about her, thinking about her, going to make sure she was OK. 'It's pretty scary in here.'

Kathleen shrugged. 'You'll be OK. It won't be for long. But best you don't mention Joe. The less anyone knows the better. He said to remember that.'

They could hear Vera Bennett's sharp step in the corridor and Kathleen hastily made her way back to her own cell. Tracey looked at the money then quickly unzipped her sponge bag and tucked it inside.

She wasn't quick enough for Vera not to have seen something that could be suspicious. But it could wait for now. Vera smiled to herself. She'd check out Daddy's little girl tomorrow.

But it was Meg who sought Tracey out in the morning. She had a dual reason. Firstly, she was curious about the girl, wanting to believe she was innocent, yet unsure; and secondly, Doreen had been released from the hospital and because she was off duties until considered fit enough, she was rather at a loose end.

Meg was hoping that since Tracey had little to fill her time, she might be some sort of company for Doreen; their age group was compatible and there was no question that Dor, for all her attempt to be cheerful, needed close watching without actually making her feel stifled. Bea was playing watchdog at every opportunity, and Lizzie, but while they were doing their daily stint in the laundry it was important that someone keep tabs on Doreen Burns.

Tracey had already sized Meg up as the nicest and by far the most lenient of the officers, and she was only too happy to chatter about her father, how busy he was, how much he travelled – always taking off to exotic places like the Far East – and he was the best dad in the world. Meg ventured to say that he was pretty upset at what had happened to his daughter. Tracey nodded vigorously; of course, he knew she'd never be in anything like that. And trust Dad, he'd have her out on bail quick smart.

The attempt to create some kind of friendship with Doreen was less successful. And it wasn't Tracey's fault: she was bored and lonely. While Judy was in the laundry she felt much more vulnerable, though not nearly so badly since Kathleen Leach had appeared. But she didn't want to sit round and watch TV all day and, after Meg had explained, Tracey felt a genuine sympathy for Doreen. The latter, however, was not interested in Tracey, or anything very much at all at this stage. She was glad to be back with Lizzie and Bea and Judy but she was well aware that everywhere she went either an officer or one of her mates was tailing her, and while she appreciated their concern, it both depressed and irritated her. And she didn't have anything in common with this girl Tracey and certainly wasn't in the mood for making new friends. Ten to one it'd go sour on her anyhow, the way everything seemed to.

Meg was confiding her concern to Erica about Doreen when Vera burst into the office, obviously excited about something. It soon came pouring out. She'd seen Morris acting suspiciously last night. So she'd taken it upon herself to do a routine search just half an hour ago. Vera held up two crisp fifty dollar notes.

'Seems she managed to get herself some protection money. I wonder where?'

Neither Meg nor Erica appreciated the triumphant gleam in Vera's eyes but they were equally concerned as to where the money could have come from.

When Erica questioned the girl she refused to talk. The knowledge that anything of this nature would not help her case made no impression at all. Vera was convinced the father had somehow got the money to her, and Meg was equally sure he was not the kind of man who would resort to subterfuge. For the moment, all they could do was punish her.

But Vera, mindful of Detective Inspector Grace's words, felt perhaps the moment had come when she could 'persuade' the girl to start taking. As Tracey laboriously scrubbed her way along the seemingly endless corridor, Vera walked beside her. The picture she painted was not a pretty one. Tracey visibly shuddered when Vera gave a graphic description of what had happened to Sharon Gilmour. She hoped when Tracey was sentenced that they didn't put her to work in the laundry. Some pretty drastic things had happened in that part of the prison while Bea Smith had been on the steam press. And had the other women told Tracey how Smith felt about pushers?

Daddy's girl had had things really easy on the outside, hadn't she? And the other women didn't take much to pampered little darlings who thought they were too good for the other inmates. Of course, she was only on remand now; it was a different story once you were sentenced – no holds barred.

Vera could see she was getting through to the girl. Her hand was clenched on the scrubbing brush as she tried to keep her panic under control.

'You've got one chance, Morris. Tell the police who set you up and you'll walk out of here tomorrow.'

She saw the quick intake of breath, the hands shaking as they wrung out the thick floor cloth. She was going to break.

'Can I make a phone call please, Miss Bennett?' It was Kathleen, smiling, polite and, coincidentally, just around the corner where she could have heard the entire conversation.

Vera frowned; what a moment for an interruption!

'Go and check with the officer of the day, Leach.'

'Thanks.' Kathleen smiled down into Tracey's upturned face.

'Going to ring my mate Joe. Give you an intro when you get out. He's the most!' She skipped off along the corridor giving Vera no hint of what her real intention had been. But she knew the moment was lost. Tracey had regained her calm. There was even a small smile playing about her lips as she slowly started to scrub the hard floor again.

The smile wasn't intact for long. Just as Tracey was getting ready for bed, Kathleen slipped into her cell and there was no sign of the friendly creature who'd slipped her the money the night before.

In a low voice, Kathleen let Tracey know the real reason she was there. Business always came first with Joe. He was paying Kath to make sure Tracey didn't talk. If she did, Kath's orders were to shut her up for good.

It was natural that Tracey, more frightened than she'd ever been before, turned to Judy for comfort. She couldn't tell her why she had this new, sudden fear but at least, in close proximity to the big, kindly woman, she felt some sense of protection. Judy was only too glad to listen and try to soothe the girl's fears. She knew for sure now that she wanted more than that from Tracey Morris, but it was too soon to even give a hint of the feelings she was arousing in Judy.

Bea noticed and commented to Lizzie that Jude had plainly got the hots for the Morris bitch. Lizzie wasn't that interested. She was still worried about Dor.

Bea had been thinking a lot about that. She was going to have a word with the Guv. In her opinion, it was time to stop molly-coddling Dor; the kid was obviously feeling suffocated and just getting more depressed. The sooner she got back to work and something like a normal routine, the better.

Erica agreed. The doctor had given Doreen a good physical report and boredom was no help for someone who'd just been through Doreen's ordeal.

But the laundry wasn't the answer.

Bea looked surprised. 'She'll be with her mates, Mrs Davidson.'

'I know.' Erica smiled. 'That's important of course. But I've decided to let her spend some time helping out in Maternity.'

Bea frowned. 'Isn't that just going to remind her of what she's lost?'

'I don't think so.' Erica's eyes were kindly. 'We've all seen what it's done for Chrissie Latham. I've had a word with her and she'd be glad of Doreen's help. I'm convinced it's the answer.'

To Bea's surprise, Doreen was over the moon. Seemed like she'd never have a kid now but it didn't mean she didn't still love bubbies. It'd probably be real beaut.

But while Erica might have come up with the right answer for Doreen she was beginning to realize that the Tracey Morris saga was getting out of hand. Vera had reported in this morning and, grim-faced, relayed a phone call she'd received the night before telling her 'lay off Tracey Morris'. Looked like someone could be starting to panic. Vera didn't mention that she'd already let Detective Inspector Grace know. He'd been delighted. Looked like they were getting closer!

Erica was curious that Vera should have been singled out. Vera shrugged: she could see the father had taken a dislike to her from the start.

Meg was outraged. A man like that wouldn't be involved in that sort of subterfuge. Vera looked very snide as she pointed out that Meg hardly knew the man unless she had had contact Vera didn't know about? Meg hotly denied it, but she had already admitted to herself in the privacy of her own home that she felt an attraction to Bob Morris. There was something so dependable and straight about him and he was also her idea of a very attractive man. Erica didn't get too heavy but she made it clear to Vera that she was not to harass the Morris girl. She didn't want one of her officers setting herself up for possible violence, and in any case, it was for the police to do the investigating on the Morris case.

Vera paid lip service, but encouraged by Grace's praise, she tried again to get the girl to talk. Tracey, terrified now of what Kathleen had threatened, had been desperately shaken. It had become the natural thing to do to turn to Judy. She was pouring out the story tearfully to Jude in her cell later that evening. Nothing about Joe or Kathleen of course, but the constant hammering and harassment she was getting from Vera Bennett and how scared she still was of Bea Smith and the other women.

Judy did her best to comfort and as Vera walked quietly past, supposedly on a routine cell inspection, she was just in time to see Judy wrap her arms around the girl's slim body while she tenderly stroked the soft fair hair. They hadn't seen her. But what a precious piece of information to pass on to the arrogant Bob Morris when he next appeared!

She had her opportunity the very next day. It was obvious to Meg as she supervised the interview that the visits were taking their toll on him. And the more Tracey played to the hilt the pathos of her position and how much she was depending on him, the more upset and concerned he became. He was getting her the best legal advice in town, everything was being done, he'd soon have her out. But the brief unhappy glance he threw at Meg told her that he was far from confident and at something of a loss to know how to help his child.

He was almost through reception when Vera inquired lightly if he felt Tracey was being treated properly, had he any complaints? He frowned, surprised that this sour looking woman should even evince concern for his daughter. But in his emotional state he did stress how important it was that Tracey's youth and innocence be remembered and that she receive as much kindness as possible.

An unpleasant smile twisted Vera's lips. Her voice was low but very clear. He had no need to worry. Since his daughter was lesbian she'd get plenty of tender, loving care. He was struck dumb for a moment then told Vera what he thought of her remark in no uncertain terms. She was unmoved, even a little amused. She herself had seen his daughter in the arms of the most notorious dyke in the prison. Seems there could be a lot he didn't know about his daughter.

Her triumph was cut short in a very unexpected fashion that evening. She'd opened the door of her unit, stepped inside and flicked the light switch. Nothing. Irritated, Vera muttered to herself about the perfidy of light bulbs in general.

A voice frighteningly close had come out of the darkness. 'You're not getting the message.' A sickening thump, and Vera's inert body slid slowly to the floor.

Twenty

Detective Inspector Grace kept his eyes riveted on Tracey's face.

'We've decided to lift the objection to your bail.'

Her first reaction was a mixture of spontaneous joy and relief. 'You really mean that?'

He nodded. 'It'll be a pretty hefty amount but I don't doubt your father can come up with it.'

'I know he will.'

Grace hesitated for a moment. 'He may have reservations. You're being released so the "interested parties" outside will think you've given us the information we wanted.'

The girl looked nervously across at Officer Barry as though looking for some kind of guidance. Joan Barry gave a small shrug to indicate that this was police business, nothing to do with her.

'How do you think your "friends" will react to that, Tracey?'

She took a deep breath and tried to look calmer than she felt. 'I just want to get out of here.'

'Perhaps when you do you'll find out who your real friends are.'

That was all he'd said but she registered the unspoken warning, a threat really.

Judy showed real concern when Tracey passed on the news. But the girl quickly reassured her. She'd panicked at the time, but Joe would look after her. Kathleen could talk till she was blue in the face, but Tracey knew in her heart that Joe loved her. Judy looked a little wistful. She'd made light overtures just two nights ago, but Tracey had made it very clear she didn't want that kind of involvement, just a friend, someone she could trust and confide in. 'But you still haven't confided in me. Who did set you up?' But Tracey was not to be coaxed. And already she was counting the hours to when her father would put up the money and get her released.

The prison was buzzing the next morning with the news about Vera. She'd been treated in casualty but had refused to stay in hospital or take more than the day off. She'd made it very clear to Meg when she'd called in to check on her that she was certain Bob Morris was behind the phone threat and the bashing. Meg held her tongue in view of Vera's white face and obviously aching head, but she'd already talked to Bob, and there was no way he was involved.

The women were thrashing out the subject in the laundry as they went about their duties. Bea was grudgingly beginning to agree with Judy that Tracey hadn't known about the heroin. You could see at breakfast when the word got out about Vera, Tracey had been really shocked. She hadn't given any details but she'd spelt it out pretty plainly to Judy that she knew she was the cause of it. And much as she hated Vera Bennett, it was awful to think of someone doing something like that.

'Lizzie reckons that old man Morris has taken a shine

273

to Mrs J.' Phyllis cackled and followed up her remark with an obscene gesture.

'More likely using her so she'll wangle privileges for Daddy's little girl.' It was Mouse, bitchy, miserable with PMT.

Judy couldn't let that pass. 'From what Tracey tells me I'd say her old man's pretty good news. Anyway, Meg Jackson's an attractive woman, why wouldn't he fancy her?'

But Bea wasn't paying attention. 'Where is bloody old Birdsworth? She went off to the toilets half an hour ago.'

Lizzie was fighting for her life. She'd popped into her cell to get a biscuit to nibble and the next thing, Kay White had sprung out of nowhere, screaming abuse at her and grabbing her by the throat with every intention of throttling her. Lizzie struggled vainly but she was no match for the obsessed creature choking the life out of her. Then suddenly, clunk, the hands fell away and White went crashing to the floor.

Still gasping, Lizzie turned, to see Linda Jones standing transfixed, staring at the body, the heavy electric jug which she'd used as a weapon still clutched in her hand.

It was Lizzie who heard the heavy footsteps approaching. Quick as a flash, she'd ordered Linda to get behind the door and shut up. Linda tried to protest but Lizzie wouldn't have a bar of it. Linda was due out tomorrow, her kid Danny was waiting for her. Lizzie was so bloody old it didn't matter and there was no one waiting for her till Josie and Ellen came back.

Jim glanced in and reacted in shock. 'What's happened here?'

He was bending over White's body, hastily checking the pulse, sickened by the pool of blood that was seeping out from the woman's skull. Lizzie looked him straight in the eye. 'I did it. It was self-defence, Mr Fletcher.' Gawd, if Linda made a sound they were gone!

Jim looked at the frail old woman and she knew he didn't believe her. But if she stuck to her story, what could he do about it?

Erica didn't believe her either. It was a mystery what White was doing in that area anyway. When her five-year sentence had come through, Erica had specifically moved her to another block. Lizzie's story about owing money for racing debts was a bit woolly, but she stuck to it and with Kay's history of fanatical gambling they had to give it some credence. But Lizzie looked too frail to lift the jug let alone lay out someone of Kay White's strength. But she couldn't be budged; it was self-defence!

Erica knew when she was up against a brick wall. There were no witnesses, Lizzie was adamant about that and Jim Fletcher had to confirm that there had been no one else in the cell when he'd found the body and Lizzie, electric jug in hand, standing over it.

'I'll have to commit you to the V.J., Lizzie, but I won't send you to solitary.' She turned to Jim Fletcher. 'Confine Birdsworth to her cell, Mr Fletcher, and let me know if any other "evidence" comes to light.'

As Lizzie confided to Bea and Doreen and Judy later, there wasn't a blind thing they could do about it whether they believed her or not. Linda came to her in tears. She couldn't let Lizzie do this. Lizzie told her to shut up. Kay White wasn't dead, Lizzie wouldn't get anything drastic from the V.J. at her age, and if Linda opened her trap and mucked up her release Lizzie would bloody well tell her kid Danny that she hadn't wanted to leave Wentworth and be with him.

Linda was terribly torn. Twice young Danny had run away from the welfare lot and he'd threatened if she didn't get out this time he'd take off for good. Bea backed Lizzie. The old girl had to fill in time till Josie and Ellen got back and she might as well stay put where Bea and Dor could look after her.

'Yeah, she'd only get back on the piss if she went outside without me.'

Linda looked doubtful but in the end, when Bea assured her they'd all back Lizzie and Linda wouldn't be able to prove a thing anyway, she gave in amidst a sea of grateful tears and emotional thanks.

When she'd gone, Bea turned to Doreen. 'We deserve a medal, volunteering to keep this silly old faggot in here for a longer stretch – snores like a bloody pig!' But Lizzie knew they were proud of her. Linda had had a hell of a time keeping her nose clean, trying to get out to her kid. And, incidentally, someone had finally given White the clobbering she deserved!

Tracey was frightened out of her wits when she heard about the 'accident'. Thank God Dad was coming in with her release! Kathleen had been mighty suspicious when she'd heard about the bail but Tracey had explained: she hadn't squealed. The laugh was on the coppers!

'I'm sorry Tracey, I can't go along with this.' She couldn't believe her ears.

'Dad, you have to get me out. You promised.'

'You're being used as bait by the police. You'll be at the mercy of thugs and killers.'

'I'll be OK, safer than in here.' The interview had ended with Tracey screaming hysterically at her father as Officer Barry took her back to her cell. Meg looked sympathetically at Bob Morris. She knew how hard it had been for him to make that decision. She'd assured him she'd try to keep an eye on Tracey. And then he broached the subject of Judy.

Meg couldn't hide her anger when he repeated Vera's words. How dare an officer make an accusation of that nature! If he but knew it, Judy Bryant was the one real friend Tracey had made in the prison and he should be darned glad of it. And Meg could assure him there was no question of a lesbian relationship. 'But, she looked him squarely in the eye, 'would you reject your daughter if you did find out she has those leanings? Surely you love her for herself, whatever her weaknesses or faults?'

He was quiet for a moment, it was clear her words had hit home and hard.

'I deserved that. I was thinking of myself not my daughter.'

Meg had apologized, felt she'd overstepped the mark, but he refused to accept that. She'd shown understanding and compassion to Tracey from the start. P'raps some time she could teach him a little more on those subjects? It wasn't an invitation in itself, but they both knew it was the first step towards their burgeoning friendship.

But that evening, Bob Morris was persuaded to change his mind. Detective Inspector Grace pointed out that Tracey would be under constant surveillance, there'd be no danger. He wasn't convinced till Grace put it bluntly to him – his daughter had been ruthlessly used by drug pushers, a quarter of a million dollars' worth of heroin involved. Were these the kind of people he wanted his daughter to spend her future with – pushers and addicts?

Grace was very vocal on the subject, and combined with the memory of Tracey's despair when he'd refused earlier, Bob felt he had no choice. He confided his dilemma to Meg when he turned up with the release for Tracey in the morning.

It had become almost automatic to turn to this like-able woman and confide his hopes and fears to her. In a roundabout way he conveyed that it might help Tracey if Meg could perhaps dine with them that even-ing, tell her enough about prison horror stories to encourage her to talk to the police. Meg declined, she couldn't associate with a prisoner on the outside. But she'd let him see that she was sorry, perhaps under different circumstances . . . ? His smile told her he understood and that there most certainly would be a future invitation.

She was still in a mellow state of mind when Erica called her and Jim Fletcher in to break the bad news. Kay White had died during the night, a blood clot on the brain. The charge against Lizzie would regrettably be more serious now.

Lizzie appeared to take the news very calmly. The big thing was that Linda had been released and was with her kid. But Bea knew the old girl was shaken – manslaughter was a whole different ball game and she could get five years, easy . . .

It was Vera's opinion that Birdsworth didn't have

the guts to take the rap for anyone else and if she'd been illegally betting, she had to take the consequences. But Meg had seen the emotional farewell between Linda Jones and Lizzie, the way Lizzie had stressed that Linda must take the best care of young Danny, and the white, strained face that Jones had presented in reception when she was signed out. Well, p'raps she was being over sensitive. In any case, making their own decisions was one freedom still left to the women, and Meg would never deprive them of that last shred of dignity.

Tracey Morris had just taken a pretty big decision herself. All too aware of the plain clothes detective on guard outside the Morris home, she'd racked her brains as to how she could escape and go to Joe. She was longing to see him, and once she did, everything would be all right again. Then she chuckled delightedly to herself as the idea came to her. She'd ring Jan, get her to come over, switch clothes and walk off, casual as you like.

It had worked like a charm. Jan bought the story that it was a bit of a lark; Tracey was sick of being cooped up. The guy outside? Just a reporter, snooping around for a story.

As Tracey mounted the stairs and knocked on the door of Joe's flat a self-satisfied smile played around her lips. Those detectives thought they were so smart! And Joe, he'd been flabbergasted! He *was* pleased? He'd actually been very taken aback, but had covered quickly, just couldn't get over how smart she was, giving the coppers the slip. And when she'd questioned him about setting her up he'd moved in physically, knowing how hooked she was, and promptly took her to bed to back up his pretty shakey explanation with the sex he knew she was aching for.

And she bought it. He'd believed the gold story too – until it was too late to stop her. They'd both been set up. But it was OK, he'd fix things, just as long as she hadn't talked to the pigs. She assured him she hadn't, the police were just trying to make it look that way, using her as a decoy. He smiled fondly at her. God he'd missed her, he was never going to let her out of his sight again. They'd get married, start again, she was the best thing that had ever happened to him.

Tracey lay contentedly stretched across the bed, glowing from the sexual satisfaction he'd brought her, and the words of love he'd poured into her ear. Someone had come to the door, Joe had told her to stay put, he'd get rid of them and he'd be right back, he couldn't wait to make love to her again.

But why was he taking so long? She got up and padded softly in bare feet to the door. And she froze as she heard Joe's voice. He was saying the most awful things about her. It was a joke, it had to be! But as she listened a cold hand clutched at her heart. It had all been lies. He'd used her. And now she was a threat, a lead to their drug operation. The boss had decided it was time for her to go. And this man, this creature Joe was talking to, was out there, getting his instructions to come in and kill her.

In her state of shock and terror she never knew how she managed to scramble into the borrowed clothes and wrench the reluctant upstairs window open. She had to get away. She had to get to the police and finally tell them what they'd wanted to know. It was her only hope.

She was through the window, scrambling down the drain pipe, and running fast from the house when Joe flung open the bedroom door and registered the open window, the shabby curtain fluttering in the breeze; a sure indication that Tracey had overheard and made her getaway. He gave a small, sneering smile to the heavy jowled man beside him.

'It's OK, Moose, the boys downstairs will get her.'

Tracey heard the running footsteps behind her. She was breathing hard, but she had to run faster, somehow get away from the two thugs who were closing in on her. She looked about wildly, turned the corner at a frantic pace, took a short cut through the lane and sped back on to the main road. She could see a telephone box; if she could reach it, call the police!

There was a sharp pain in her chest as she fought for breath. She had the door open, her hands were shaking as she lifted the receiver, started to dial . . .

A hand was clapped over her mouth without ceremony. She was aware a second hand had broken the connection, snatched the receiver out of her hand.

With one last superhuman effort she grabbed the hand that covered her face and bit it hard. As her assailant fell back with a screech of pain, she'd ducked under his arm and was running again for dear life.

There was an alleyway, she'd be safer there. She turned into it at a frantic pace and instantly, at the other end of the narrow lane, she saw the two burly figures.

A bullet whistled over her head. She dived to the ground and from behind her another shot was fired.

She watched as one of the burly figures toppled to the ground. God, it was a nightmare and she was caught in the middle. Another shot and the man at the other end of the lane turned and ran off quickly. She was lying there, trembling from head to foot. It was all over now. She felt a strong hand under her arm, lifting her up.

'You're all right now, Miss Morris.'

She turned a frightened face towards the man.

'Detective Evans.' He flashed his identification in her direction. 'I think p'raps you might be ready to have a little chat with us, right?'

She nodded, dumbly, still confused. She'd been running away from the men trying to protect her. She gave a stifled sob. What a fool she'd been! All this time, believing she must cover up for Joe because he loved her. Well, she'd never make that mistake again. And she'd make sure he got just what was coming to him!

Kathleen Leach reacted nervously when Tracey was returned into protective custody at Wentworth. And when Tracey told her what had happened with Joe and her subsequent talk with the police, she was even more apprehensive. She knew what happened to anyone who squawked, there was no knowing what the boss might be planning for Tracey Morris. She wanted no part of that heavy stuff. She'd be out of Wentworth in a week. She wasn't going to cop a life sentence in this joint. But what the hell was she going to do if they put the hard word on her to get rid of Tracey Morris?

She didn't have long to wait. She knew when she walked into the interview room the thug who'd passed himself off as her boyfriend had come straight from McNelty, the big boss. He'd slipped her a cigarette –

Barfield probably saw but what was one fag after all? – and the note had been inside. A delivery at the rubbish tip next morning.

It had come, right on time. She'd opened the small paper-wrapped parcel. An evil looking flick knife with just two words on the attached note, 'USE IT'.

It took a moment for the panic inside her to die down. God, if she knifed Tracey she could get life. If she didn't, they'd get her.

She made an excuse to visit the toilets and instead hurried down the corridor leading to the laundry. Judy looked at her rather curiously as she sidled over to Bea Smith. She was the Queen Bea, the one who really ran this joint. And she'd seen it all. She'd know what to do. In a low voice, Kathleen told Bea the score. There was a look of revulsion on Bea's face.

'In with the same bunch of ratbags are you? Why would I help a pusher?'

'I'm not. I didn't know what I was getting into. They paid me a lot of money to make sure Morris didn't talk. You can have it all!'

Bea looked hard at the fear stricken face in front of her. She knew now that Tracey was no pusher, doubted if this kid was. If she did nothing, it was as good as murdering Tracey Morris. Did she want that on her conscience?

'Take that sheet out of the press while I think about it.' Kathleen nodded, she needed this woman's help desperately.

But as she reached out to remove the sheet, Bea sent the steam press crashing down on her hands with a violence that made the women round her shudder. They'd be a long time remembering the agonizing screams that were torn out of Kathleen as the boiling steam scorched her mangled hands.

Twenty-one

'I'm suspicious of that twinkle in your eye, Jim Fletcher.'

Jim looked up from the rosters he was amending and smiled. 'Is that so?'

Meg grinned. 'You've just agreed to fill in for Vera and do a double shift, and you're actually happy about it.'

He shrugged. 'Not much good complaining.'

'Come clean.'

Meg was teasing, but she'd noticed for the last week that there was something very different about Jim and she hoped her suspicions were correct. He'd had a hell of a time, it would be great if he'd met someone. And she couldn't help adding to herself, like I have. Things were bubbling along very nicely with Bob Morris, a delightful dinner, phone calls, several pleasant chats in the prison garden when he'd come to visit Tracey.

'I know what you're hinting at, Meg, and yes, you're quite right. Her name is Sarah; we met two weeks ago at a party and I'm hoping to see a lot more of her.'

Meg chuckled. 'Literally?'

Jim gave her a mock stern look. 'You're beginning to sound as crude as the inmates.'

Meg smiled, but after a moment's hesitation she

285

decided to confide in him. She'd been worried about Vera lately. She'd been furious with her over the Bob Morris lesbian thing and since then they'd had very little social contact. So last night, Meg had dropped in and Vera had been pretty sloshed. She hadn't been drinking on duty of course, but the morning headaches had been all too frequent, and Meg strongly suspected Vera was seeking the Scotch bottle as an antidote to loneliness.

Jim wasn't as surprised as she'd expected. He'd called around himself a few nights ago. They'd had a bit of a brush at work and he decided maybe he'd been a bit rough, better apologize.

She'd heard him out, but she wouldn't invite him in. And he was certain she'd already swallowed a fair amount of whisky; he could smell it for one, and she'd already sounded a bit slurred, certainly not the Vera who turned up at work.

Meg was thoughtful as she went on her rounds. It was hard to know how to help. And if both she and Jim were on the brink of finding some kind of emotional happiness, it would be a bitter pill for the lonely Vera.

The same thoughts were passing through Vera's mind. And the prisoners would have been startled to see the tousled figure crouched on the settee, nursing an aching head and trying hard to resist a hair of the dog as she stared at the full Scotch bottle on her sideboard and willed herself not to get up and open it. She lost the battle. What the hell was the use of resisting? She'd just have one, to pull herself together. But she knew she wouldn't be able to stop. It had started gradually, a couple of drinks to cheer her up when she came home worn out from work: singles, then doubles, then to hell with counting. It made her feel better for a little while and she desperately needed something.

She'd registered what was going on with Meg and that arrogant Bob Morris. And you didn't have to be too smart to see that Jim Fletcher was walking around like the tom cat who'd just drunk the cream. Well, she'd let him know she didn't need his patronizing company, and she wasn't going to stick her neck out and ask Meg Jackson round again. She knew full well the last two times Meg had refused that she was just making up excuses. To hell with the lot of them. Her hand was shaking as she lifted the half-full tumbler of Scotch to her lips. She took a sip, the neat spirit was sharp on her throat. So what, who the hell needed water? That was strictly for washing. Vera gave a small crack of laughter at her own little joke, then broke off abruptly as she put a hand to her throbbing temple.

What had she been thinking about when she was sitting there, just now? She screwed up her face, trying to focus her thoughts. Oh yes! The familiar sneer was back on her thin lips. That bloody Bea Smith! How could the Governor go on and on buying her stories about 'accidents'. She'd set Leach up, no question – then why was Leach backing Smith's story? Vera shrugged bony shoulders. Who bloody cares?

Judy had reacted very differently to Bea's violence. But when she heard the full story she was aghast at the danger Tracey was still in, and agreed that Bea had had no option but to put Kathleen out of action and out of danger. They'd have to keep a close eye on Tracey, and as Bea pointed out, keep their eyes open. You could bet those bloody pushers would get another plant into Wentworth once they knew Leach was off the job.

Tracey, oblivious at the moment to what had really happened, was in a much happier frame of mind. Meg was supervising her father's visit and as they strolled through the garden, the girl felt a sense of peace and security she hadn't enjoyed for a long time. It would be a new beginning for them, he was going to make sure he gave her more of his time when she came home again. They'd make all sorts of plans. She didn't notice the quick glance he sent in Meg's direction as he spoke. Meg smiled and he knew from her eyes that she had understood and was happy about it.

'Let's go over to the rose garden.' Tracey indicated the roses blooming a little near to the tall wire fence. She looked questioningly at Meg, who nodded.

'They're my favourite flowers, too.'

They were walking three abreast as they moved leisurely across the garden. And then Tracey saw the butterfly. Like a small child, she gave a cry of delight and ran forward.

In that instant, the bullet was on its way. The telescopic sight had been trained on Tracey but her sudden movement had foiled the sniper. Bob Morris gave a strange muffled cry as his body jerked around, the bullet grazing his shoulder and throwing him to the ground. As Tracey uttered a long, terrified scream, Meg was already shouting at her.

'Get down.'

The girl stared at her, uncomprehending. Meg literally threw herself at her and tumbled her to the ground, unhurt. But as Meg began to duck, the second bullet was on its way. There was a look of quick surprise as she clutched her side and fell slowly to the ground.

The women knew something pretty big had happened. They'd heard the wail of the ambulance; Lizzie, on trolley duty, had seen Detective Inspector Grace and his mob scream into reception in a panic, and they'd all heard Tracey's hysterical screams as she was bundled off to the infirmary and given a sedative.

They fired questions at the officers but no one would tell them any more than that an officer had been shot and taken to hospital. It was after the evening meal, when Tracey had been returned to her cell and the women were gradually moving into their own dormitories, that they'd got the answer. Tracey, listening to the cross-fire of questions and conjecture, could stand it no longer.

'They were after me but they shot Meg Jackson instead.' The words came out in a burst of hysteria, and the women fell quiet.

As Bea confided to Doreen and Lizzie, it was a nice state of affairs when the bloody crims were taking on the prisoners! And it was beginning to look like no one was safe as long as Tracey Morris was kept inside. Someone was really out to get that girl.

They were relieved next morning to learn that the bullet had passed through Meg's body and although she'd lost a lot of blood, only minor surgery had been needed. Bob Morris's shoulder had only been grazed by the bullet but the shock of what had happened to Meg had shaken him badly. He'd spent half the night at the hospital and come back in the morning, pleading to at least sit with Meg for a short time. He was told 'five minutes only' in a firm tone, but the nurse smiled sympathetically as she indicated the chair beside the bed. Meg was lying very still and the face on the pillow framed by the thick cap of golden hair was very pale. This woman had saved his daughter's life, but at what cost to her own?

He heard a small sound from the other patient in the two-bed ward. She was beckoning to him, smiling encouragingly. He rose and walked softly towards her.

'She doesn't look too good, but she's going to be fine. I heard them talking.'

She was a much older woman than Meg, and obviously a long-term patient.

'Thank you.' He managed a smile.

'Are you her husband?' It wasn't prying, just a natural assumption. He explained that he was just a friend but even as he said it, he realized almost with a shock how deeply upset he was about Meg, and he knew it wasn't simply gratitude. With a smile and a further murmur of thanks, he moved back to Meg's bedside and sat down. For a fleeting moment she opened her eyes and he saw the flicker of recognition, the merest hint of a smile, then she lapsed back into sleep.

He'd already talked to the doctor, knew the facts, but he couldn't stop himself from thinking how close to death this woman had come – and what a brave, unselfish thing she had done. He would never forget it. He would make it up to her somehow. And he knew even as he thought of it that it was not just born out of gratitude. He wanted this woman in his life. Dare he hope she might feel the same?

With Meg out of action, Jim had explained to Vera

and the other officers that he would have to adjust shifts and certainly some overtime would be inevitable. Vera was shocked at what had happened to Meg, but she'd made it clear to Jim that she was not to be considered, automatically, as the patsy who'd happily cop the double shifts.

It was uncharacteristic of Vera, and Jim, remembering the talk he'd had with Meg, began to wonder how serious Vera Bennett's booze problem had become. For the moment, he'd pushed it to the back of his mind. He was meeting Sarah Forrest for lunch and he wasn't going to allow anything to spoil that. Their friendship was blossoming into romance and he found himself counting the hours until he'd see her again.

He knew she was equally attracted, but would she be if he hadn't lied about his work? He hadn't meant to, but when they'd met that first night he'd so wanted to make a good impression on her, and he knew from past experience what the sight of a prison warder's uniform did to attempted friendships. Women, in particular, just didn't want to know!

So he'd told her he was a building contractor. She was in partnership in an interior design business. She'd worked with Julian Phillips for some time and then he'd decided that she was the real talent, and that they should be on an even footing in status and finance. She loved the work, and as she laughingly put it 'she loved Julian to bits'.

Jim had been surprised at his rush of jealousy, but she'd laughed and assured him that Julian wasn't interested in her or any other woman in that way. When he met him, Jim knew she was speaking the truth. There was something markedly effeminate in both voice and manner; but there was also a slightly sharp and suspicious air about him as he sized Jim up.

Sarah didn't seem to notice it. She'd already confided to Jim that in order to expand the business, they'd decided to offer a third partnership which would inject capital and give them a much needed cash flow. And now, sitting across from her at lunch, he'd surprised himself by saying he could be interested in the partnership. He could see she was genuinely delighted. But he hastily added that his idea would be to invest say ten thousand or so, and remain a silent partner. That surprised her a little but she said she'd talk it over with Julian.

Julian was against the idea. It was quite obvious that Jim and Sarah were in love. But Julian had never seen a building contractor with hands as smooth as Jim Fletcher's, and something about him just didn't ring true. As for Sarah, his love for her was very sincere and he'd developed a highly protective attitude towards her over the years. After the hell she'd already endured, he wasn't going to see her go through any emotional agony if he could help it.

Jim was aware that either Julian was jealous of his friendship with Sarah, or the man had taken a dislike to him on sight. But he kept these thoughts to himself as he sat beside Meg's bedside. She was looking much more her old self and, of course, making light of what had happened.

She asked a bit anxiously after Tracey. Bob had told her she seemed all right, a bit subdued; what did Jim think? He'd go along with that, though he didn't doubt the girl was still scared stiff of what might happen next. But the women had done a turn around, acting quite protectively towards her and Erica had decided she shouldn't be left alone. They'd moved her in with Bryant – and Jim definitely didn't approve of that.

Meg grinned; of course he wouldn't. Bob Morris wouldn't be too thrilled either. But they were both wrong. Bryant had no predatory leanings and she'd been a darn good friend to Tracey from the start. What about Vera? Was she still giving the girl a hard time? Jim shrugged, not that he knew of. But he was worried about Bennett, Meg had been right; she was definitely hitting the booze. He'd rung her two nights ago to see if she could come back for a couple of hours and there was no question – she'd said she wasn't well, but she'd sounded drunk.

He gave Meg a wry smile. 'You haven't helped either.'

'I didn't choose to come here!'

He shook his head. It wasn't that. Apparently Vera had twice come to the hospital to see Meg and, to her disgust, seen that Bob Morris was already there behaving in a very possessive manner and making it clear that he was all the company Meg needed.

Meg gave a rueful grin. 'It wasn't quite like that, but it was a bit awkward and I could see Vera was put out.'

Jim gave her a measuring glance. 'You two are getting serious, aren't you?'

'Let's just say things are progressing rather nicely.' Meg raised an eyebrow. 'How about you?'

Jim didn't take much encouraging. And Meg knew from the way he spoke about Sarah and the glow that lit his face as he talked about her that Jim had indeed found someone to care about. She was glad for him.

He'd been dealt such a terrible blow and his life must have been very empty since he'd lost his two little boys. Perhaps both Jim and herself were really going to find happiness again.

She was not to know that Vera Bennett, bitter and jealous, had already sown the seed to undermine Meg's hopes. She'd been locking Tracey and Judy in for the night, making her usual snide comments about how they would spend the night, which bed would they fancy this time, when Tracey had turned on her and given her a mouthful of cheek. Well, she'd hit back and hard, let the little bitch know her father was all set to have an affair with heroic Meg Jackson, so she needn't expect big Daddy to waste his time on Tracey when she got out.

Tracey had been terribly upset. Judy had tried to make her see reason; she liked Meg, and of course her father needed someone in his life. But when Bob had come to visit the next day, the girl's jealousy was at fever pitch and she'd positively spat the words at him – he could make his choice, that conniving prison officer or her. Bob had been shocked, and bewildered. Meg had saved her life, didn't she realize that? Tracey did, and now she knew why! There was no reasoning with her. He drove Meg home from the hospital the next day and she knew immediately something was bothering him.

When the cheerful old soul who'd shared her ward said goodbye to them, she'd added, 'And every happiness in the future', spelling out that she for one could see they were headed for the altar. Meg had laughed but been a little surprised to see Bob's serious expression. Had she taken too much for granted? Was it simply gratitude? Worst of all, had Vera been right when she'd hinted that Bob Morris was using her to make sure his kid got special treatment?

He helped her to settle in, made her coffee and was very solicitous for her comfort, but there was an awkwardness, a constraint she'd never felt with him.

'What's bothering you? Has something happened to Tracey?'

He hesitated for a moment, then he told her what had happened on his last prison visit.

Meg sighed, no doubt Vera was the informant, she knew from Jim how resentful she was about Meg's association with Bob. Poor Tracey, to hear about their friendship like that!

He gave her a long, admiring glance. What a special creature she was. No condemnation, no resentment – just understanding for his daughter.

'She was told it was much more than a friendship.' He moved to the easy chair where he'd ensconsed her and sat on the arm and took her hand. 'I'd like it to be, Meg.'

She had her answer in that moment. He loved her. He wasn't playing games or using her. He'd been told to make a choice and he'd made it clear: he wanted Meg. His daughter would, in due course, have to accept that. She squeezed his hand gently.

'So would I, Bob. But,' there was a note of hesitancy in her voice, 'we mustn't rush things. I won't have you making that kind of choice.'

He nodded. He didn't want to estrange himself from his only child. And God, she was still in danger from one day to the next.

*

A scream of terror was ringing through Tracey's cell at that very moment. She'd been chatting to old Lizzie who'd just got back from court, very happy with her eighteen-month sentence (just be out in time to meet Josie and Ellen).

Lizzie had been trying to cheer her up and talking ten to the dozen about Meg and what a beaut person she was. Tracey knew that. She regretted the way she'd spoken to her father. She was so scared, she didn't know what she thought about anything any more. Lizzie advised her to ring her dad next day and say she was sorry. Tracey had agreed and given Lizzie's wrinkled old cheek a quick kiss. She was grateful for the chat and the advice. Then she'd gone to the cell and seen the envelope lying on the bed.

Lizzie came rushing in. Tracey was standing in the middle of the room, the envelope in one hand, the note in the other.

'Tracey! Whatever's up?'

The girl turned a terrified face to her. 'Read that.'

Lizzie took the note and screwed up her eyes so she could make out the words 'TESTIFY AND YOU'RE DEAD.'

Frightened sobs broke from Tracey. 'Someone in this prison put that on my bed! Someone in here's going to kill me.'

Lizzie slid an arm around the shaking shoulders. It was a frightening bloody thought all right! And for sure it looked like there *was* another 'plant' in Wentworth.

'Wentworth!' Julian looked stunned. 'He's an officer there?'

Sarah's face was white and tense. She'd gone to

296

dinner with Jim last night. Then they'd gone back to his flat. They both knew the moment had come and she'd fallen into his arms as though it was the most natural thing in the world. They had made love, a long, lingering, tender affair that had been wonderful for both of them. And then, the awful truth!

She'd slipped out of bed when the alarm went off. Jim had still been sleeping. She'd looked around for a bathrobe and when she couldn't see one, she'd opened the wardrobe. And there it was: his uniform. She'd stood stock still, shocked out of her mind. She'd prayed she would never see that dreaded uniform again!

Twenty-two

'What do you mean she won't see me?'

Jim glared angrily at Julian Phillips. He'd heard Sarah's voice from the back of the shop just as he walked in.

'Exactly that.' Julian shut the big book of design patterns and slammed it on the desk. 'If you care a rap about her, Fletcher, you'll get out of her life and stay out of it.'

Jim had realized when he finally woke and saw the open wardrobe door what had happened. Obviously Sarah had seen his uniform. It was vital he explain to her why he'd lied about his work.

Julian was watching him shrewdly and had obviously read his thoughts. 'Oh yes, she knows you're not a building contractor. I knew it from the start.' His eyes were snapping angrily. 'We don't want your money and we don't want you around here.'

Jim hesitated for a moment, then turned on his heel and walked quickly out of the shop. He had to talk to Sarah. He'd come back later when Julian wasn't around. After last night, there was no way he was going to let Sarah just walk away; she'd let him know she cared every bit as much as he did. She just needed a little time. She knew they had a future together just as well as he did.

Meg could see the moment he signed in for duty at the prison that something had upset him but he bit her head off when she ventured to ask if he was all right. Well, he'd get around to talking when he was ready. Meantime there was the business of the threatening note to Tracey to worry about.

The girl had talked to her lawyer that morning but his assurance that if she could just hang on until she was put in the witness box then she should be safe was pretty cold comfort. She'd told him about the note, but he'd brushed that aside as police business and hurried off to another appointment.

Judy had tried to comfort her. She'd done the right thing telling the Governor, and Lizzie had reported that Inspector Grace had already called to see Erica. They'd have been less impressed if they'd heard what went on between them. Grace had been very critical of the security in Wentworth – how could a note like that get inside? And what about the shooting incident? Erica had pointed out that the rifle had been fired from outside the prison and no arrest had been made as yet; not to mention that one of her officers had almost lost her life protecting Grace's witness. He'd shrugged it off. Meg Jackson was just doing her job, he and his men had to take those kind of risks every day.

He'd ended the interview with a terse suggestion that she keep security tight because he had no doubt there'd be another attempt on Morris's life.

At least the mystery as to how the note was delivered was soon cleared up. Doreen had been helping Chrissie Latham change baby Elizabeth's nappy, and prattling on about Tracey and the new threat. Chrissie had gone quite pale. She'd had someone come to visit, didn't know the guy. He'd been really nice, said it was important he get a note to his girlfriend and he'd given Chrissie twenty dollars to deliver it. She'd had no idea what was inside the envelope.

'We'd better let Bea know.' It was automatic for Doreen to go to Bea as the person who'd take charge, tell them what to do. Chrissie looked shaken.

'She'll beat the shit out of me!' Bea wasn't impressed, but apart from warning Chrissie not to be so bloody greedy in future, she was relieved at least to know that the note had come from outside, and she was quick to let the Governor know.

Tracey found the hearing an ordeal. She told Judy afterwards that she could tell the jury despised her, and Joe had got up, staring straight at her, and told them she'd known she was carrying heroin all along. Why would he do that?

Judy's smile was cynical. 'He tried to have you killed, hon. Why would he protect you now?'

Tracey looked wistful. 'I know; it's just,' she searched for the word, 'I really did love him and I thought, in spite of everything, maybe he'd show me that he had at least cared a bit.'

She put her head in her hands for a moment. 'Dad looked so awful, so white and strained and sad.' She'd felt her heart would break when they wouldn't even let her touch him. She'd asked Meg Jackson to go and see him; it was still hard to think of her dad taking on another woman, let alone a prison officer, but he needed someone right now and she was still stuck in this awful place.

There were some pretty unkind things printed in the evening paper, but when the women settled down in the recreation room to watch the TV news, she could feel a wave of sympathy towards her when they showed her scurrying from the court, hiding her face, trying to dodge the reporters who descended on her like vultures. Vera was on guard at the doorway and there was an unpleasant smirk as she listened to the reporters hounding Tracey and asking her if she really was a runner for the mob. Judy nudged Bea.

'Get the look on old Vinegar Tits. If my dog had a face like that, I'd shave its backside and teach it to walk backwards.'

Bea collapsed into laughter and even Tracey managed a small smile.

Lizzie cackled. 'I'll drink to that!'

'You'll drink to anything, you old bugger.' It was Mouse joining in the effort to try and cheer Tracey up.

McNelty was making very different plans for her as he spat out orders to his thugs and made it clear once and for all that Tracey Morris was not to testify.

The following day in court was desperately harrowing for the girl, but it was after she was leaving that the confusion started. She was bundled into the back of the police car with Policewoman Saunders, a friendly young woman who was doing her best to reassure Tracey that things were going all right for her. Their car was just picking up speed when a huge van backed out from an alleyway and drove between them and the second police car. In a moment, Tracey's car had turned into a side street, abandoning the motor cycle escort.

'What's going on?' Saunders tapped the shoulder of

the uniformed man in the front passenger seat. In a moment, he turned around, an ugly scowl on his face and a gun pointed directly at her.

'Sit back and shut up. The pair of you.' Tracey looked at Saunders, the horror of what was happening dawning in her eyes.

'They're not policemen.'

The thug gave her a nasty smile. 'Special Branch, under orders from Mr McNelty.'

'You stole those uniforms. What happened to the men you took them from?' Saunders was keeping her cool, trying frantically to think of some move she could make to get Morris to safety.

'Just shut up and don't make trouble or you'll get it.' He was fumbling with the police jacket with his one free hand as he talked, the gun still firmly trained on them.

'Shit!'

The car jerked as the driver saw the broken down vehicle stuck in the middle of the road dead ahead of them, and wrenched the wheel, swerving to pass the stalled car. In that second, the car dropped speed, attention was diverted for one split second, and Saunders had lunged forward, knocking the hand holding the gun towards the roof.

'Jump, Morris.'

Tracey was scared but she needed no second telling. She wrenched the door open and threw herself forward, hitting the ground with a thud. And then it all happened like some terrible nightmare. She heard the gun shot as she scrambled to her feet, and the car screamed to a halt.

The limp body of Policewoman Saunders fell out

from the opened door of the car, and the two thugs were coming at her, firing wildly. She dashed behind a parked car, a sob of fear escaping her. There was nowhere else to hide. And then she heard the scream of the sirens and the two motorbike cops had rounded the corner. The rest was almost a blur. The thugs firing at the police, the second car screeching to a halt and Detective Inspector Grace flinging himself out of it and rushing to where the inert body of the policewoman lay. He'd yelled for an ambulance – she was still alive – and then he'd been at a shaking Tracey's side, the now familiar ironical smile on his face.

'Nice friends you've got, Miss Morris.'

She could only stare at where one of the officers was kneeling beside Saunders, talking softly, loosening her collar.

'Why did she do it?'

His voice was matter of fact. 'She wouldn't have had much future after they'd bumped you off.'

'Will she be all right?'

He looked toward's Saunders and his face softened for a moment. 'Let's hope so.' But there was very little hope in his voice.

And all too soon, when Tracey had been readmitted to Wentworth and a sympathetic Meg was taking her back to her cell, the news came through. Saunders had died. Grace was certain there'd be no more trouble for Tracey, but as she explained to Judy, it was a relief, but she still couldn't believe it and she'd never forget the sight of the young policewoman lying in the road. Meg had saved her life the first time but, thank God, she hadn't been badly hurt. Now this. If Judy had any

303

sense she'd keep her distance. It wasn't safe to be Tracey's friend.

When the news came through on the TV later that Joe had been found in his cell – he'd hung himself – Tracey was almost too overwhelmed by earlier events to register it. She simply confided to Judy, in a voice almost devoid of emotion, that she had her doubts that he'd done it himself. And sooner or later, they'd still get her. She was almost past caring.

Meg was concerned about her. She'd tried to reassure Bob. He'd wanted to see his daughter but regulations wouldn't allow it, and regretfully all Meg could do was say she'd keep an eye on Tracey and do what she could to comfort her. He was just as concerned about Meg. He'd begged her not to go back to work so soon after being hospitalized, but Officer Powell was off sick, Carter's leave had come up, and Jim obviously had a lot of personal pressure on himself at the moment and she didn't want to aggravate that.

As for Vera, she was sure the heavy drinking was still going on – the same pattern, the headaches, the reluctance to work extra hours, and she was even more aggro with the women than usual. Meg knew too that she was desperately jealous as it became more and more obvious that wedding bells were not too far off for Meg – yet another thorn in her side that intensified her own lonely existence.

For once, Jim was sharing some of Vera's bitter state of mind. He'd phoned, called at the shop, left notes, tried everything. Sarah refused to see him. And finally, his feelings got the better of him and it all came pouring out into Meg's sympathetic ear.

She watched his face as he talked, sensing how deep

was the hurt. Sarah Forrest had meant a great deal to him, he'd hoped he'd found a lasting relationship, a new start. She felt almost guilty about her own happiness and, as she confided to Erica later (though of course she didn't betray his confidence), it seemed so hard on Jim, after all he'd been through. Erica thought a little wistfully of Andrew Reynolds, and the hopes she'd had that something lasting might have come out of the relationship. But she was very interested to know the kind of work in which Sarah Forrest was engaged. She'd been feeling so fed up with things lately that she'd decided perhaps a face-lift to her apartment might cheer her up. She'd get Jim to speak to his friend, and she added lightly, 'I might even be the catalyst that smooths things over between them.'

But Jim reacted rather oddly to Erica's suggestion that he ask Sarah Forrest to make contact, even going so far as to say he wasn't sure Sarah's standard of work would come up to Erica's expectations. She put it down to perhaps a lover's tiff and decided to check out the place for herself.

Sarah made a very good impression; Erica thought her quite charming and secretly decided Jim was showing very good taste. But the moment she mentioned who she was and where she worked, Sarah seemed to clam up. She claimed to be snowed under with contracts and when Erica became a little more insistent, she told her almost abruptly that her partner Julian Phillips specialized in the kind of decor Erica wanted, and she would get him to contact her and follow through with the work.

Erica was puzzled, even more so by a nagging thread of memory. She'd seen this woman before. For the moment she couldn't quite place where, but one thing she was certain of – it was in connection with the prison!

Twenty-three

'I'm sorry, Jim... I've checked the records. Sarah Forrest's real name is Jackie Nolan; she escaped from Barnshurst prison some years ago.'

Jim's face was ashen. Why the hell had he ever confided in Meg, talked about Sarah? That had set Erica off, wanting to get her bloody interior decorating done: and God, what had he done? What would happen to Sarah now.

'Are you saying I knew this all along?'

'Of course not.' Erica felt desperately sorry for him. 'But now that you do know, I'm afraid the association is out of the question, for a start.'

His face was grim. 'That's not a problem. Sarah,' he almost stumbled over the name in the light of this new development. 'She's ended the relationship.'

'Now you know why.' She hadn't meant it to sound cruel, but she regretted she hadn't said it more tactfully.

Jim turned on her angrily. 'You're always talking about rehabilitation. Well, Sarah's done that, made a success of her life. And your reaction is to put her back behind bars just as fast as you can. You don't practise what you preach, do you?' He'd slammed out of the

307

office and gone straight through to Vera in reception. He informed her tersely that she'd have to take over for an hour. He'd make it up to her later. He had an urgent appointment.

Vera was furious. She'd been on since early morning. The fact that she had a crashing hangover didn't help. She knew she'd have to do something about the drinking, but every day she'd made the resolution to go on the wagon the next day – and then she'd get home, tired and miserable, and promise herself just one drink. And the inevitable pattern followed. She knew it was making her edgy. She found herself watching the women furtively – did they know, had one of those filthy bitches started rumours behind her back?

Meg was distributing mail in the dining room when she caught up with her. Vera stood for a moment, watching the easy, friendly way Meg chatted and exchanged badinage with the women. So many times she'd wished she could be more like that, but the only attempts she'd made had been treated with distrust or contempt by the prisoners. They didn't want to know her sad life story – they all had their own problems, and they'd decided long ago that old Vinegar Tits was the pits.

Oh yes, she knew they called her that. She remembered the first time she'd heard it. The pain, the humiliation – the feeling that they'd taken away her last shred of femininity. She'd covered those emotions with anger but it still cut deep, haunted her in her lonely hours.

'Letter for you, Judy.' Meg held it out and Judy looked surprised as she opened the envelope. Meg smiled as she saw Lizzie already eagerly devouring the contents of her letter from Ellen, and she wasn't fooled by Bea's offhand manner when she'd handed her the letter from Ken Pearce. That relationship might be the thing Bea needed in her life to give it some direction and help her tone down her aggressive attitude in the time left for her to serve.

'What do you know!' Judy's face was alight with happiness. 'My Pop named me as chief beneficiary in his will.'

'Another rich bitch!' But Bea was pleased for her. The money wouldn't be the main thing for Judy. It would be the fact that he'd gone on believing in her and let her know by this final gesture.

'My sisters are contesting it, of course.' Judy shrugged. 'Who cares, it's the thought that counts.'

Her eyes met Bea's; an almost imperceptible nod from the latter; Judy knew she understood.

'Jim Fletcher's taken off in one hell of a hurry.' Vera kept her voice low as she moved up to Meg.

'Had a barney with Erica I'd say. I got lumbered with staying on, of course.'

Meg looked concerned. 'He's got a few problems at the moment.'

'So let him solve them in his own time.'

Jim was trying to do just that. But Sarah, white faced and tense, wouldn't listen to him. She was not going to give herself up and go through that hell again!

'I'll decide what's best for Sarah.'

It was Julian, tightlipped, giving Jim a look of pure loathing. Jim understood that look. He might hate Julian's guts but one thing he had learned. The man's loyalty and dedication to Sarah was absolute. He was the one who'd stood by her, given her a chance, a new

309

life. Then Jim had come along and blasted the scene wide open. He was entitled to his deep dislike.

There was no point in trying to say any more. A customer had entered the shop and Sarah had quickly pulled herself together, adopted her professional manner of charm and ease. He'd no option but to walk out.

The moment he'd gone, as Sarah turned to select a book of designs, Julian had hissed in her ear. 'Don't worry darl. We'll skip the country. Trust me.'

She'd turned calmly back to the customer, but the speaking glance she gave him told him he'd given her new hope.

But later, when they'd closed the shop and were enjoying a quiet drink together, she told him she'd thought it over, appreciated his support and caring, but she was sick of running. She'd decided to give herself up.

In vain did Julian rant and rave and try every kind of persuasion on her. She shook her head. She'd been lucky to get away with it for so long. The time had come to face the music.

Julian cursed the day Jim Fletcher had ever come into their lives, but Sarah couldn't go along with that. It was useless, hopeless, but she was in love with Jim. All right, he'd deceived her about his job, but she understood that. She'd heard the derogatory things women said about prison officers. And she'd been living an even bigger lie.

Julian was quiet for a moment. He looked at this woman he'd come to care about so deeply, his best friend, so talented, so warm and loving and loyal. He'd move heaven and earth for her, they'd get her out in no time! And tonight, he'd buy her the best damned dinner she'd ever eaten!

He chose a beautiful, candle-lit restaurant and they made a pact that they wouldn't talk about the future, tonight was for good wine and happy memories and, for Sarah, the final taste of freedom.

Jim was trying to lift his own spirits as he signed out in reception. But Erica's words were ringing in his ears.

'If she doesn't give herself up by tomorrow I have no choice but to ring the police.'

God, what a mess! He was still in shock, couldn't believe that Sarah was an escaped prisoner – he couldn't bear to use the word criminal. Meg was ready to knock off, too. He watched with envy as a smiling Bob Morris took her hand and smiled down at her. Why couldn't things have worked out for him the way they were doing for Meg? He didn't begrudge her, but he felt a surge of bitter envy as they left the building together, their happiness patent for all the world to see.

Well, they'd have their problems. Tracey Morris wasn't out of the woods yet. And for all Meg's protestations, Jim was absolutely convinced that Tracey was having a lesbian affair with Judy Bryant. Let Morris sort that one out! He imagined he'd be as sickened and disgusted as Jim at the very idea of it.

Officer Barry was signing in as he took out his car keys and headed for the door. 'Have a good night, Mr Fletcher.'

He turned an unsmiling face towards her. 'You'd better hope you do.'

He turned and walked out abruptly. Joan Barry was a bit surprised, she usually got along very well with

Jim. Was he letting her know there was some sort of trouble in the offing? She hoped not, she most certainly wasn't in the mood. Officer Barfield was coughing her head off and didn't look as if she'd last her shift. And Barry herself was limping around on an ingrown toenail that was doing very little for her usual happy-go-lucky approach.

Initially when she did her rounds things seemed to be pretty normal. Lizzie and Doreen were joking with Judy about how wealthy they'd all be soon, with Bea and Mouse and the rest of their group joining in good-naturedly.

The Morris girl was still looking pretty down in the dumps; Barry felt sorry for her. She agreed with Meg that Tracey had simply been misled – apparently the father had been away a lot on business and the girl had got into the wrong company. Well, when Meg married Bob Morris (and Barry was thrilled her old friend had found such a nice, steady man) she'd be a real mother to Tracey and they'd get things sorted out. And meantime, it must be hard for the kid to see her father so happy and still be locked up in Wentworth, not knowing what the future really held for her.

'I got a beaut letter today, Mrs Barry.' Lizzie patted her pocket – she carried her letters around for weeks after they came. 'Me granddaughter's doing real well over there in Chicago.'

'I'm pleased to hear it.' Barry gave the old girl a friendly smile.

'Officer Barfield's as sick as a horse. I reckon she ought to go home.'

Joan Barry hid a smile. Really, Bea Smith was so

used to being top dog with the prisoners, she sometimes sounded more in charge than the Governor.

'I know.' Joan Barry moved towards the door. She'd better let Barfield go home but they were short staffed and she'd have to call someone in.

She'd tried three officers, including Jim, before she decided to ring Vera. Barry didn't feel Bennett had been looking all that crash hot lately but she had to have someone. Vera's voice sounded rather strange when she spoke to her. But Barry stressed the urgency of the position and although Vera had said she was a bit tired – and she sounded it – she eventually agreed to get there as soon as she could.

Apart from the fact that Vera almost forgot to pick up her keys, Barry hadn't picked up anything special about her. Vera had resented coming in, but Joan had assured her everything was fine, should be a nice quiet shift and Barfield had simply had to go off duty. Vera nodded and went through to the main building. She paused for a moment, took a deep breath. She'd poured a pint of black coffee down her throat before she took off. Pity she'd had that extra drink before the phone rang. But she was OK. Out of habit, she smoothed her hands over her uniform, straightened her shoulders and made for the recreation room. Those lazy bitches were probably all sitting around like morons, staring at the television or cheating on each other at cards.

She paused in the doorway and looked them over. What a scruffy looking lot they were. Not worth two bob the lot of them. Why Erica Davidson wasted her breath trying to talk to them about rehabilitation and persevered with the training and work release schemes, she'd never know. They were here because they'd committed crimes. And most of them were just biding their time, waiting to get out there and do it all over again!

'Oh Gawd, there goes the neighbourhood!'

The others followed Bea's gaze. Vera was standing in the doorway, and in spite of how carefully she'd put on her uniform, the knot of her tie wasn't quite right and one strand of mousey coloured hair was hanging down from under her cap. But she was standing poker straight, feet apart to make sure she was steady; and there was a snide smile on her lips.

'Didn't expect to see you in here without your fancy girl, Bryant.' She moved a little way into the room. 'Better watch it. Morris might find herself something a bit younger.'

'Lay off, Miss Bennett.' Judy's face was tight and angry. Vera ventured a little closer.

'I'll say what I like to you, Bryant. I can say whatever I like to all of you. And there's nothing you can do about it. Because when I'm on duty, I'll run the prison the way it should be run!'

And then to the women's absolute astonishment, Vera reached into her pocket, drew out a packet of cigarettes and a lighter, and proceeded to light up.

Lizzie moved closer to Bea and whispered. 'Strewth! She's smokin' a fag!'

Vera felt their eyes fixed on her and took a long drag on her cigarette. 'What are you staring at?' She looked slowly from one face to the other. 'Oh yes, I know how much you all hate me. Well, I wouldn't want scum like you to feel any different, and the feeling is mutual. You're inside because you're criminals.'

Bea was watching her thoughtfully, but she kept her

voice casual. 'This is a concentration camp not a holiday resort, isn't that how it goes, Vera?'

'You'll refer to me as Officer Bennett.' Vera ground the cigarette out under her heel. 'This place is a pig sty. I want it cleaned up.'

Bea gave the other women a quick wink and, almost as one, they stood up and went into action, emptying ashtrays, straightening the book shelves, setting the chairs to rights. Mouse scurried out with Phyllis and they were quickly back with a very full bucket of water and two mops.

'That's it.' Vera's voice was not quite clear in spite of her efforts. 'When I say jump, you jump!' Almost without thinking, she helped herself to another cigarette but before she could reach for the lighter in her pocket, Lizzie had dashed across and lit a match. She moved as close to Vera as she could possibly get as she lit her fag, and Bea hid a grin as she watched Lizzie sniffing noiselessly.

'That OK, Miss Bennett?'

'Thank you Birdsworth.'

Vera inhaled deeply as Lizzie turned and made the thumbs-up sign to Bea. Vera was drunk; they'd suspected it but it had been up to Lizzie to get smart enough to make sure, by getting a really good whiff of Vera's breath. Lizzie leaned close to Bea.

'Gawd, I could let her breathe on me for hours! She's had a skin full.'

The word was quickly whispered around. The women had created plenty of diversions in their time but this was even more fun than usual! As Lizzie dropped an ashtray, Mouse clanged the bucket, Judy dropped a heavy book and Phyllis made all the noise she could, clumsily dropping her mop. They'd planned to try and disorientate Vera, and it worked. Her reflexes had slowed considerably and she found herself turning in a circle, her feet not quite in synchronization with her head.

'What are you doing? Clumsy idiots!'

She made an effort to right herself and threw her cigarette on the floor. 'Pick that up, Bryant.' Judy made as if to move forward but, quick as a flash, Mouse and Phyllis had lifted the full bucket of now dirty water and with an excellent pretence of slipping, managed to slosh the water all over Vera's skirt, drenching her legs and feet at the same time. She let out a yell of dismay and immediately Lizzie and Mouse were apologizing, wiping her down with a none too clean cloth and Lizzie was patting, brushing, seemingly straightening her jacket and trying to make amends.

'Stop that, you fools! Get your hands off me.' Vera was trying to pull herself together, flailing at the hands, trying to step out of the pool of water at her feet.

'Yes, Miss Bennett. Sorry, Miss Bennett.'

Bea could hardly hide a laugh as Lizzie bared her teeth in the most ingratiating of smiles. Vera, trying hard to hang on to her dignity in her wet skirt and squelching shoes, made an unsteady path to the door.

The moment she was outside, Lizzie turned with a cackle of triumph and held up the bunch of keys which she'd 'lifted' from Vera's belt.

'Got 'em.'

The other women yelled their approval, then Bea told them to settle down and listen. She had a plan – at last they were going to get even with Vinegar Tits!

And it was so simple. Doreen had agreed to hide

316

the keys in Maternity – no one was likely to start checking baby cots! Barry had locked them in their cells and said a pleasant goodnight, then Doreen had scooted back and let them out.

Bea handed over the keys to Lizzie. 'Don't bugger it up.'

Doreen protested. 'You can't let Lizzie go to the Governor's office. One sniff of that booze and that'll be the end of it.'

Lizzie looked hurt. 'Pinched the keys didn't I? 'Course I won't stuff it up.'

She hurried on her way. Bea knew Vera would go to the staff room to clean her skirt and try to sober up.

And that was precisely what she did. And to make a call to Meg. She'd discovered the keys were missing, and she was distraught.

'You've got to tell the other officers immediately.' Vera didn't answer directly.

'Could you come over, Meg? I need your help. I could lose my job over this.' Meg hung up the phone and turned to Bob.

'I'm sorry. I have to go back to work.'

She explained what had happened and he made it pretty clear that, in his opinion, the sooner Vera Bennett was out of Wentworth the better. But Meg was insistent, and reluctantly he let the lovely, intimate atmosphere that had been between them slip away, as he collected his car keys, insisting on driving Meg.

She was mystified when she arrived to see no sign of Vera, and Barry, busy with an induction, couldn't throw any light on it. And why had Meg come in? She made a hasty excuse and hurried to the staff room.

317

Meg found her where the women had left her. They had finally got their revenge.

It had been a simple thing for Bea and Margot to creep up on Vera in the staff room. In her dazed state, she'd offered little resistance. True to her word, Lizzie had come bustling in with the decanter of Scotch from Erica's office. She was loath to waste such good booze but Doreen assured her it was in a good cause. Vera began to realize what they had in mind but there was nothing she could do about it. The years of humiliation and anger came welling out of the women. She'd broken too many hearts, too many brave spirits, over the years – now it was her turn.

As Judy and Bea held her fast, Margot had yanked back her head and forced her mouth open. With just a touch of reluctance, Lizzie poured the neat spirit down Vera's throat. She coughed and spluttered but they were relentless. The alcohol ran down her chin and into her collar and seeped down over the once immaculate uniform.

'Wonder what the Guv will say when she finds out you were boozed on the job, Vera, eh?'

There was hate in Bea's face as she looked down on Vera, the eyes closed as the neat spirit burned into her throat and dribbles of alcohol ran unheeded down her chin.

'It's a wicked waste!' from Lizzie, 'but, I reckon it's worth it.'

By the time they'd finished, Vera was a snivelling, drunken heap and she'd be out of it any moment. They'd hurried back to their cells, got Chrissie from Maternity to lock them in, and settled down for the night, waiting eagerly for what was to come.

Chrissie had locked the last cell then thrown the keys on the corridor floor as far away as she could manage; then she'd scuttled off to her quarters, glad to be out of it, scared if she was involved it might endanger her and her little baby daughter.

Meg was stunned, as she looked at the figure slumped in the chair, reeking of alcohol and almost incoherent. God, Vera had finally cracked and started drinking on the job! But she would never let herself get into this state. Joan Barry popped her head in and reported that they'd done a quick head count and no one was missing. She looked at Vera, hardly able to believe her eyes.

'What do you make of it, Meg?'

Meg shook her head. 'I don't think she managed to get into this state on her own.'

At that moment, Officer Read walked in, jangling Vera's keys.

'Found these in the corridor. I don't know how Vera could have missed them.'

But then she looked at Vera Bennett and realized what a state she was in. Well, Read had no time for the woman, a bully who made life as unbearable for the prisoners as she possibly could. About time someone taught her a lesson.

Vera was muttering to herself: 'Animals, that's all they are! Animals!'

The speech was slurred but they could sense the pent-up emotion behind it.

Barry gave Meg a very direct look. 'It'll have to be reported.'

'I know.' In spite of everything Meg felt a rush of

319

compassion. This could mean Vera's job; and what else did she have to live for?

Erica realized that too, but she was absolutely outraged when the incident was reported to her. Vera had tried to bluff her way through, laying the blame heavily on the women, stressing the kind of punishment that should be handed out to them.

Erica's voice was icy. 'I have no intention of punishing the women for an officer's dangerous mistake and stupidity, Miss Bennett. They could have escaped, rioted, people could have been injured. I want an explanation as to why you did not immediately report your keys missing.'

Vera knew she was defeated. She'd been drunk on duty, careless, allowed that scum to bamboozle her and steal her keys. She put her chin up and tried to quell the awful sinking feeling in her stomach.

'I think the only thing I can do is resign.'

Erica's clear blue eyes were totally unforgiving. 'I'll expect your resignation in writing.'

Although Meg had expected the Governor would react that way, she was still shocked.

'I've been aware of her problem. If I'd been of more help this probably wouldn't have happened. Erica was unrelenting. They were in enough trouble with the Department now. Imagine if they heard about this fiasco! Meg accepted the facts but she was worried. As she confided to Joan Barry, from their own experience they knew what people did when they felt that life wasn't worth living.

'You don't think Vera would try suicide?'

Barry was horrified.

Meg didn't reply, but the concern in her eyes was answer enough.

Twenty-four

'I'm a really smart bastard.' Jackie looked at the group of women, staring at her with a mixture of curiosity and hostility. 'Married a bloke who screwed up my life by turning to armed robbery and taking me along for the ride. Then I fall for a prison screw, and end up in here.'

She'd decided to meet the other prisoners head on. The officers in reception had noticed Jim's misery during her induction. The women would find out soon enough that there was something between them.

'You saying Jim Fletcher dobbed you in?'

'No.' She managed a rueful smile. 'Your Governor, being a pretty smart cookie with a memory like an elephant, checked me out.'

There was no denying the women were impressed with Jackie Nolan. To have escaped from Barnshurst, fooled the coppers for so long, and set up successfully in business – boy, that took some doing. And you could understand old Fletch the Letch getting the hots for her. She had it all – class, brains, sex appeal, and a smashing figure that even a prison uniform couldn't conceal.

'Bea's Queen Bea around here, Jackie.'

It was good old loyal Doreen, making sure Jackie

didn't get any ideas. She made it very clear she had no such aspirations. Lizzie had a bit of trouble understanding that high falutin' talk but Dor assured her it just meant Jackie didn't want no part of being top dog and Bea'd run things as usual.

It was Jackie's reaction to Judy and Tracey that puzzled the women. Big Margot had made a bloody tactless remark about Jude being the lady to like if you liked ladies, and followed through with a pretty lewd crack about Tracey being Jude's new sweetie. Jackie had got really uptight and made it clear she wanted nothing to do with either of them.

'Over-reacting a bit, aren't you?'

Bea wasn't going to let this new bitch piss on big Jude. Then the explanation had come out and Jude agreed with the rest of them that she could understand Jackie's attitude. The reason she'd broken out of Barnshurst was because there'd been a bloody great dyke of an officer who wouldn't leave her alone, made her life a nightmare.

'Well, that's something you and Fletch have got in common.' Bea gave a tight smile. 'Got a real thing about lesbians. The trouble is he can't seem to work out the difference between the real thing and a straight down the line friendship. Right Jude?'

Judy nodded. 'Young Tracey's had a hell of a time. I've just tried to be there for her. We're not lovers. But try telling him that!'

Meg was having much the same trouble with Bob Morris. He hadn't forgotten what she'd said to him earlier, but Jim had stirred a bit the last time Bob had visited the prison. And then he'd seen them, Tracey and Judy, walking in the garden, their arms around each other. He'd been sickened and much as he tried to go along with Meg's theory he wasn't convinced, and he ached to get his daughter out and away from that Bryant woman.

Unfortunately he'd broached the subject with Tracey at the same time as he had told her that Meg had finally and officially agreed to marry him. He knew it had been a clumsy, tactless thing to do but those damned visits with an officer breathing down your neck, and so little time to say things the way you meant to! The upshot had been that Tracey had slammed out of the interview room, and he knew he'd damaged the friendship which had been very gradually forming between his daughter and the woman he intended to marry.

Bob had done a lot more than that. Tracey had wept bitterly after he'd gone. Judy had comforted her as best she could but in the end suggested she ask for a move. If Tracey wasn't sharing her cell maybe that would calm things down with her father, and Jim Fletcher!

Although the other women were friendlier to her now, Tracey still looked on Judy as her only real friend, the one person who was trying to protect her and help her stay sane in that awful place. Judy had gone off to the recreation room and Tracey had been sitting on her bunk lost in a sea of unhappy thoughts. The voices had been indistinct at first, then she'd realized it was Jim Fletcher talking to Jackie Nolan. And what she heard had sickened her. He was telling Jackie not to swallow that hogwash about Morris and Bryant, they were on together all right and their behaviour was disgusting. Jackie had murmured something about keeping her distance and Jim Fletcher was moving off with her when he made a final crack about how sorry he was for Bob Morris, a hell of a nice chap who was heartbroken that his kid had turned lesbian.

It was too much. There was nothing left. Joe had hung himself. Her father hated her and he'd lied all along; he wasn't going to spend more time with her, try to make things better. He was going to get married and she could like it or lump it. And everyone in this awful bloody place had branded her as a lesbian. Twice she'd nearly been killed. Well, why not save them all the trouble? She was shaking with pent-up emotion as she moved quickly across the cell to the small mirror on the cabinet. She picked it up and hurled it to the ground, then feverishly scrabbled around for the sharpest piece she could find. She put the jagged edge to her wrist.

'Tracey – no!'

Meg had leapt forward as she spoke, sending the sliver of glass flying and grabbing Tracey hard by the wrist.

'That isn't the answer and you know it.'

The girl's eyes were wild. 'Why would you care? You'd have my father all to yourself. You've already taken him away from me. This'd make it easier for everyone.'

But she was crying now, young and vulnerable and desperately upset.

'Listen to me, Tracey. Your father loves you, lives for you. He sacrificed everything to give you a good start in life. Does he have to spoon feed you forever?'

Tracey looked taken aback. Subconsciously she'd expected the kind of sympathy she'd have got from Judy.

'I know it will take you time to get used to the idea of my marrying your father. That's completely understandable. But you're young, you have so much to look forward to. You mustn't even think about doing something like this.'

Tracey's smile was cynical.

'Like spending the rest of my life in this place?'

'That's not going to happen. But while you are here, I think you should try to stop feeling quite so sorry for yourself and see things as they really are. Your father is a wonderful man and it's about time you earned his love.'

Meg hadn't enjoyed speaking so strongly to Tracey but she hoped it might stir the girl out of her apathetic state of mind. Later, she told Bob what had happened. He was terribly shocked, his daughter attempting to take her own life! Meg didn't mince words with him. Didn't he realize that his daughter's life was in turmoil? That it was a living hell for her being in prison, no matter how hard Meg or anyone else might try to soften the blow? To blithely visit Tracey and talk about getting married was enough to push the child over the edge.

As for the Judy Bryant affair, Meg was disappointed in him. She thought she'd spelt it out loud and clear that there was no question of Tracey being involved in a lesbian relationship. Bob was very contrite and knew better than to bring up the subject of Meg resigning when they got married. She'd been adamant about going on working. After the shooting episode he'd felt even more strongly about it. But for the moment he'd have to settle for Meg's accepting his proposal and hope perhaps later she would change her mind.

Erica was very gratified that Meg would stay on. She was happy to arrange time out for the wedding and honeymoon but it would have been a great disappointment if Meg had resigned. She'd have lost not only a fine officer, but one of her best friends.

Meg gently broached the subject of Vera. She'd called in to see her a couple of days ago. Meg didn't enlighten Erica with the facts she'd learned. Vera, drunker than she'd ever been before, had taken home a derelict old woman and gone on and on drinking with her. The upshot had been that Vera had passed out, the woman had stolen anything and everything of value, and the police had to be brought in.

'How did the Department react to her resignation?'

A tiny flush of embarrassment crept into Erica's cheeks. 'I never sent it on.'

Meg's face registered her astonishment.

Erica had given the matter a lot of thought after Meg had told her Vera's life story. She hadn't known about the sad, unrewarding life that lay behind the brittle facade that was Vera Bennett. When she did, she'd sat there weighing things up for a long time. What would become of the woman if she lost the one thing left to her – her work? So Erica had put the envelope in her drawer and, instead, arranged for Vera to take sick leave. She'd give her one more chance. Didn't everyone deserve that?

These were the very sentiments that Julian Phillips was pouring into the ears of an attentive reporter, Michael Graeme. He'd given him the whole story of

Jackie's rehabilitation. All the talk about trying to get the criminals and misfits back into useful activity in the outside world, and what did it all amount to? A lot of do-gooders and Departmental bigwigs preaching a theory they didn't practise for a moment.

Michael Graeme could smell a good story. He had a political contact, Anthony Vickers, looking for a specific platform, interested in prison reform. This could be just the hook he needed to hang his hat on.

Julian was well pleased with the interview but disappointed in Jackie's reaction. She was resigned to serving the two years still hanging over her and she didn't want to be used by some MP so he could get re-elected and she could be hounded to death by the media.

She felt rather differently when she received her sentence; and Jim was stunned. She was to serve out the original two years without benefit of parole, with another fifteen months for escaping lawful custody, a total of three years and three months.

'I thought you had every chance.'

Her mouth was grim and she refused to read the concern in Jim's eyes.

'That magistrate wanted an eye for an eye. I should have taken Julian's advice and run, shouldn't I?'

He had no answer to that.

Erica urged her to appeal but Jackie wasn't interested. She was bitter as she told Jim how the magistrate had served sentence, then had the gall to say he hoped in time she would once again become a useful member of the community! Well, she'd been there, done that. Now she would accept the fact that she'd been treated like a criminal, was a criminal, and would act accordingly.

Jim was terribly saddened by her bitter attitude. He protested to Erica; surely they could do something. The Governor was sympathetic but her hands were tied if Jackie wouldn't appeal. And she ended with a gentle but firm warning to Jim about getting further involved now that Nolan would be staying on at Wentworth.

But Jim was simply unable to walk away. He still felt an immense sense of guilt for what had happened. If he and Jackie hadn't met, who knows? The police might never have caught up with her. And whether a man in his work should be thinking that way or not, he was sickened at the thought that a woman of her calibre who'd carved out a useful career and proved herself eminently worthy of being part of society should still be treated as a criminal.

So when Myra Desmond had suggested he attend the meeting of the Prison Reform Group he'd accepted eagerly and determined he'd use them as an avenue to try and get at least some leniency towards Jackie's sentence.

The women were beginning to be pretty impressed at all the action on Nolan's behalf. Initially they'd thought she was a bit of a rare bird anyway, escaping, changing her name, going into business. Now, with MP's jumping up and down about her and the PRG chucking up banners left right and centre, she was fast becoming a celebrity. The only person not impressed was Jackie herself. She knew that Julian meant well, and Jim, but in her bitterness she couldn't help but suspect that both sides were simply using her, a convenient stepping stone.

Vera Bennett certainly didn't approve of all the publicity and the glamorizing of an ordinary, common criminal. She might feel a bit shaky, first day back on the job, and knowing she was being watched pretty closely by the staff and women alike; but the leopard couldn't change its spots. She soon let Jackie Nolan know she was not impressed. As for Jim Fletcher and the way he was mooning over the creature, it was disgraceful, the woman should be transferred at once.

But the greatest thorn in Vera's side was Tracey Morris. She'd heard all about the wedding plans and when she'd learned that Meg would continue to work at Wentworth, she'd been disgusted. That little bitch would get plenty of privileges with her stepmother on the spot! She'd lost no time in baiting Tracey until the girl had answered her back and Vera had had the perfect excuse to punish her. She set her to scrubbing the corridors after the evening meal. She'd let her know she was in prison, not just filling in time until her rich daddy could take her home and spoil her rotten again.

But she'd reckoned without the other women. They'd told Meg Jackson how Vera had heckled Tracey till the kid answered her back, and even then it had been pretty mild. But old Vinegar Tits had jumped on her and the kid would be on her knees till dawn trying to clean up that lot.

There had been a twinkle in Meg's eye as she'd wondered out loud if anyone had thought of volunteering to help Tracey? They weren't that thrilled at the idea of the extra duties, but as Lizzie put it 'nothing much on telly, girls', and a nod from Bea, and that had been all it took.

Vera was fuming the following morning when she found out what had happened but Erica paid little attention to her complaint. Vera had only just resumed duties and the Governor hoped she wasn't going to overstep the mark or victimize a prisoner while she was being assessed as capable of working again.

Tracey was very grateful to the women but they laughed it off, and while they were going through the usual routine of laundry duties, they got around to discussing Meg's wedding.

'How do you feel about it, Trace?'

Bea was curious. The kid had been up and down like a yoyo for yonks, and the idea of her dad marrying a screw, even one as beaut as Meg Jackson, was probably pretty hard to swallow.

'I was a bit mixed up for a while.' Tracey flushed, embarrassed. 'But Jude's straightened me out. I guess I'm glad Dad's found someone as nice as her. But,' she hesitated, 'the only thing is — is Vera Bennett going to make things even rougher once Meg really is my stepmother? I don't think I could take that.'

Bea nodded. 'Know what you mean. But I reckon you can leave that to us. Vera won't be wanting a repeat of the last lesson we taught her.'

'Have you applied for leave to go to the wedding, Tracey?' It was Doreen, who, for all her ups and downs, and still some pretty low times when she thought about Kev, was still a romantic at heart and would love to have been going along herself.

'Can I do that?'

'Course.' Bea thumped the steam press down with a thwack. 'Talk to the Gov. It'll be OK.'

'Eh,' Lizzie tapped the sheet she'd just folded. 'I got an idea for a wedding present.'

Bea winked at Doreen. 'This'll be good. Pearls from the lips of the old and wise one.'

'Shut your trap, Bea.' Lizzie grinned at Tracey. 'If we could get our hands on some cotton material we could make them a pair of sheets and pillow cases to match. What do you reckon?'

'Beaut.' Doreen beamed at Lizzie. 'And we could embroider something on them, you know, like "His and Hers".'

'Or "To whom it may concern".' Bea chuckled at her own wit. Phyllis wasn't going to be outdone. 'Or "This end up".'

Tracey was looking embarrassed and Bea called the women to order; they were talking about her old man after all. But how did they get their hands on the material?

Lizzie shook her head at them; Gawd they were thick. 'Nick it from the store of course.'

Bea laughed, but their mood was cut short as Jim Fletcher appeared in the doorway and told Jackie Nolan she had a visitor. He walked beside her along the corridor, and tried again to understand why she had insisted on replacing Bryant in the laundry. There were less unpleasant duties. But she'd been obstinate. When Bryant moved out of Tracey's cell and requested a change of duties as well, Jim had rostered Judy to the workshop and another pair of hands had to be delegated to the laundry. And Jackie was still as determined to stay there.

She'd imagined her visitor would be Julian Phillips, and Jim watched the lack of interest in her face as she listened to the plans he was pouring out – the contracts made, the words in the right places – the continuing media interest. Jim had tried to have a few words with Phillips before he brought Jackie through, but he'd been up against a brick wall. Julian was appalled at the idea of getting together with the PRG – a bunch of ex-con ratbags who weren't capable of campaigning for anything more than a few extra bits of meat in the prison stew. He'd ended up by accusing Jim of wanting the kudos for getting Jackie out.

'You're the bastard who put her in here. Now you want to whitewash yourself by getting mixed up with a group of ex-criminals who'd be more likely to put people's backs up than achieve anything for Jackie.'

There was no point in continuing the conversation. And now as he stood in the interview room, obliged to listen to the conversation between Jackie and Julian, he was having a hard time keeping out of it. Julian was impressing on her that she stood a very good chance of a vice-regal pardon if they could keep ratbags like the PRG out of the way. Those sort of people would just ruin the image he and the press were building up around Jackie.

There was a lot more of the same, a lot of name dropping and a smugness about Julian Phillips that sickened Jim. He'd been so sure the man was dedicated to Jackie, but now he wondered. She was the one with the real talent; was Julian perhaps just trying to salvage his business regardless of what the publicity did to her?

He said as much, in guarded terms, as he walked her back to the laundry. She'd turned on him angrily. She just wanted the whole lot of them to drop it! She didn't want to know about MP's, reporters, prison reform groups or any other damned thing. Jim was hurt but he still cared deeply about her and he touched her gently on the arm just before she moved into the laundry.

'Please don't shut me out, Sarah.' The name slipped out involuntarily.

He saw the pain in her eyes, the slight sag of her shoulders as she let herself remember for a fleeting moment.

'There is no Sarah, Jim.' But when she raised her face to his, there was a warmth in her eyes that told him she would never forget their time together.

'I still care a great deal.'

She knew he meant it. She still cared about him . . . enough to know that the best thing for him was to forget the woman he'd known as Sarah. It would be hard, but from now on, she'd only let him see Jackie Nolan – a prisoner who would accept no special favours, from him or anyone else.

The subject of favouritism was being hotly discussed at that moment in the Governor's office. Meg had found Tracey in tears. Vera had taken great delight in jumping the gun on the official announcement that Tracey was to be transferred to Barnshurst. Meg had been furious, firstly at the way the news had been broken, and secondly, that Erica had chosen to take that step at all.

'I've weighed it up very carefully, Meg. I had no choice.'

Meg put forward every argument in the book but she knew in her heart that Erica wasn't persecuting her or Tracey. It was standard procedure. Meg would be legally the girl's stepmother and the situation wasn't tenable, would affect the other women no matter how carefully Meg tried to tread the fine line between authority and personal emotions.

Bob was equally upset. He hadn't wanted Meg to go on working but at least while she was around he knew Tracey was safe. What would happen to her in a strange prison where very likely there were a dozen Vera Bennetts?

Vera was at that moment putting a strong case forward to Erica Davidson regarding the transfer of Jackie Nolan to Barnhurst. The thought had obviously crossed Erica's mind; the woman's prior involvement with Jim Fletcher couldn't be overlooked. And she also suspected that a number of the women saw Nolan as something of a heroine – the woman who'd escaped from Barnshurst, managed to stay out for six years, and now had a national media campaign working on her behalf for release. That sort of thing could lead to trouble.

Jim registered Erica's reaction and knew he had to talk, even though he knew Jackie would hate the story coming out in front of Vera Bennett. Briefly and succinctly he told the Governor about the lesbian warder who'd molested Nolan. The officer had constantly fabricated reports to prevent Nolan getting parole and had made her life so unbearable that she'd escaped out of sheer desperation.

Erica was appalled; why hadn't Nolan reported the matter? Jim's smile was very bitter.

'A prisoner's word against an officer?' They all knew about that. And probably no one would do a damned thing about it till one of the prisoners hung themselves and the truth finally came out.

Even Vera was taken aback. She might be officious and at times heavy handed, but there was no way she could condone that kind of behaviour.

As it turned out, Julian Phillips' prediction was correct. He denied the PRG had been of any help, but the combined effect of his efforts and theirs had been successful. A pardon had been granted to Jackie Nolan.

The women were delighted for her and when they saw her back in civvies and looking a million dollars they could see why old Fletch had gone for her. She really was a knockout.

Jim was at the gate when she and Julian Phillips met an excited reception. Reporters and television cameras were all over the place but they wouldn't be able to get to her till she passed through the gate. She saw him. Then she turned to Julian, spoke briefly, and, a bit reluctantly, he passed out of the prison to join the throng of media and well-wishers outside the gates.

'I guess this is goodbye, Jim.' She held out her hand and he took it tightly in his.

'Thank you seems so inadequate for all you gave to me!' She heard the tremor of emotion in his voice as he spoke.

'It was short, but it was sweet.' It was all she could manage to say but she smiled very directly into his eyes and that said it all. It wasn't much to cling to, but he'd remember that look forever.